SKELETONS

OTHER BOOKS BY ERIC SAUTER

Hunter

Predators

ERIC SAUTER

SKELETONS

DUTTON
NEW YORK

DUTTON

Published by the Penguin Group
Penguin Books USA Inc., 375 Hudson Street,
New York, New York 10014 U.S.A.
Penguin Books Ltd, 27 Wrights Lane,
London W8 5TZ, England
Penguin Books Australia Ltd, Ringwood,
Victoria, Australia
Penguin Books Canada Ltd, 2801 John Street,
Markham, Ontario, Canada L3R 1B4
Penguin Books (N.Z.) Ltd, 182–190 Wairau Road,
Auckland 10, New Zealand

Penguin Books Ltd, Registered Offices:
Harmondsworth, Middlesex, England

First published by Dutton, an imprint of Penguin Books USA Inc.
Published simultaneously in Canada by Fitzhenry & Whiteside, Limited.

First printing, June, 1990

1 3 5 7 9 10 8 6 4 2

Library of Congress Cataloging-in-Publication Data

Sauter, Eric.
Skeletons / Eric Sauter. — 1st ed.
p.   cm.
ISBN 0-525-24874-9
I. Title.
PS3569.A8215S5   1990
813'.54—dc20   89-23808
                                                            CIP

Printed in the United States of America
Set in New Baskerville

Designed by Steven N. Stathakis

For Beth and Molly

I want to thank Dick Marek for his wise and generous help in completing this book.

Note: Various aspects of the city including geography, streets and landmarks, have been altered to suit the purposes of the story.

SKELETONS

Prologue

JUNE

It was the third break-in in a little over five weeks and the worst so far. Paige wanted a few minutes alone in the apartment before the scene car got there, so he asked Cooper to take the hysterical young couple out into the hall to question them.

No wonder they were hysterical. They'd come home at seven-thirty—they worked for the same law firm—and found their apartment had been destroyed.

Paige listened to the woman's sobbing and the man's terrified bluster for a moment and then closed the door behind him. Once inside, the detective closed his eyes and listened. There was chamber music, a piano trio, the soft churning of notes drifting into the background as he stepped into the apartment. The break-in was exactly like the first two. The skin on the back of Paige's neck began to tingle.

He opened his eyes and moved to the center of the living room, adjusting his vision to the room's strange light. A tall corner lamp with a red shade lay on its side across the arms of a chair. A rose-colored blossom of light spread across the wall behind it. On the other side of the room, beneath a window

1

that looked out onto Spruce Street, someone had balanced a small round table lamp between the legs of an overturned coffee table and switched it on. The shade on the table lamp was turned up, the rest of the room awash in its harsh white light.

Paige was careful not to focus on any one object but to see everything as a kind of tableau, an abstract pattern that would eventually suggest the general sweep of the destruction the longer he looked at it. His first impression was that it had begun in the far right-hand corner near the window; all the objects in the room seemed to fall back toward that corner as if the burglar had moved clockwise from that point, building up layer after layer of debris as he tossed everything behind him.

Paige walked the perimeter of the room, stopping every few feet to picture it in his mind. He found a clean corner of the couch and sat on it. No, he thought, after a few minutes, there was no pattern to the destruction. It was completely random and without any apparent purpose. That was the same as the last two; even the first one, where the damage was so slight that he'd almost overlooked it at first. It was like a bizarre aberration, a quick lashing out that was over as suddenly as it had begun.

There were a few things Paige had figured out so far.

The burglar was probably white and well-educated; in all three apartments the radio had been tuned to the public radio station. Only one of the victims said they listened to it regularly, which meant that the burglar had selected it.

Paige figured the burglar was strong and careful about his weight. He had to be reasonably strong to turn over that much furniture, and while he always helped himself to the food in the refrigerator, he never ate anything heavy. Usually it was a salad or a few slices of cold meat, a piece of chicken. If there were diet sodas, he usually drank one of those.

He wore leather gloves the entire time in the apartment, even when he ate. The crime lab people had found glove smears on a plate from the first apartment. In the second apartment, they found a similar smear on a bathroom glass; similar but not an exact match. That meant he changed gloves with each new job.

The burglar spent several hours in each apartment, enough time so that he got hungry. He also knew that each apartment

2

would be vacant for an extended period during the day, and that meant he had probably been watching each building for some time. He went in during midday, probably somewhere between 10 A.M. and 11 A.M. and stayed for several hours, ate something, and then left. For each apartment, he selected the best method of entry. There were no false starts.

In the first one, an apartment near South Street, he came in through the roof. He popped the roof door off its hinges and then crawled around the heating ducts to an opening in the hall ceiling near the elevator shaft.

To enter the second one, a town house on the same side of Society Hill near Sixth and Walnut, he walked up to the front door and popped the spring in the lock with a pair of channel grips. One good wrench and he was inside in less than fifteen seconds. He changed exits each time. For the first one, he used a back fire escape; for the second, he went out a window and down a utility pipe. Since he went in through the front door this time, Paige guessed he went out through a back window or climbed out onto the roof.

All the apartments had dead bolts. The burglar worked a straight edge behind the molding on the jamb, pushed back the bolt, and then worked the door open with a hard shove. He didn't try to rock the door frame with a screwdriver or a pry bar. He went in quickly and carefully. After that, Paige's ideas on the burglar stopped. He didn't want to think anymore. He wanted to walk through the apartment, try to get a better feel of something he had already begun to suspect.

Paige stepped around the shattered frame of a large flower print, a pale Georgia O'Keeffe orchid, white against a washed-out blue background, in the doorway. To his left was a short hallway that led to the bedroom and bath. The kitchen was on his right, a few steps away. Paige wanted to save the kitchen for last. The music came from the bedroom, so he walked in that direction, pacing himself, making sure that he had everything under control.

The bedroom wasn't as bad as the living room. Clothes were strewn across the floor and the bed. The burglar had swept the top of the dresser clean. A jewelry box, several small vials of perfume, a photograph in a burnished silver frame, and one or two jars of hand lotion were scattered in a wide arc alongside

3

the dresser. The bed was untouched except for a small indentation near the end. The radio lay on its side next to the head of the bed, the toppled nightstand beside it. Paige stared at the impression on the bed for several minutes, then went to look at the kitchen.

It was a narrow room with a small island in the center of the room between the stove and the sink. The island had a Formica countertop that looked like butcher block. The countertop was clean except for a can of Diet Coke, a jar of imported mustard, and a partially eaten chicken leg on a small white salad plate.

The burglar had emptied the cupboards onto the floor. Flour covered the stove and the range hood. The bag lay crumpled like a drunken dancer in the far corner of the room. Cans of tomato paste and soup, crushed boxes of cereal and pasta, formed a lumpy carpet on the floor. The burglar had poured the spices out next to the sink; they formed a distinct pattern, a multi-colored snake of red, yellow, and green powders that curled around itself and then trailed over the edge of the counter onto the floor. The burglar had grown tired of his design and dumped them all together. Some he had thrown down hard. The jars were smashed, and the floor glittered with broken glass.

But the island in the center of the room was left undisturbed.

Paige went back to the living room and noticed the same effect. The center of the room, where Paige had stood just minutes before, was clean.

Paige closed his eyes and imagined the burglar standing in his place, gazing at his work, his performance. The word stuck. Paige opened his eyes.

"I know you," he said out loud.

Paige thought it out. Once inside, the burglar went through the apartment carefully. He took his time. No one was expected home, so why not? After that, he went to the kitchen to find something to eat. In this case, some chicken, a soda, nothing much different from the first two places. But he didn't eat right then.

Instead he went berserk. In the first apartment, he kept his frenzy well under control. He broke a pair of expensive antique

4

Flemish plates, knocked over a chair in the dining room. It seemed so accidental that Paige almost missed it. The second time, the burglar dismantled the kitchen, tossing the contents of the refrigerator and cupboards all over the walls but kept the table meticulously clear where he ate, as if protecting his sanctuary.

In both cases, he left no evidence behind, no torn pieces of clothing, no shoe prints in the debris, nothing. He also didn't take very much. Paige didn't know about this time, but he was willing to bet only a few items would turn up missing. Theft seemed a secondary consideration. It provided an excuse to invade.

Outside, the burglar was in control, coolly professional, the best Paige had ever seen. But then something happened to him. Each time the burglar stepped into a new apartment, his control slipped one more notch, the grip on his splintering personality weakened and the performance itself took over.

That's why he stood in the center of each room when he finished, Paige thought, to see not only what it would look like but also to make certain it was as good as everything else he'd done. The burglar was a perfectionist, even while he was going insane.

Paige returned to the bedroom and checked the windows. All of them were locked. But the bathroom window wasn't, and there was a small scuff mark on the ledge. Paige opened it carefully and looked down. Ten feet below was part of a garage roof. The burglar had jumped. Paige could just make out the spot where he'd landed.

The door to the apartment opened; voices broke into his concentration. He watched the young couple as they stepped into the living room, embarrassed by what had become of their apartment. Like people who have contracted a terminal disease, they seemed to think it was their fault, that something about their lives had attracted it.

They looked at Paige and smiled, shrugged and looked away again. The man shook his head at a pile of ripped and torn books. The young woman put her hands to her face and breathed through her mouth. Paige could hear it above the music, the rush as it passed between her open fingers. Her husband put his hands on her shoulders and squeezed gently.

5

One of the other detectives called from the landing to some-one at the bottom of the stairs. Paige heard the sound of feet treading heavily up the steps, the crime scene unit come to look things over. Paige didn't want to be there when they did their work. He didn't feel comfortable around them; not that he felt comfortable around anybody in the department.

He watched the couple and realized what a sad audience they were, how unprepared they had been for this strange and frightening performance. What they could never hope to un-derstand was that it hadn't been for them at all.

It was for Paige.

He stepped aside to let the crime scene crew into the apart-ment. Now, suddenly, it seemed crowded and claustrophobic, the sound of voices grated on his ears, the light hurt his eyes. The place was no longer his, and he slipped past Cooper down the stairs and out into the street. There would be a house-to-house to see if anyone had seen anything, but Paige knew that nothing would come of it, just as nothing had come of the others. The burglar was like a ghost, invisible to everyone except Paige.

After the second break-in, Paige had asked for additional patrols in Society Hill, an area of expensive apartment buildings and red brick row houses that covered an area of approximately eighty-five square blocks alongside the river. They had come up with nothing.

Society Hill, a slum in the early sixties, was now a rich and respectable area. It ran from Penn's Landing, a brick-walked promenade along the river, past Independence Mall. On the north side, it ended at Market Street. Its southern border was South Street, a narrow strip of shops and restaurants and bars, squeezed by tourists and teenagers during the warm months, a place so bizarre that at times it seemed not to be part of the old city at all. You could disappear on South Street in seconds.

Paige thought of stopping to see Julia; he hadn't seen her in more than two months. It wasn't a good idea, he decided. She hated when he showed up unexpectedly. He'd done it once and she had reacted with extreme irritation and asked him to leave after a few intensely awkward moments. Paige had not done it again. In fact, he remembered now, that incident was the beginning of the end of the relationship. He realized he had no real claim on her time and that they both preferred it that way. She hated surprises, so did he; they were alike in that respect.

He felt anxious, impatient to get moving. But he forced himself to wait. That was the key. No false moves this time, no near misses. There'd be another performance, Paige was certain of it. The burglar's control would slip another notch. Next time, he'd leave something behind and Paige would find it. He had no name, no description, only his own belief that the phantom he had been hunting for years was real, and now he was certain of it.

1

Getting in was never the problem, especially this time. Grant had the key. Getting out would be just as easy. He had removed the inside lock on the roof door several weeks ago. She rarely, if ever, went up there anymore.

He closed the front door behind him, gently easing it shut, and stopped to let the stillness of the house settle over him. It was like a secret sound, a cloak that he could wrap around himself and disappear, like a shadow vanishing into a web of vaporous light. The silence changed, broke; a car rushed past outside the door and he heard the distant clatter of horses' hoofs from a hackney carriage, the hollow splatter of water dripping slowly from the leaky faucet in the kitchen at the end of the front hallway.

Grant stepped past the living room and toward the kitchen. Her study was to the right, off the living room, a small room lined with bookshelves and a small rosewood desk and chair. The desk sat at a slight angle to the door so she could watch the television in the living room while she went over her bills and notes.

9

He wanted to hear her voice.

On the desk was a combination phone and answering machine. A small red button in one corner blinked frantically, as if the machine itself were crying for help. Grant switched it to "play." His hands were narrow, the fingers, long and delicate like a woman's, covered in elegant black leather gloves. He owned several dozen pairs, bought at various times throughout the city, usually during the holidays. If a pair were ever found, that would make it difficult, actually almost impossible, to trace. He pressed the outgoing-message button. The machine clicked and whirred and then he heard her voice.

"Hello, this is Dr. Weinstein. I'm unable to take your call at the moment but if you leave your name, the time of your call, and a brief message, I'll return your call. If this is an emergency, please try my office. That number is 998-9222. Thank you."

She sounded very much the way she appeared to be, controlled, precise, filled with a kind of exactness that tolerated no emotional ambiguity except, perhaps, that of her patients. It showed in her house—plain white curtains neatly pulled back, window shades exactly halfway down in every room. Magazines neatly stacked in a brass stand beside the living room couch. He pressed the message button. Another voice came on the machine. Grant listened. It was one of her patients, obviously troubled. Psychiatrist's patients were always troubled, she remarked once; a psychologist's patients only had problems. Grant turned the machine back to the "answer" position and the voice disappeared in a sudden squeal.

Grant spent the next half an hour going through her study. He'd done some preliminary searching before but always at night and always restricted. Now he was free to take his time, to sift through her life, to see her as she really was, vulnerable and unguarded. It was the feeling of power he enjoyed, something separate from everything else, a kind of sexual trance. The blood pulsed through his veins, his face became flushed, he could feel the sweat on his skin. He had to consciously slow himself down to keep from rushing forward. As always, there were revelations. Even if he thought he knew everything, there was always something new to be learned about each one.

In one of her desk drawers, for instance, he found an exquisitely bound book of Japanese erotic drawings from the fifteenth century. In that same drawer, he found a brown leather box filled with several dozen gold coins, illegal South African Krugerrands, some still in their plastic after having been shrink wrapped. Grant set the coin box aside and flipped through the book, noticing once again the strange attraction Japanese erotic artists had for outlandish male organs. They were enlarged beyond all physical proportion, cocks as big as a man's arm. The women seemed to ride them in a swoon, legs and bodies twisted into nearly fetal position, the slits in their bodies open like great red wounds. Their sense of perversion, so close to reality yet so grotesque at the same time, was almost irresistible.

He turned a page. There was a picture of a woman being strangled to death with a white silk scarf. Her eyes had become clear white orbs and her hands trembled exotically at her sides. The man rode on her back, forcing her down with one knee.

Grant forced himself to close the book, unable to go on. He'd grown hard looking at the picture, thinking about her, but that wasn't all. His nerves had taken on a sharp edge, a quick fast twitch. His fingers were nimble, and moved with great speed, snapping the book shut, pushing it away from him. He closed his eyes and waited for it to pass. Each time it seemed to take longer and longer.

His hand curled around the book and he ran the palm down the spine. She had a radio on one of the shelves. He switched it on and found the public radio station. Light classical music filled the room. For a few moments, he held the book close to him and swept around the study in a kind of moody dance, losing himself in movement, forgetting for a moment the reason he was there. He stopped suddenly, caught and held by a memory.

Runyon would not have approved of his behavior. Runyon taught him that speed and discipline were what counted on the job. He had three rules and he drilled them into Grant's skull: always know what you wanted, get in fast, get out faster.

But Runyon was gone and he was dancing.

The thought pulled him up abruptly. He was there to steal whatever he could from her. He turned off the radio and returned to her desk.

Beginning with the left side, he went through the contents

11

of each drawer. The doctor was quite frugal. Aside from the house, she owed less than a thousand dollars between several credit cards. A great many of those charges were from book-stores. In a small security box, he found nearly four thousand dollars in cash and her passport. He put the money in his pocket.

Next, he sorted through her investments. There were the fully paid-up IRA accounts, several hundred shares of stock in two large mutual funds, part ownership in an apartment build-ing near Ninth and Bainbridge. He found himself fascinated by her choices, approving her competence.

The afternoon passed quickly. By six-thirty he had collected everything that he wanted from the downstairs. There was the money, the gold coins, and an Edwardian pen-and-ink drawing in a lovely antique wooden frame that he had noticed when he had made his first examination of the house, only a few days after they'd met. He put them all in a brown grocery bag and left it in the kitchen.

After that, he moved upstairs to her bedroom and was surprised to find several condoms in the drawer of her night-stand, each one wrapped in gold foil like an exotic present. Grant sat down on the bed and fingered the tiny packets, feeling just a twinge of sexual fear, a brief sanitary admission of it, wondering how he had missed this particular facet of her, won-dering why she felt compelled to hide it from him when she had shown him so much else.

When they'd first met, she had been standing by herself at the refreshment stand during an intermission at the Academy of Music, the red brick throwback to gentility on Broad Street where orchestras that were passing through on their way to Washington from New York might stop for a night or two to play. He preferred the smaller orchestras, liked chamber music best of all, and never went to see the Philadelphia Orchestra, not with that arrogant Italian at the helm.

She liked Muti, she had told him, but could only listen to so many symphonies before they all started to sound alike. She was drinking a glass of wine, her back to the crowd, but turning every now and then to look at the people. Grant realized that she was looking to see if anyone else caught her eye. The eve-ning was a quality pickup for her and she was making sure that

Grant was the best the place had to offer. It turned out that he was.

He looked different that night. Green contacts darkened his eyes until they were nearly black and he'd rinsed his hair several times with lemon juice to bring out the blond highlights. It was March, and he wore a slightly padded jacket of heavy corduroy that added a few pounds to his thin frame. A slight bit of rouge on his cheeks and he appeared quite happy and prosperous. Looking at himself in the mirror before leaving his apartment, Grant would have said advertising, or a professor of communications arts.

Afterward, they went across the street to the Hershey Hotel. He paid cash for the room and they spent several hours together. That was where he learned about what she liked in bed.

In bed, she gave up all control, seemed to revel in her own submission. It was such a classic transformation that it would have been comical if it weren't for her seriousness. She was a determined slave; acceptance became her great strength. What she liked most was being tied facedown to the bed, hands bound together and tied to the headboard so that her face was pressed into the pillow. She wanted her ankles tied as well, one to each bedpost by a long piece of cord, not quite as tightly as her hands because she liked to move, too.

If she wanted, she could rise up on her knees and look back at him, her features blank except for her eyes, which glimmered in a kind of easy hatred as he would thrust into her, his hands gripping her ass so hard that the surrounding skin would turn white. If it wasn't hard enough she would tell him so, whisper hoarsely what she wanted him to do, demand that he use his fingers to fill the rest of her up. Later, when she brought him to her house, she gave him things to help him do it, all of which she kept in her dresser drawer. The image seemed frozen in his memory, along with so many others.

She went home by herself that first time, remarking that she kept her mornings to herself. Grant didn't mind. While she was in the bathroom, he made an impression of her house key with a piece of modeler's clay that he carried in his pocket.

He remembered that first time with her in such detail because a few days later Runyon, his old teacher, had been killed, a stupid and senseless murder, and then several months later, he discovered that she was seeing someone else, a detective named Patrick Paige. At first, Grant thought that it was no coincidence at all and that the detective had engineered it from the start. The idea was terrifyingly real, that Paige had somehow found him. But soon he realized that Paige was the one who had been found instead. She had never told the detective about Grant; he was her one great secret.

In the same way that Paige was now his.

He learned about Paige by accident. One night he had taken himself out to dinner at a small restaurant, a quiet place just a block from the lunacy of South Street. He was out of sorts and looking for silence. The waitress gave him a table in the back, away from the front room and the bar, brought him a half bottle of wine, took his order, and left him alone. When he finished, he started to walk directly home. At the last moment, he changed his mind and decided to make a slight detour past the doctor's house. He was on the other side of the street, half a block from her door, when he saw Paige. The detective stood beside her and waited while she unlocked the front door.

He wanted to turn and run but forced himself to keep walking, to make sure that it wasn't some kind of illusion. No, it was Paige. In fact, the detective turned to look at Grant just before he stepped inside, an automatic gesture, no more than a passing glance. Grant was in the shadows, away from the streetlight, and Paige couldn't have seen his face anyway. Still, it was frightening and unnerving and Grant hurried away.

The last time he'd been that close to the detective, a lot closer now that he remembered it, Paige had been waiting to arrest him. It had been one of his first jobs, one of a series of practice runs that Runyon had set up for him. Nothing complicated, some small homes in Elkins Park just across the city line. Get in, get out, keep careful track of the time.

He went in through the roof, an open dormer window in the attic, the way he always did in those days, spent less than ten minutes inside, and then started out the same way.

Something stopped him. He moved away from the window quickly, falling back into the darkness of the attic and looked out into the yard. It took a few minutes but Grant saw him. Paige sat in the notch of a tree near the center of the yard, one more shadow among a dozen others. Grant saw the shadow move but only slightly. Grant was impressed. Any cop who could climb a tree and sit there without making a sound had to be pretty good.

Grant left by the front door and added another rule to Runyon's original three.

Never leave the same way you went in.

Runyon had found out Paige's name a few days later. Grant wanted to know something about him. "He's pretty good," Runyon had said. "Stay away from him." As far as Runyon was concerned, that was all Grant needed to know.

That was nearly seven years ago and now the circle had come around again. A look of irritation crossed his face and he continued his search through the bedroom.

He found his second surprise beneath the bed. She'd bought a gun, a .22 automatic with a cheap plastic grip, and hidden it in a cardboard box near her nightstand. He removed the gun and, with his fingertips, pushed the empty box back underneath the bed toward the center, just out of her reach.

The gun was light in his hand, like a toy. Grant disliked guns, had never carried one, and thought them dangerous. Especially ones like this, the kind manufactured for amateurs; a gun made them think they were braver than they really were and that made them dangerous. He removed the clip, slipped it into his pocket, and smoothed down the bed.

What was she going to do with a gun? He had no answer for the question and it annoyed him the same way that Paige's sudden appearance annoyed him. They were unexpected flaws in a plan that he'd worked on for nearly a year and he was uncertain how they might affect it. It was possible they didn't mean anything at all, that they were just bits of chaff blowing through his life.

On the other hand, now that he had decided to leave the city and move his business to Houston, he wasn't certain he wanted to take that chance. Why couldn't she just leave him alone? That was why he'd been so angry and distracted lately.

He was angry right now and getting angrier.

Grant slipped the condoms back into the nightstand and closed the drawer, pulling back from the edge and focusing instead on the work at hand. In the top drawer of the dresser

15

he found what he was looking for, a full-head black leather mask with a silver zipper for a mouth, and hidden below that, next to a dark green travel bag, a small wooden box. From inside the box, he took out an ivory carving and held it up. A man was sodomizing a woman from behind. The woman seemed to be laughing.

Grant closed his hand around the carving and squeezed until he could feel it dig into his skin. He held it like that for a few minutes. When he let go, he noticed that the palm of his hand was bleeding.

He closed the drawer and returned to the kitchen to get something to eat, adding the carving to what he already had in the bag.

From the refrigerator he selected one or two pieces of cold roast beef. Standing up, he ate them with some mustard and a small glass of milk. He read a magazine while he ate. Afterward, he still felt hungry, so he ate a container of coffee yogurt as well.

Grant washed his dishes but made certain to leave the ones in the sink that Julia had put there in the morning. When he was satisfied that everything looked right, he spent a few minutes at the junction box in her basement, making sure he knew the circuit layout so he could work the right sequence in the dark. While he was there, he also found the rest of what he needed, a ball of heavy twine and a hammer. He hefted the hammer, decided that it was the right weight, and took it upstairs to the kitchen and laid it on the counter. He wrapped the head carefully with a dish towel and tied it tightly with the twine.

Then he returned to the bedroom to set her radio alarm clock and to take a small tape recorder from his pocket and place it beneath the bed. While he was there, he also cut the line to her phone. Outside, the street lamps came on, hanging circles of pale light against an orange-colored sky. Grant checked his watch. It was seven-thirty. Unless there was an emergency, another forty-five minutes and she would be home.

Dr. Julia Weinstein left Pennsylvania Hospital at Eighth and Spruce streets and walked the four blocks through Society Hill to her house near the corner of Fourth and Pine. The house was east of the hospital toward the river, a three-story red brick town house built in 1801 that she purchased in 1981 and then spent several years having restored, at least the first two floors. The third would have to wait. By now she felt comfortable with the house. It gave her no surprises.

Like a smooth stone with all the sharp edges rubbed away, she knew its surface, each worn crevice and plane; when she walked into her house, the illusion of certainty made her feel she was in control again. So much of her life seemed out of control these days that the house had become her last refuge.

She walked along the sidewalk with practiced steps, aware that she had been taking the exact same steps for slightly less than ten years now. Each one seemed like an old friend, and she did not bother to think that they were among the few she had acquired over the years. She was in her late thirties with straight brown hair. Her figure hadn't changed much in twenty years except that now her thinness seemed less appealing to her than it once had. She made acquaintances easily; friendships were harder and she had given up working at them.

She crossed Spruce and hurried along through the fading evening light. A block behind her a few customers from the grocery store where she usually shopped were struggling with overloaded bags, anxious to get home. It was a Friday night, time to make dinner. There was some leftover roast beef in the refrigerator and that would do nicely.

The street and sidewalk were littered with paper and dirt. A bit of newspaper caught on the toe of her shoe. She tried to kick it away but it refused to move. It scratched noisily at her shoe and ankle as she walked, like a small angry creature ready to attack her.

She stopped, bent down, and removed the paper, tossing it in the gutter. Everything was filthy everywhere she looked. Philadelphia seemed to attract dirt, she thought. Even New York never looked this dirty.

The weather was warm, the oppressive humidity of summer settling over the city like a rag. Her dress was soaked with perspiration and her hair hung damp along the back of her neck. She would run the air conditioner tonight, she decided.

She climbed the three short steps to her house, worked the

17

key into the door, and stepped inside, staring for a moment out into the street. Then she closed the door behind her and stood quite still in the dark cool hallway.

She thought she heard something move inside the house and the shock of it stopped her breath. It came so suddenly that it was like a hand closing around her throat.

She stood in the hallway, her back against the door and peered into the empty house. One of her hands slithered down the jamb toward the knob, grasped it, and turned slowly. The door opened an inch, letting in a warm jet of night air. A car drove by, scattering the papers on the sidewalk. They clattered against the door as if they, too, wanted to get inside. She turned on the light in the hall. From there, she could see the living room and part of her study. Both were deserted. She waited until her eyes were fully adjusted to the light and looked again. Nothing seemed out of place. A car horn made her jump. She looked into the living room once again and shut the door.

I should have left some lights on this morning, she thought, and dropped her briefcase in the hall. My brain is a sieve these days. Still shaken, she turned on the lights as she made her way through the first floor, the living room, study, and kitchen, and then back again to the study.

Once there, she turned on the answering machine, grew quickly annoyed by the message, and snapped it off instead. The clock next to the machine showed her the time in crisp black numerals. It was 8:19. She laid her briefcase on the desk and went upstairs to change her clothes and turn on the air conditioner to cool her room.

Her bedroom was painted an off-white with rose highlights on the windows, woodwork, and in the master bath. It lent the room a gentle air, she thought, and the color was soft on her eyes. It was like her room in her parents' house in Rochester, soft and serene. She spent her days with people whose problems she was no longer interested in solving, if she ever thought she could. More and more these days, she resented their intrusion into her life. She had her own problems and nobody wanted to help her with them. Maybe she needed a vacation. Maybe she just needed a long bath. She looked at the phone by the bed, wanting to call Grant but afraid to annoy him again. She had called twice that day and left messages on his machine, but he hadn't called back. God she wanted to see him, to feel him inside of her. She touched a finger to her mouth, closed her eyes, and thought she could still taste him on her tongue.

She undressed in front of the mirror, imagining how she must look to his eyes. Her hips were too narrow, she thought, and her breasts were too large for the rest of her. She held each one in her hands, pushing the soft flesh up. They were beginning to sag. She could see the minute stretch lines on each side, like tiny cracks in her skin. There were several small bruises around each nipple and, when she turned slightly, several more across her back. She looked at them and smiled, the memory so close again that she wanted to touch it.

She cupped one breast in her hand and brought the nipple to her lips, bringing her teeth down on it, gently at first, then much harder. The pain spread down across her stomach to her groin. Her legs felt weak and she leaned one shoulder into the wall for support. She lost herself in the pain, stretched out along it like heat pushing through a wire. Her legs felt like they were on fire. She brought two fingers between her legs and rubbed herself, moving the wet folds of flesh slowly back and forth, then harder and faster as the sensation took hold. She screamed into her own skin, and when she finally released the nipple, raking her teeth across it as she pulled it away, the dark skin glistened like wet marble.

She sat down on the floor and sobbed, drawing her breath deeply and holding it until her throat tightened and doing it again until her heart stopped pounding and the pain in her breast was reduced to a gentle throbbing.

God, she thought, turning away from the mirror, I'm as bad as my patients.

The clock on her nightstand read 8:26. Maybe she should take that bath now. She slipped into the bathroom and turned on the water, kneeling down next to the tub to splash some in her face. She ran her wet fingers through her hair, shaking the strands loose as she walked back into the bedroom to turn on some music.

One by one, the lights went out downstairs. The chain reaction climbed up the stairs toward her and plunged the house into darkness. She whirled around and took a few steps toward the open bedroom door. The house remained silent and still as if someone had pulled a shroud over it. She peered down the stairs, hoping to catch a glimpse of something, anything; a ghost wrapped in a shroud would have been better than what she feared.

The radio came on. It screamed at her and she jumped, her heart pounding out of her chest, a sudden intake of breath as sharp as a knife, the skin on her face and hands turning suddenly warm and sticky. The music seemed to grow louder. In her confusion, she reached first for the radio to turn it down, changed her mind, and grabbed for the edge of the door to swing it closed. Her hand reached the knob, holding it tighter and tighter, until she thought her fingers would break. She slammed the door shut.

She turned and slapped at the radio, knocking it off the nightstand. It bounced away from her on the carpet. She got down on her knees and dragged it toward her by the cord, the black box tumbling over and over until it banged into her knee. She yanked hard on the cord. The music died as quickly as the lights.

She grabbed for the phone by the bed and it tumbled off the nightstand. She yanked on the phone and the end of the cord slithered against her leg. It had been cut. She threw the phone against the wall.

She swung one hand across the carpet toward where she'd hidden the tiny gun she'd bought last month. The dealer said it was a .22, a woman's gun, small enough to fit into her purse if she needed it, which she never had. Until now. Her fingers groped for the box.

It was gone. She bent down lower to see. The box was stuck near the center of the bed, well out of her reach. She sprawled on her stomach, using one of her shoes to reach the box. With her arm extended out as far as it would go, she hooked the heel into the box and hauled it toward her. She tossed the shoe away and reached inside. The box was empty.

She looked under the bed for the gun, thinking it had fallen out. There was something else there, near the foot of the bed. A tape recorder. What the hell was a tape recorder doing there? She reached for the recorder and dragged it out.

Someone had turned it on.

She put her head down and screamed the word "No!" The lights in the bedroom went out the moment her lips touched the carpet. She dropped the recorder and pushed herself back against the bed.

When she heard the footfall on the stairs, she got up and threw herself at the door, trying to hold it shut while her fingers fumbled for the lock. Something slammed into the other side of the door and knocked her backward. Her head struck the corner of the bed frame and she sat down hard. She tried frantically to get to her feet but the pain kept her down. When it finally subsided, and her vision cleared, she looked up to see a man standing over her. She sat up as quickly as she could and pushed herself away from him. Her hands groped along the carpet for anything she could use against him. She looked up to see him tilt his head toward her. Without thinking, she reached out with her hand to scratch him but he caught her wrist and squeezed hard. The pain brought flashes of light to her eyes.

He bent closer to her and she saw the side of his face. It was caught briefly in one of the pale white ribbons of light from the street lamp that streamed from the other side of the bedroom curtains. One of them cut a thin line down his face, exposing an eye, a glistening blue orb. The light moved down the bridge of his nose and then to the flat even line of his mouth.

She knew him. The relief of it took her breath away. *I know him.*

"My God," she said, thinking it was some sort of joke, unaware that she was speaking out loud, "it's you." She began to move toward him.

He was holding something in his hand that she couldn't see.

The last moments of her life were crowded with thoughts. They came to her randomly, like bits of wind-blown debris. He had on women's gloves. They were made of smooth black leather that stretched over his wrist. Her eyes shifted. His chest was all white. She realized with a start that he was wearing one of her aprons. It was tied up tight around his neck. He's going to hit me, she thought and she waited for the pain, hungered for it with eyes closed. When the blow never came, she opened

21

her eyes and saw that he held one hand high over his head. As it came down, she saw what it was; a hammer, one end of it covered with a dish towel and tied with twine.

I should scream, she thought next, as he brought the hand down toward her face. Then, realizing it was too late for any of that, she thought, I'm going to die.

Grant brought the hammer down, once, twice, then several more times, so many that he finally lost count.

He sat by her bed in one of the kitchen chairs, careful not to step in the large bloodstain, a dark tear-shaped puddle near the nightstand, and listened to her screams, then the sound of the hammer coming down. When it was over, he rewound the tape and listened again. The sounds had resonance and depth, like something orchestral, that was how he thought of them. They were much better than the tapes he had made in the other apartments when he had turned his anger loose, mesmerized by his own power.

He glanced down at the blood and made another curious discovery.

In the dark it had no color, though it did give off a faint metallic odor. He turned away to look at her. She lay with her head on the pillow, propped up slightly so that her chin rested on her chest, her face turned toward Grant.

Except it was no longer her face. It did not resemble a human face at all. The black leather hood fit snugly over her head and covered her entire face except for her eyes. Grant could barely see them in the room's dreary light. They were swollen and lifeless as they peered out through the eyeholes. Blood smeared down the side of the leather, marking it like some tribal mask.

The hood belonged to her. Grant had taken it that morning. She had used it once or twice, almost always on herself. He had no idea how he was going to use it when he took it, only that he would. He had come to the conclusion that even then he had known what its final use would be.

Grant took the chair and the recorder and left the room. He put the chair back in the kitchen and, after returning the circuit box to its original condition, checked the house one final time. In the study, he made certain that the desk was straight.

22

When he stepped back to look, his elbow struck a small white porcelain vase. He tried to catch it as it fell but it caught the edge of the bottom shelf, tumbled out of his reach, and smashed on the hardwood floor.

The sound was like a flash of current ringing through his veins. Grant spun away from the shattered vase as though it were radioactive, forcing himself out of the room. The urge to destroy was that strong. He felt himself getting caught up in it again, that exhilarating sensation of power and freedom that had overtaken him in the last apartment, the same way it had overtaken him upstairs. He brought the hammer down on her again and again and discovered that he could not stop himself. He didn't want to stop. What finally brought the killing to a halt was simple exhaustion. His muscles weakened and slowed. He remembered letting his arm drop. His hand ached and the muscles that ran along the back of his arm and across his shoulder were numb. But he felt alive. His senses were sharp, marvelously acute, a feeling he hadn't known for years.

But now, standing in her study, the feeling was just as strong, perhaps stronger, a clean white fire that would quickly burn out of control if he let it.

He grabbed the paper bag and was prepared to run from the house when he forced himself to stop. This is your worst enemy, he told himself, this is the thing that will destroy you. The words came to him in Runyon's tired and knowing voice. If you lose control, the voice told him, you lose everything.

When the old man had sent him on one of his first real jobs, he'd stood in a darkened corner of a bedroom and watched a man and woman make love for nearly an hour. They were drunk and it took a long time. He thought they were asleep but something had woken them up, probably his presence in the room. But they were more interested in themselves than the shadowy figure standing just twenty feet away watching them. The woman finally ended up masturbating the man and they rolled over and went back to sleep. Grant waited another half hour before continuing with his work. He remembered that when he got outside, his face and hands felt cold and lifeless to the touch.

That's what he wanted to do now. He stood in the darkened living room and willed his control to return. But ten minutes

23

later the feeling of urgency was still strong. He could no longer stand to be in the house. Grant took one last look around and went out the front in a quick, easy motion, closing the door behind him and walking swiftly away. There were a few people on the street. He blended with them effortlessly until he felt himself vanish in their midst, forgetting as he moved away that he had broken one of his own rules.

2

Paige was at his desk when Cooper brought him the news. It was early afternoon and through the row of windows above the desk he could see the cars already lined up to get on the Ben Franklin Bridge for the short trip back to New Jersey. Four lanes of traffic merged awkwardly into two heading onto the bridge. The day was warm, the sky hazy. Waves of heat rose with the exhaust fumes. In the heat, the city was like an old man dying of emphysema.

There was a knock on one of the metal cabinets that surrounded his desk on two sides and he turned around. Cooper stood there squinting at him. He always squinted and Paige could never figure out why.

"They got a body," Cooper said. He had a piece of paper in his hand. "A town house, Fourth and Pine." Cooper held out the paper for him. Paige took but didn't bother to read it. Instead, he crumpled it up and dropped it on the floor. "That's the address," Cooper said.

Paige swung his feet off the desk. He stood up and felt his heart quicken.

"A name?" he asked.

"Female," Cooper started to answer. But Paige was moving before he could finish. "White," Cooper said as Paige rushed past him. "Didn't get her name," he said but Paige was gone. Cooper picked up the crumpled piece of paper and smoothed it between his fingers before dropping it in the wastebasket on his way out.

Paige drove without stopping, using his horn to force his way through the dozen or more intersections between the Roundhouse—police headquarters—and Pine Street. He pulled out of the parking lot onto Race, made a right turn without looking, and drove down a block, made another right onto Sixth Street and sped up, racing alongside Independence Mall. The Mall was crowded with visitors, out to see the sights or take a stroll on a warm Saturday afternoon. There were lines of tourists at the Liberty Bell. A young couple with a stroller stepped off the curb at Chestnut Street, half a block from the Bell. Paige laid on the horn. The husband looked up wide-eyed and grabbed the stroller, yanking it back on the curb as Paige flashed by. Paige stepped on the accelerator and aimed the car down the center of a one-way street.

His mind was clear and precise; a mechanism connected to the steering wheel and the brakes. A Cadillac stuck its nose out at Sixth and Walnut. Paige hit the horn and swerved to the left. The Cadillac missed him by a yard. He slowed down and rolled through a yellow light at Locust and another one at Spruce. Pine was next.

He turned left at the corner of Sixth and Pine and stopped. The street was blocked by a blue and white police car. Paige held out his shield, the cop nodded and motioned for him to pull over to the side.

Paige parked and walked past the police car. There were barricades up, light blue sawhorses that straddled the street at odd angles. Paige moved slowly, wiping whatever shock he felt from his mind, like clearing a table with a swing of his arm. He kept his feelings off his face as well. A black uniformed official stood out front to keep track of everyone going in and out. Paige was an unfamiliar face. He held up his hand.

"Who's running the job?" Paige asked before the cop had a chance to question him.

"Lieutenant Sloat," he said. The cop hooked his thumbs in his belt.

Paige held up his shield so the black cop could see it. "Tell the lieutenant I know her," Paige said to him.

"Know who?" the black cop asked casually.

"The dead woman," Paige answered.

"Wait one second." The cop stepped into the apartment. Paige glanced briefly at the door. The keyhole was unmarked.

The cop returned. A heavyset detective with curly black hair stood behind him in the doorway.

"You know her?" he asked. Paige nodded. "Let him in. I'll go find the lieutenant."

The black cop shrugged and stepped aside.

Paige followed the detective down the hall toward the stairs in the back of the house. They were going upstairs because that's where she was.

He slowed down as he passed the living room and the study. His mind registered the fact that the room was undisturbed. He saw someone bent over a broken vase on the floor beside the desk and wanted to stop, but the detective in front of him looked back to make sure he didn't linger. Once the lieutenant passed him on, Paige could do what he wanted as long as he didn't get in the way. Until then, he was trespassing. Crime scenes were proprietary by nature. Tourists were not encouraged.

Paige fought to detach himself from his surroundings, from the feel of the apartment, from objects and scenes that were like partially developed photographs, half-remembered, half-imagined. He hadn't been there for two months and it felt now as if he had been someone else. Paige knew what he was doing. *Disengagement* was the word the police psychologist had used. It worked, Paige had learned. He abstracted everything, people, places, memories. Especially those. The past ceased to exist, the present became an elaborate game. He no longer thought about the future. Instead, he concentrated on now.

You think you can keep the game going forever, that's what the psychologist had said to him, but you can't. The past will always catch up with you and then things will happen you're not going to like. No, Paige had told him, those things had already happened to him.

27

As Paige walked behind the detective, he saw some heads turn toward him in recognition. Maybe Sloat thought it was a burglary gone bad. Maybe it was one of the reasons Sloat let him inside. He didn't let the thought get to him. They knew each other in a passing sort of way. Sloat was already a detective in Fishtown when Paige started working there. Paige thought through the brief chronology of his life. He joined the force in 1978, he was assigned to the burglary team, his wife had died, he'd made detective, and now he was walking through the house of a dead woman who until two months ago had been his part-time lover. There seemed to be a certain twisted logic to it. He let his thoughts and memories slip away where they couldn't touch him anymore.

"In the bedroom."

Paige heard Sloat's voice and followed it to the top of the stairs. Sloat stood there with his jacket on, tie undone, both hands in his pockets. He was of average build, maybe a little on the thin side. He had thick brown hair that was combed straight back off his forehead, and he rocked gently on his heels as though Paige had kept him waiting. He didn't bother to shake hands when the detective made it up the short flight of stairs.

"I'm glad you're here," Sloat said and walked toward the bedroom. Sloat stopped him at the door. "How well did you know her?" he asked.

"We saw each other off and on," Paige said. "Not for a few months."

Sloat was making certain he was going to be all right.

"I'll be fine," Paige said. He could hear himself speaking. It sounded like his voice was coming at him through a long tube.

"Okay," Sloat said and opened the door. Paige took it all in at once. The body was in the center of the bed, her arms at her sides. There was something dreadfully wrong with her face. Paige let his eyes move on quickly. All the curtains were open and the shades pulled up to let in the late afternoon light. A line from somewhere came back to him, something he'd read, *certain evidence that cannot be discerned in artificial light shows up quite clearly in daylight.* Paige closed his eyes briefly.

On the right-hand side of the bed, near the nightstand, was a large pool of blood. It was shaped like a tear. A white line snaked through the center of the tear. Paige looked for the phone but it was gone. There were blood spatters on the nightstand and the wall behind it. Paige looked up. They were on the ceiling as well. The bathroom door was open. The closet door next to it was also open. On the opposite wall, several drawers of the dresser had been pulled out.

Paige heard a noise behind him. A crime scene detective stood in the corner just behind the door making a sketch of the room. At his feet was a small cardboard box. Inside he could see the phone and the blood-covered cord. Next to the box was a medium-size grocery bag, folded neatly at the top and stapled to it, a white identification tag.

Paige turned to look at her again and saw the black leather hood. He stared at the blood-stained image until he could disconnect it from Julia Weinstein. She no longer existed. An apparition had taken her place.

"We don't think she was wearing it when she died," Sloat said. "He probably put it on her afterward. Guy's got a strange sense of humor." Sloat moved toward the open bathroom door and the closet just on the other side of it. "We know he touched the mask and the phone and probably a small gun box that we found underneath the bed. Did she own a gun?"

"I don't know," Paige said. He remembered her mentioning to him that she was thinking about buying one. She worked at the hospital. Somebody might think she kept drugs at home. Paige remembered that he had told her he thought it was a good idea and suggested a .22. She could handle it without much trouble and it was fine for close range. He told her he could help her with it once she got it, but she had never asked.

Something at the edge of the tear-shaped pool caught his eye and Paige moved closer to look. It appeared to be a half-moon-shaped indentation along the edge, a shallow scoop taken out of the stain itself. He found it curious and moved closer. There was something else, a small indentation near the foot of the bed, maybe four or five inches square. It was similar to the one in the last apartment. What the hell was it?

He looked at her face once more. Her eyes were open. They stared straight at the bathroom door. The right eye drooped somewhat, as if she had started to doze.

There were bloodstains on the hood around her eyes and

29

some smaller ones on the pillow. She had bled mostly on the floor. He suddenly wanted to see her face behind the mask, to see if it might tell him something. The black leather gleamed like ebony and hid everything.

Not like his wife's face. Hers was so white that her skin looked like polished alabaster, pale and translucent. Except when he saw the blood.

The thought came suddenly out of nowhere and Paige shut it off before it had a chance to grow. He had the urge to flee the room and fought that, too.

"How often did you see her?"

"A few times," Paige said absently. He let reality pull him back down and returned to the indentation on the bed, trying to figure out what had been there.

"When did you see her last?"

"About two months ago," Paige said. "I don't remember the exact date."

"Was she upset by anything?"

"No," Paige said and looked at Sloat. The homicide lieutenant nodded and opened the closet door. "She was always pretty even tempered, at least the few times I saw her."

They had kept their distance, he remembered. They didn't reveal their secrets to each other and they didn't brood in each other's company. The fact that she was dead seemed to glance off of him. She had not been a complication in his life while she was living. He was still waiting to see what she might mean to him now that she was gone.

The detective who had led him into the house entered the bedroom. He began examining her dresser, going systematically through each drawer.

"Did she say anything about any of her patients?" Sloat asked.

"No. She never talked about her work."

"What did she talk about?"

What did she talk about? "Herself," Paige said.

"Did you sleep with her?" the detective asked.

"Jesus, Leiberman, what the hell kind of question is that?" Sloat said.

Paige straightened up. He wasn't certain why the detective had asked the question, but he wasn't going to answer him.

When he turned around, Leiberman was standing next to the dresser.

"I just thought you could tell me about these," Leiberman said. He motioned toward the bottom drawer.

Paige came over to see what the detective was pointing at. Sloat looked over his shoulder.

Inside the drawer was a green travel bag, about the size of a hardcover book but much thicker. Without saying a word, Leiberman opened it up. Nestled at one end of the bag like several small coiled snakes were four or five long pieces of black nylon cord. Most of them had adjustable loops at one end, large enough to fit around someone's wrists and ankles. Leiberman removed a pencil from his pocket and lifted up the cords.

Carefully laid out underneath were a number of interesting items: a large flesh-colored dildo, a smaller silver-colored one, one or two long pieces of cotton cloth, another plastic device with two stiff narrow prongs jutting out from the handle in a small v-shape, one of the prongs studded with what looked like tiny pink bacilli; a tube of lubricant that smelled like ripe strawberries; a black leather hood similar to the one the doctor wore in death except there was no zipper for a mouth. Leiberman pointed to it and then looked at Paige.

"I can't help you with this," Paige said evenly.

"I didn't think so," Leiberman said and put the nylon cords back into the bag. "She had an interesting sex life," he said. "Too bad you weren't part of it."

That was true, Paige thought. They had sex but nothing like this. Paige felt cheated somehow.

"We can check for latents," Sloat said. "But I don't think we'll find any. This stuff looks like it's been washed."

Leiberman closed the bag. "I thought only raccoons did that kind of thing," he said.

Paige ignored him and moved toward the bedroom door and looked back into the room. He had this image of a man standing with his face in the shadows. He was tall and strong, he had to be strong to lift her onto the bed. Paige could not see his hands except that they were covered in leather gloves and holding a small box that he was about to place at the end of the bed.

Who are you? The man offered no answers.

Sloat interrupted his thoughts. "I'd like you to look around."

"If it isn't going to be a problem," Paige said.

"It's not a problem. I hope you can help," Sloat said.

"Did you check the roof?" Paige said.

"Not yet. I didn't see any signs of forced entry. Maybe he knew her."

"Maybe," Paige said.

"But you don't think so?"

"I don't really know," Paige said. "I want to see the roof first."

Julia had left the rooms on the third floor unfinished and they were as Paige remembered them, the walls covered with water stains, the floors littered with dust and bits of paint that had peeled away exposing layers of wallpaper and dirt. The stairs to the roof were in the back of the house.

The lock was missing on the roof door.

Paige took out his gun and pushed the door with the toe of his shoe and let it slam open. Warm air blew against his cheek. He scanned the black tarred roof, his eyes looking for something out of place. When he found nothing, he stepped onto the roof. Then he shut the door behind him and examined it closely.

There were several small scratches on the handle, like tiny rows of teeth. They weren't new; most of them were rusted. There were pry marks on the door jamb as well. Paige felt the first jolt of recognition. He searched the area directly below and found some small slivers of metal and wood. Somebody had tried to come in through the roof but didn't want to break the lock, probably because of the noise. They might've taken the door off its hinges but that would have been risky as well.

So he used a key for the front door and removed the lock for the roof door from the inside in case he needed the roof exit. But where did he get the key?

The obvious answer was from Julia Weinstein.

Paige returned to the second floor and told Sloat what he'd found. He forced himself to stare at the body on the bed when it struck him that if he wanted to spend more time there he would need a chair. He looked at the indentation next to the bed and decided that's what the killer had done. Paige went downstairs to look for a chair with blood on one leg.

He found the chair in the kitchen. One of the other detectives was standing on it, examining the top of the cabinets. Paige could see the ring of blood around the left front leg, like waterlines on a pier. It was clear to him now. After he killed her and placed her on the bed, he sat down beside the bed, the perfect vantage point to admire his work. And do what?

Listen to it, of course. The son of a bitch had taped it. The indentation was from a tape recorder. Paige tried to imagine the sounds and stopped. He didn't want to go that far.

He was left with only one conclusion. This was exactly like the other three break-ins, only this time the violence had been carefully directed. That meant the burglar was getting better at it. And he was starting to enjoy it.

"How's it going?" Paige asked the detective.

"It's not," the detective replied and kept looking.

Paige reached underneath the bottom of the cabinet and ran his fingers down toward the corner until he found her keys, a spare set she had hidden there. Paige discovered them one night while he was getting something to drink. He'd been through each room of her house like that. In her desk, he found a photograph of her and took it. He couldn't help himself. It was just a quick frisk, nothing personal.

There were three keys on the tiny metal ring, he remembered; one for the house, her hospital office, and one for her private office in the medical arts building across the street from the main hospital entrance.

He palmed the keys and slipped them into his jacket pocket. The detective on the chair was still examining the top of the cupboards.

Paige wanted to look at her study before he left. She had a small notebook with a light blue cover where she wrote down her personal engagements. She usually kept it with her regular datebook right on top of the desk. He'd looked through it casually before, now he wanted to go over it in detail.

In the study, the crime scene detective was still collecting

33

shards from the shattered vase. Paige saw Julia's regular date-book but couldn't see her personal one. He moved some papers around, checking for it.

"We haven't gone through that stuff yet," the detective said.

Paige held up his hands. It didn't matter. Her notebook wasn't there. The killer had taken it.

Or Julia had.

That was the thought that moved him out of the study, through the living room, and out the front door. The black cop moved out of his way.

"Short reunion?" the black cop said. Paige ignored him and hurried up the street.

The medical arts building was across the street from the hospital and next to the oldest Jewish cemetery in Philadelphia. It was a gray brick building with a pharmacy on the first floor and some mosaic work around the front door, an unpleasant mélange of turquoise sprinkled with dark blue flecks. Her office was on the third floor. There was one large room in the back, a reception area, coat closet, a window in the large room overlooking the cemetery.

Paige rode the elevator alone to the third floor, remembering that there was a stairwell at the far end of the corridor. If he saw anybody, he could just keep on going. Unless there was somebody waiting in the stairwell. Or in the office. Not this soon, Paige thought. The elevator was big and slow. It ground its way to the third floor and stopped.

The hallway in front of the elevator doors was empty. Paige looked to his left. Empty, too. He moved quickly. Her office was the first door on the right. He fingered the keys. No hesitation, he thought. Paige found the right key and slid it into the lock.

He swung open the door. The small reception room was deserted. Paige strode through it to her office. The door hesitated, then gave way as Paige pushed it open with his foot. The furnishings were sparse, a small desk, a pair of office chairs with black leather seat cushions, an innocuous print on the wall. From the window, Paige could see the pikes on the high wrought-iron fence that surrounded the cemetery next door. A gold Star of David shone on top of one of the faded gravestones.

Paige used a handkerchief to open the desk and went

through it rapidly. He started with the bottom right-hand drawer and worked his way up. The bottom drawer was empty. The next one contained a thermos, a paperback novel, and some empty file folders. The top one was filled with stationery. That left the center drawer. Paige pulled out the drawer and set it on top of the desk. He sifted through it until he found the notebook stuck under a stack of folders. Paige started to slide the center drawer back into place when he saw something behind a box of paper clips.

He took out a small ivory carving and held it in the palm of his hand. The carving was round and slightly larger than a golf ball. He rolled it from one hand to the other, looking at it closely. Two women were making love to each other, their hands and feet bound together. The work was intricate and graphic and Paige found himself fascinated by it. He dropped it into his pocket and slid the center drawer back into place.

Mentally, he was counting the seconds he'd been inside. He hit the count of one hundred and fifty as he shut the office door behind and without looking back walked swiftly toward the exit at the end of the hall. If there was somebody behind him, Paige didn't want to give him a clear glimpse of his face. He was through the door and down the stairs in less than ten seconds and out the front door in less than five. If he counted the elevator ride, the whole thing had taken him just under three minutes.

3

The day after the murder, Grant lay on his bed and dreamed. The exhilaration of it had left him and he spent his time at home in a kind of gluttonous languor, like a big cat that had eaten too much. When dusk finally came, he mixed himself a gin and tonic and moved from the coolness of the house to the patio in the backyard. The patio itself was small and cloistered, surrounded by tall Douglas firs, their branches outstretched, hanging limp and frail like the arms of old women. Grant sat on the stone bench and sipped his drink, watching the night fall all around him in infinitesimal degrees.

His house, an expansive three-story Victorian made of gray and black quarry stone and dark cedar, was in Chestnut Hill, an expensive neighborhood that pushed its way north to City Line, as if trying desperately to get as far away from the rest of Philadelphia as possible. Fairmount Park, a greenbelt that started in Center City and then meandered north, was its western border. The park thinned out along the banks of the Wissahickon Creek until it disappeared completely at the city line. Montgomery County bordered it on the east. The rest of Philadelphia hung beneath it like an empty apron.

The drink made him hungry. He went inside to the kitchen and cooked an omelet with Swiss cheese and fresh mushrooms. Eating seemed to slow him down even more, and afterward he strolled contentedly through the dimly lit house, locking the front door and checking the windows like a watchman making his evening rounds. There were two sets of dead bolts on the front and back doors and pin-set locks on all the windows. Beyond that, he didn't bother. If a burglar wanted to get into the house, he would, and there was very little Grant could do to stop him.

When Grant finished on the first floor, he climbed the wide oak staircase to his bedroom and lay down fully dressed on the bed and closed his eyes.

In the beginning, he had been nothing more than a raggedy kid who liked to sneak around. That was how Runyon had found him in the first place. Why he had picked the old man's house to break into was something of a mystery to him. It was never a mystery to Runyon, who had answered plainly when Grant asked him about it. "These things happen." That was how Grant liked to think of it now.

Grant had no idea what he was looking for when he broke into Runyon's two-story frame house a couple blocks off Germantown Avenue in the Germantown section of the city. The front door was locked and no one was at home, so it seemed the most natural thing in the world to him to slide around back and climb through the open dormer window on the second floor.

It reminded him of his grandfather's home, a place dark and claustrophobic, a place so filled with the past that it seemed to deny the existence of the present, a mausoleum of old furniture and photographs, dusty lace curtains and brittle piles of newspaper, a place that drew him in deep and held him there. He let the mystery of the house consume him.

One of its mysteries, one of the things Grant found amazing, were the three dozen color television sets stacked up in the back bedroom.

The family returned to the house an hour later. Grant heard their voices and hid himself near the top of the stairs in a narrow hall closet that smelled of mothballs and old wool. At first he could barely hear their voices. As they got closer, coming up the stairs, he thought he recognized one as speaking Russian, the other a kind of polyglot of English and Russian. Both voices were male and they sounded strained, as if they were carrying something heavy. In a few minutes, they stopped speaking and returned downstairs. Right after that, the front door slammed shut.

He returned to the room with the television sets. There were two new sets stacked against one wall, each still in its box. While he was looking at one, trying to figure out a way to get it out of the house without being seen, he heard behind him the raw sound of a match scraping on wood. He spun around too quickly, tense, scared, and nearly fell.

There was a flash of light as the man in the doorway lit his cigarette with a match and watched Grant. "So how did you get in here?" the man asked. His accent was uneven; some of the words spoken quite clearly while the others came out as bent and broken noises.

Grant had nothing to say. The man continued to block the doorway, staring at him calmly. As he waited for him to do something, it came to Grant that the man really expected him to answer, that it was a serious question, not something to pass the time before he pounded him into the floor. The man was large enough to do it. He wore a white short-sleeve shirt that showed a pair of thick beefy arms. There was a dark shadow of beard across a heavily rounded chin. He had the calm patience of a born teacher, watching Grant with solemn watery eyes.

"Please," he said. "I would like to know."

"Through the dormer window," Grant said, relaxing slightly. "It was open."

The man shook his head. "That's very high up," he said. It was a neutral observation; he might have said that the earth was round.

"I climbed the tree and swung over. It wasn't that hard."

"You like it up there?" the man asked. "Up in the sky, away from the noise and the people."

"Yes," Grant said. It was something he hadn't known about himself and now realized was true.

"That's good," the man said. Then he said something that took Grant completely by surprise. "May I see you do it again?"

It became a tutorial that lasted years. Runyon made him

work. He learned to take locks apart blindfolded and put them back together one piece at a time until his fingers bled. He learned to separate in seconds serious gems from those that were merely adequate; he knew how to mount jewelry, altering the shape of the metal setting enough so that even the owner wouldn't recognize the stone. He could refine gold and twist silver into delicate thread. He knew the routine of the diamond sellers, what kind of cars they liked to drive, where they ate, where they stayed. He could climb up the side of any building or slip silently through a house filled with sleeping strangers without waking a soul.

Jack Runyon taught him everything, and Grant became his best student.

Grant looked around his bedroom and wondered what Runyon would have said to him now. He could not believe how much he missed the old man. Jack Runyon had been born in Lodz, a Polish Jew named Jacob Ruyowski. He had managed to escape Hitler only to run into Stalin and only survived him through cunning and his quick, clever hands.

He owned his own pawn shop on the fringes of Fishtown and kept it there for thirty years, long after the neighborhood cracked and splintered. For most of those thirty years, Runyon had been the best fence in Philadelphia. In addition to the shop, he had houses all over the city, basements and attics, filled with what he called "my inventory," each one holding different items. The houses belonged to his relatives, an aunt here or an uncle there, cousins everywhere. Runyon could remember the inventory as far back as necessary, and nobody ever argued with his memory. He was so good, somebody said, he could weigh gold with his eyes.

He was a large man with delicate hands, slow to anger, devoid of jealousy and envy. He had no children and no family at home anymore. His wife had died from breast cancer a week after their thirtieth anniversary. He went to ball games in the summer. He liked the ballet. He read a lot of history. He learned to speak a little Spanish, enough to keep up with his new customers. He kept a 12-gauge shotgun mounted beneath the cash register in his pawn shop with an eight-inch jerk wire attached to the trigger that could take out the front of the plywood counter and anyone standing in front of it, which was the idea.

He was sympathetic to his new customers but not overly sentimental about them.

After a few years of work and practice, Runyon put him to work. Grant moved out to Havertown, near the state mental hospital, into a small apartment, less than fifteen minutes from Bryn Mawr and Villanova and the rest of the Main Line.

He worked the big homes carefully, hitting them at the end of the week, Thursday or Friday, when the husbands stayed late and invited their wives into Center City for dinner and drinks. There was a certain sameness to the homes he robbed. They all had heavy copper drain pipes that he used to reach the second-floor balconies. More often than not, there were French doors off the balconies leading into the house, the wood around the panes of glass so old and weak that he could usually pop the glass out whole.

Grant worked alternate weeks, shifting towns every other month. On the odd weeks, he would move out to the rural estates near Chadds Ford. Those were slow jobs. He would spend days scouting until he found a place he liked. Then he would drive back into town and return with his bike. In the spring and summer, the roads were filled with bicyclists and he was just one of dozens with a backpack and a picnic lunch. He could eat by the side of the road and watch the house until he knew the daily routines of its occupants.

When he got inside, he stayed with the jewelry and the money and the gold. Safes were hardly a problem, since most of them were freestanding, the kind he could work with a square piece of steel plate about an inch thick that fit over the knob and spindle. In each corner of the plate there were threaded bolts that fit flush with the safe door. It would take only a few minutes to tighten the bolts and rip the knob and spindle out. The plate went back under his bicycle seat where it looked like just another bike part.

Grant never bothered with what he found in ornate jewelry cases on the dresser tops; that was mostly costume jewelry and of little value. Usually he looked in the bottom of dresser drawers or along the backs of the closet shelves or sometimes underneath the bed in small plain cases that were not supposed to attract any attention. Runyon told Grant he was the best he'd ever seen.

40

Years later, Grant had tried to persuade the old man to quit, to take the money he had and retire. Runyon had looked at him with his sad angry eyes and said, "At my age, where would I go? I don't like the beach. I like my work." A few months later, he was dead. Grant was surprised to see Paige at the cemetery. The detective came alone, paused for a few moments beside the casket. Grant watched him through binoculars from a nearby hill and waited until everyone had left before he went down to the grave. Few had come to the old man's funeral anyway. They were burying a dinosaur. Nobody ever showed up for things like that.

Lying on the bed, drifting through his past, Grant tried to imagine Runyon's sad and tired face. Instead, he saw Julia Weinstein's contorted features covered with the black leather mask. It brought him fully awake. There was something he'd forgotten to do.

The ivory carving was still in the bag. He held it in his hand, weighing it, feeling the sharp edges. Memories flooded through him. For a moment he felt himself losing control, but it returned quickly.

He placed the carving on the second shelf of the living room cabinet with the others and retreated once again to his bedroom.

Grant lay on the bed for a long time, listening to the sound of his own heart. What, he wondered, did Paige dream about?

4

Paige sat alone on the roof of his house, savoring the cool evening and made a list of places and names from Julia Weinstein's notebook. Everything in the notebook was in initials or half words, not a code really, just her own private language.

Paige had some of it figured out. For instance, "A of M" was easy—the Academy of Music. "PP" was even easier—Patrick Paige. As he read through the notebook, his initials appeared less and less frequently; it was as if he were slowly disappearing, bit by bit, until finally, he vanished completely. During the last two months of her life, his initials did not appear at all.

He reached down beside himself and pulled up a can of beer, his third since he'd been home. After he'd gotten the notebook and his car, he'd stopped on South Street and picked up a couple of cheesesteaks for dinner. He'd eaten half of one on the way home, finished the other half standing over the sink to let the grease drip directly into the drain, with a can of beer in his other hand to wash it down. He took the second one and the rest of the six-pack of Rolling Rock from the refrigerator up to the roof with him. He didn't want to stay in the house.

It was close to midnight. He'd been working on her notebook for nearly five hours and was finally making some progress deciphering it.

Paige's house was in Queen Village, a stub of a neighborhood that butted up against I-95, just south of Society Hill. It was a mix of older homes and new condos built on vacant lots and, occasionally, the broken bones of abandoned storefronts. A few years before, the place had been discovered and Paige watched in amazement while the prices went totally berserk.

He liked the house. It was smaller than most of the other houses around him, a simple red brick three-story row house, like thousands of others in the city, but it suited him. The size was right, two bedrooms, a bath, a nice kitchen and a living room with a fireplace, which he'd never used.

The house was at the end of a street with no official name, just a crooked little alley. Someone had given it one—Desolation Row—and painted the name on an adjacent wall. Paige thought it was funny. Next door to his house was an empty lot that everybody used to grow vegetables except for Paige, who didn't have the inclination. He had started to remodel the house but managed to finish only the first floor, his bedroom, and half of the basement.

The roof was where he liked to be. The old owner had raised rabbits on it, and their empty cages, compact little warrens built from two-by-fours and turkey wire, were still standing. They formed a kind of barricade around the narrow rooftop. The guy had even rigged up a string of lights around the top of the cages.

Paige let the bulbs burn out except where he liked to sit, close to the edge, his chair tilted back against the abandoned cages. With the lights on, Paige wondered how the rabbits got any sleep. He finished the rest of the beer and tossed the can in the pile with the others and what was left of the second cheesesteak.

The list he had compiled wasn't as definitive as he'd hoped, but it was a start. As far as he could figure it, she'd begun seeing someone with the initials "EG" about the same time she'd begun dating him. Paige felt a momentary quiver in his ego, remembered the detective's remark about her sex life, and moved on from there. Apparently she'd also been seeing someone else.

43

His initials were "HH" and they appeared on the same page with "A of M." Sometimes she got the initials mixed up, at least that's the way it seemed; "EG" sometimes appeared on the same page with "HH," sometimes on the opposite page. Paige couldn't understand why she had mixed them up as much as she did.

The final entry in the book was less than a week away, a Friday night. For that one, only "HH" and "A of M" appeared along with the time, "8 P.M." Paige planned on being there.

The rest of the notebook was filled with notes to herself, to pick up the laundry, shopping lists, a reminder to tape a television program, nothing that seemed connected with the Academy or the man she was supposed to meet.

Did "EG" and "HH" have to be men? Maybe they were women. Paige thought about the stuff in her dresser drawer and the carving and could not shrug away the thought completely. He tried to picture Julia in bed with another woman but the vision didn't seem right. But then how the hell would he know? Paige tossed the pad of paper on the asphalt roof and opened his fourth can of beer. The ivory carving was downstairs. He'd spent half an hour examining it but could not figure out its significance, if it had any at all. It might have been a curiosity that she'd picked up and that now belonged to him. But why keep it in her office? Why not at home?

He drank quietly for a while, then got up and unscrewed the remaining light bulb, the only way he had to turn it out. The sudden darkness was like a vacuum. It seemed to pull the rest of the city toward him. Paige stepped around the cages to the edge of the roof. He heard music coming at him from the street below, the sound of a car radio played too loud, fading slowly as it drove away. Along the river, he could see the glow of the lights from the ships moored at Penn's Landing.

In the distance, a plane made its final approach to the airport, skimming in over the river. Paige wanted to be on it so he could see the exhaust fires from the refineries on the southern edge of the city. Sometimes, even on the roof, he felt earthbound and sluggish.

Mostly Paige wanted to be out there because that's where *he* was right now. Paige knew it. The feeling had haunted him from the moment he got home. That was why he'd chosen the roof instead of working at the kitchen table, which is what he usually did.

The question he faced now, the one he faced every time he went on the roof, was: will tonight be the night he would make that last jump? Now that he asked the question, he'd have to find out.

He climbed up and walked along the edge of the roof, a little unsteady from the beer but nothing he couldn't handle. From the corner of the house, he looked down into the shadow between the houses. The next house was four feet away, a little less. From that roof, his gaze moved to the next one, and the next and the next, each one a little farther apart than the one before it. Until he came to the last one. The last jump was nearly eight feet across. Paige had never tried it.

Paige jumped. He made the first jump easily and landed on the next roof. Without stopping, he ran across the roof toward the next one. His foot hit the edge of the roof and he leaped into black space. He closed his eyes briefly, felt a surge of exhilaration, then opened them again as he came down on the gravel rooftop.

Paige took the next two roofs the same way. He waited before trying the last one. "Come on," he whispered to himself. "Just one more." The space between the rooftops lay straight ahead of him, a black mouth waiting to swallow him up. If he missed, it was fifty feet down to the street. He crouched down, dug his foot into the gravel and started his run, arms and legs pumping hard. He was going to make it this time.

He pulled up at the last moment, the fear taking hold as it always did, and he stumbled to a halt at the edge of the roof. Fifty feet down he could see the cracked paving and the piles of garbage that lined the narrow alley. Briefly, he saw himself lying there among them.

Tom Ferris and I used to do this crazy shit all the time, he thought. *I* used to do this all the time. The thought came to him like a stray neutron careening through space. But instead of pushing the thoughts away this time, he welcomed them. He opened the doors and let them come, one memory colliding into the next in a chain reaction.

What he remembered was the waiting. Sometimes that was the best part of the night. Ferris stayed on the ground. He was big and always a little overweight and felt awkward climbing around rooftops. Not Paige. Paige loved heights. As a kid, his parents couldn't get him out of the big elm that grew in the yard. When the tree finally died with all the rest of the elms in the neighborhood, Paige watched stoically while they cut it down and then hid in his room and wept.

While Paige watched from above, Ferris slid through the shadows between the buildings. He was as good on the ground as Paige was dodging across rooftops. That's why the partnership worked. Each one had worked what they knew best. It had been the same even when they worked informants. They never had to guess their roles, each one knew instinctively how to play it, how to shift from one tactic to another with just a glance, a shrug of the shoulder.

He liked to think that he and Ferris began together, even though Ferris was already half a decade ahead of him. Sometimes, when he looked back, his life seemed like a series of unexpected explosions, each one pushing him further away from the life he once thought was going to be his.

He had gone to college at Penn State, went into the service, came back and married, got on the force. He managed to slip past the Affirmative Action quotas. His father had pulled in some favors for him. Everybody knew who he was and how he'd gotten in and it made things difficult at first, something he had to work hard to overcome, and maybe that had been part of the old man's plan, too. He rode the streets in Fishtown for a year and a half and then joined the burglary team there with Tom Ferris. A year after that, the explosions came one right after the other and his life seemed to blow away. Connie was killed, then Tom Ferris killed the man who did it, Paige became a detective, his father died and left him the old house.

His mother wrote him from Israel, where she lived and taught school, and said she would not be coming home for the funeral. She had married Paige's father when she was fresh from Girls' High and stayed with him for twenty-five years. Their religious differences were never a problem. At first. Then they became overwhelming. His father's true religion was politics and he always managed to find an excuse not to be around when she lit the Friday candles or when she needed a ride to services. So, when Paige graduated from Penn State, she divorced his father and moved to Israel.

She had slipped out of his father's grasp but was still so afraid of his reach that she would not risk coming back for his funeral, for fear, she wrote Paige, that he might somehow change his mind and come back from the dead to find her.

His father's funeral was an event among the politicians in the city, a charmingly overbearing piece of entertainment not to be avoided. His father would have enjoyed it. Paige did his best to see it through his eyes and found that he actually enjoyed himself when he did. The old man must have known something.

Now he had to deal with another kind of death. Why murder Julia Weinstein? It could have been a warning for Paige but he never seriously believed it. That put the emphasis in the wrong place. It assumed that the burglar's fury was controlled by outside forces, and Paige did not believe that. The burglar had somehow chosen the moment to let loose of his control. Or it had been a combination of causes, a mixture of opportunity and motive that might never be repeated. That was why it would be so hard to catch him. Unless it happened again, the man would sink back into the void. Paige would be left once again with nothing.

He wanted to get to it. He would start in the morning with the Academy of Music to see if he could find somebody who remembered seeing her with either of the two people whose initials appeared in her notebook.

Paige sat down on the edge of the roof. A breeze cut through the darkness and he shivered as it passed over the skin of his arms. His hands were slippery with sweat and the hair stuck to the back of his neck. Paige wiped his hands on his pants, closed his eyes, and drank in the silence.

Waiting.

The images came suddenly, the way they always did. He saw Julia Weinstein's battered face and then Connie's and he remembered everything at once. His breath swelled inside of him and he felt as if a cold hand were pressing against his chest, sinking through his skin and freezing the air in his lungs. His brain seemed too small to contain everything.

When the feeling came over him like this, Paige knew

enough not to fight it. He pulled all the bad things he could remember about her death toward him in a dark and cold embrace, and when they were close and he could see them and touch them and smell them, he would begin to kill them one by one and they would slip away again.

But not here. He opened his eyes. He needed a place to go. Paige returned to his own roof, taking the jumps at a slow easy pace this time.

Downstairs he slipped on his light blue jacket and tucked his gun into the right-hand pocket. He picked up his car keys and locked the front door behind him. The street in front of the apartment was empty. Paige got in his car and headed for the expressway.

He drove north on the Schuylkill, comfortable inside the car, the wind cutting across his face through the open window. The motion slowed him down. He willed his mind blank. The only feeling he had left by the time he pulled off the expressway onto the Wissahickon was the mechanical thrust of hands and feet, shifting and accelerating.

He drove for more than a mile until he reached the street, turned right, drove three more blocks, slowed the car down, still foolishly afraid that somehow he might have forgotten which house but, no, it was still there, on the left in the middle of the block, set back behind the two big oaks that seemed to hide it in a special kind of darkness.

Paige pulled over, close to the curb. Since he'd been there last, the lawn had been cut, some of the bushes near the high spiked metal fence had been trimmed. When he and Connie had lived there, he didn't want any shrubs in the front, only some flower beds, maybe just some ivy, but she had persisted, saying the yard looked too empty without something alongside the walk.

He had the first-floor windows boarded up and the doors double-locked, mostly to keep the neighborhood kids out. A window had been broken on the second floor, in the back bedroom that had belonged to them.

A light went on in the house on the other side of the street. He glanced at it, saw a curtain open and flutter shut. The neighborhood had grown more wary since he had lived in it. There were Neighborhood Watch signs everywhere, and strangers were no longer ignored. Paige closed his eyes and let the empty feeling inside take him away.

The memories welcomed him back. It was Christmas when Connie died, fresh snow had fallen, the first time it had snowed on Christmas for years that he could remember. He left a trail of footsteps behind him up the walk as he carried an armful of presents to the front door. Rows of colored lights sparkled all around the porch. His father had one of the city's road crews put them up and Paige had little to say about it. The front door was locked. Paige thought it was strange, but instead of knocking, he went around to the backdoor.

The backdoor was open. There was a pot boiling on the stove, he could see the steam rising from it through the glass. But he couldn't see Connie. Maybe she had gone upstairs for something. He stepped inside, put his packages down on the table, and went to the stove.

Brussels sprouts. She was cooking Brussels sprouts and the water had nearly boiled away. A feeling of alarm swept over him. He wanted to run through the house to find her, to make certain she was all right. Maybe she was upstairs on the phone and had forgotten about them. There was a phone next to the refrigerator. He picked up the receiver, heard the dial tone like a warning siren in his ear, and set it back quietly in its cradle.

Before heading upstairs, Paige turned off the stove.

In the living room, the ironing board was tipped over against the coffee table. The iron had burned a hole in the carpet. It smoldered in the middle of the floor and Paige wanted to scream. He walked like a tin man, keeping himself so rigid that he thought his bones would snap. He waited until the pounding in his head dimmed and walked toward the stairs, gun at his side, the lights of the Christmas tree blinking furiously in his wake.

He heard something from the top of the stairs, a clatter that came and went like the sound of footsteps echoing through a tunnel. At the top of the stairs, he hesitated, then made his way toward their bedroom at the end of the hall. The door was partially open.

He saw her leg first and pressed himself against the wall because he was afraid right then to go any farther, to see anything more than what he had already seen. Her leg was twisted

49

at an odd angle, inward, the heel tucked up against the sole of her other foot.

Paige thought he might be sick and breathed through his mouth, hot air fanning out across the skin of his hands. He stepped closer and pushed the door open.

There was blood on the ceiling. His eyes went there first and he saw the splatter, a thin red wave running up from the top of the window curtains halfway across the ceiling. When he looked down, he realized she was naked and that he couldn't see her face because of the blood and because someone had smashed it beyond recognition.

After that, the images came very fast. He ran outside and threw up in the yard while white snowflakes fluttered all around him, landing like crisp white angels on his hands and face. Then he sat down and sobbed until he felt numb and empty and alone and by that time his neighbor had somehow seen him and was standing over him and Paige told him to call the police and he was still there in the snow when the first cars began to pull up. Paige saw his father get out of one and found that he couldn't speak and felt relief that he had gone mute.

Time and images contract now and congeal into a single moment. His fists are like hammers, pounding into one of his snitches, beating him, breaking him. Paige doesn't know which one, can't remember his face, chooses instead not to see it and doesn't care. His voice follows each blow. It is the voice of a madman.

Tell me who did it. Tell me or I'll kill you. Tell me who did it to her or I'll break your fucking neck.

Then Ferris is there, pulling him off, yelling at him to stop, asking him if he's crazy. Paige stands numb and mute, retreats into silence because he doesn't want to tell him the truth.

A month later, Tom Ferris shot the man who killed his wife, a petty thief and junkie by the name of Sonny Ray, shot him three times, Ferris told him, once in the kidney, twice in the chest and watched him tumble down half a flight of stairs before he shot him a fourth time because he wanted to make sure the little greaser stayed down.

His father attended Sonny Ray's funeral. There were few other mourners in the little ghetto church besides his father, and he hadn't exactly come to mourn. He marched up the aisle toward the open casket with half a dozen cops behind him. When he got to Sonny Ray, he leaned down and spit in the dead man's face, turned defiantly to see who might challenge him, and when no one bothered, he did it once more and marched back out with his teeth clenched.

Six months later, his father was dead and the house was boarded up but not sold, and Paige came there whenever he needed.

A patrol car pulled up behind him. Paige watched it in the rearview mirror. The officer inside was bent over the radio, calling in Paige's license number. Paige decided to save him some trouble. He held his shield out the window so the cop could put his search beam on it. After a minute or so, the cop got out and walked over to the car. He was young and his voice was filled with relief.

"We got a call about a suspicious car," he told Paige. "You need any help?"

"No, I just stopped for a minute. I was tired. I'm all right now."

A light came on over the front door in the house across the street and a man stepped out on the porch to watch them. Paige thought his name was Kaufman but that was all he could remember.

The Kaufmans had moved in after Paige had left. Another five minutes and half the neighborhood would be out on their steps, wondering what all the commotion was about.

"What should I tell him?" the cop asked.

"Tell them I was looking for a stolen car," Paige said. "That way everybody will sleep better."

"Why aren't you home with the wife and kids?" the cop asked him.

Paige started the car. The cop stepped back so Paige could pull out.

"Don't have any," Paige said.

"Too bad," the cop said. "You can't beat it."

"So I've heard," Paige said. It was an easy answer. Somewhere on the way back, the thought came to him that he'd just about run out of them.

5

Paige was at the Academy of Music business office fifteen minutes before it opened. He brought coffee and a bag of glazed donuts with him and ate breakfast in his car. The coffee was hot and slightly bitter. After a few minutes, he could feel the caffeine bite into his bloodstream.

He ate two of the donuts and read the *Inquirer* and tried to keep the paper from clinging to his sticky fingers as he flipped the pages. The murder made the front page of the Metro section. They had her picture from her hospital identification card. She appeared cool and professional, the way she looked most of the time. That was how she had been for him; that was how he had been for her. They had sex but no passion; she had saved her passion for someone else. He looked at her picture again and noticed something odd about her eyes, something he hadn't really seen before.

He took out the small color photograph, the one he had taken from her desk, and compared it to the black-and-white newspaper photo. There was an interesting difference between the two pictures. The color photo had muted the intensity of her eyes; the contrast of the black and white brought it out, focused it clearly. Paige saw what he had missed when she was alive, the depth of her secretiveness. His own lack of interest in her appalled him. I might as well have been asleep, he thought.

An older woman in a light blue summer dress and carrying a large straw purse turned the corner at Locust and fumbled with her keys at the office door. Her hair was grayish blond and combed up off the back of her neck. Paige poured the rest of his coffee out on the street and followed her inside.

At first, she seemed to regard him as some sort of predatory invader and refused to speak to him until she had straightened out her desk to get ready for another day. Her name plate said she was Mrs. Alice King. Next to her name was a small ceramic statue, a cartoon couple locked in a comical embrace. The caption read GRANDMOTHERS LOVE DIRTY OLD MEN.

"Now," she said when she finished, "how may I help you?" She pronounced the words precisely, with just the right inflection, and clicked her nails together when she spoke, emphasizing each syllable. Her nails were the color of arterial blood. Paige took out his shield and held it up for her to see. She nodded her approval.

"I need to speak to your ushers," he said. "Also the people who work the box office."

At first, she seemed baffled by the request, then concerned.

"No one's done anything wrong," Paige said quietly. "I'm just looking for possible witnesses."

"To what?" Mrs. King asked, obviously interested and wanting to be let in on the secret.

"Anyone who might remember seeing this woman at one of your concerts." Paige held up the small color photograph. Mrs. King leaned across the desk to look at it more carefully.

"What did she do?"

"She was murdered," Paige said and put it away.

Mrs. King looked more intrigued than alarmed, as if she were trying to figure out exactly what getting murdered might entail. Paige felt himself growing impatient with her, wondering just how much work it was going to take to get what he wanted. A badge didn't always do it for the average citizen these days, you had to work for your information. You had to give them the details, show the pictures, pretend it was television, or they didn't think it was important enough to get excited about. Without a show, they wouldn't waste their time. Paige didn't want to give her a show. He wanted this to be strictly low-profile.

"Can I speak to the manager?" he asked.

Mrs. King shrugged. "He called in sick and won't be here until tomorrow." She gazed at Paige through her considerable lashes, sizing him up. "Let me see that picture again," she said. He handed it over.

Show time.

Twenty minutes later, he emerged with a list of the eleven names and addresses of the ushers who had worked the concerts Julia Weinstein had attended. Paige decided to start with the ushers first; the person he needed to see at the box office would be there later in the afternoon. Most of the ushers lived in Center City, two were Penn students and there were two more in Jenkintown, nothing too far away. If he hustled, he could be back by noon.

By noon, Paige had finished with everybody in Center City. The two Penn students were out. He left his card with his home phone number on it. Nobody remembered Julia Weinstein or her date. Only one remembered her as the dead woman whose picture they'd seen on television. A few looked at Paige as if he'd lost his mind. They couldn't remember what they had for breakfast, let alone somebody they handed a program to a month ago. Paige expected the same results from the students when they called back.

He drove out Broad Street to Elkins Park, where he met with the same blank faces, the same puzzled stares, the same apologies. Jenkintown was the same. Nobody remembered Julia Weinstein. She had ceased to exist. Paige stopped at a Wendy's and ate a hamburger before he drove back home to see if there were any messages for him from the students. One had called. So had Tom Ferris. Paige listened briefly to the detective's beery squawk and shut off his answering machine. Ferris wanted to see him and asked Paige to call.

The student who called didn't remember Julia Weinstein, either. Paige took a chance and dropped by to see the other one. She was a Thai medical student and was busy eating her lunch, a salad made from rice, red peppers, and shredded pieces of chicken that she held together between her fingers and dipped in a thick greenish paste. Paige had never seen anything like it. She was short and homely and very serious; she studied while she ate. An anatomy book lay open on the table next to her plate, an illustration showing the muscles of the upper back. They looked like overlapping brush strokes spread across the shoulder blades. She seemed irritated by his presence.

He held up the photograph. She stared at it and shook her head. He asked her again, in a different way. She told him that she could not remember the woman at all. Paige asked her what her lunch tasted like.

"Very hot," she said in her clipped singsong voice. "I doubt you would like it at all."

Paige parked on Broad Street and walked up the steps to the main entrance of the Academy. The box office was right inside the door. He wanted to avoid Mrs. King and her curiosity again. The man at the box office was named Dickens. He was bald and cheerful and wore a crisp white shirt and tie and white cotton gloves. Paige introduced himself and slid Julia Weinstein's picture across the counter to him.

He looked at it carefully and said, "Yes, I remember her. I was so sorry when I read about her in the paper. The name struck me right off. She picked up her tickets here before each performance. That's how I remember."

"Do you remember if there was anyone with her?"

"Not really," Dickens said. "But there must have been someone, because she always bought two tickets. I just don't remember ever seeing them. There's usually quite a large crowd here before a performance. It's hard to see anybody."

"Did she say anything about a friend?"

"She might have but I don't remember it right now."

"What about the concert on Friday?" Paige looked up at the poster next to the box office. "The Cleveland Symphony."

"There are still some seats available," Dickens told him.

"Are you holding tickets for her?"

"Oh, I see," Dickens said brightly and checked the rack behind him. "Yes, we are." He held up two pink tickets.

"If anyone asks about them, I want you to get their name and give me a call. Are you working the rest of the week?"

"Every day except Wednesday."

"Tell whoever's working that day what I said, okay?" Paige gave Dickens his card and said that if he remembered anything more about Julia Weinstein to call him at home or leave a message at his office. Just leave his name and a number to reach him, that was all, Paige would know what it was about. "What time do people usually start showing up?"

"For the concerts? Oh, I'd say seven or seven-thirty. Probably closer to seven for this one. People like to get here early for the symphony. Do you want a ticket?"

"Not right now. What happens if nobody claims her tickets before the concert?"

"Nothing. They're hers. If she calls and asks us to sell them, she gets a refund but most of the time we just throw them away. I don't know what to do now. We don't have any rules for murdered people, at least none that I know about." Dickens stopped and shook his head slowly. "What am I saying?" he asked suddenly. "I forgot. I'm sorry."

Which, Paige thought, makes you no different from anybody else today.

Paige walked a block to the newsstand at Walnut and Broad, across the street from the old Bellevue Stratford Hotel, and tried to buy a pack of cigarettes. It had been over ten years since he smoked. He'd quit just before joining the department.

He had no idea what he was going to do with them but wanted to buy a pack anyway, just to hold them; it seemed like a harmless impulse. Now he couldn't decide which kind to buy. Three or four people waited impatiently behind him. The guy in the newsstand told Paige to buy a pack or get the hell out of the way.

"You don't look like no smoker to me, pal," the guy said to Paige. He spoke with a cigarette hanging from his lip, his head tilted back, and tried unsuccessfully to keep the smoke out of his rheumy eyes. "Forget it. It ain't worth it, believe me."

"What do I look like?" Paige asked. He waited for the punch line.

The guy started to cough. "You look like a cop," he said, spraying smoke and spit with each word. "You act like one, too."

"What if I said I was a doctor?"

The guy looked him up and down. "Not in that suit you ain't," he said.

Paige laughed and bought a pack of gum instead. He sat down on the front steps of the Academy of Music and chewed a piece. Across the street to the left was a health food store. To his right was the Hershey Hotel.

Paige stood up suddenly, realizing at once what his mistake had been, and started across Broad Street before he had it completely thought out. A horn blared. Paige stopped to let the car pass.

Julia's notes hadn't made sense to him because he hadn't read them right.

"HH" wasn't a person at all. It was a hotel.

6

Grant was at his Broad Street
bank in the morning to drop off the coins and the cash in his
safety-deposit box. He might have gone to a bank closer to his
home—he had at least four different accounts scattered
throughout the city—but he had something to do at the library
later and thought he might eat a late lunch at a new Italian
restaurant in Center City that he'd read about.

The bank clerk verified his signature and led him to a
cubicle. Grant waited while the box was brought to him.

"I'll wait outside," the clerk said. She was a young woman
who smiled too much, Grant thought.

"This may take several minutes."

"No problem," she said and stepped away.

Grant reached into his briefcase and took out the Krugerrands, the cash, and a calculator. He counted the bills once
more and then pulled back the lid of the steel deposit box.

Two thirds of the box was filled with cash. At one end was
another steel box. Grant opened that and removed a small
ledger book and turned to the fourth page. He took out that
morning's *Wall Street Journal* from his briefcase and turned to

the gold prices, up twenty-six cents an ounce. Grant counted the coins again and put them in the box.

Grant didn't care all that much for gold. It was bulky and unstable and the market for it was hamstrung with speculators and regulations. But right now he needed all the money he could get, and while it might be difficult selling the illegal coins, he was certain he could get rid of them quickly if he needed to, especially in Texas.

Runyon liked gold; Grant liked cash. He had nearly one hundred thousand dollars in cash in front of him, close to half a million between all four deposit boxes. He marked down the new cash deposit in the ledger and counted up the total again.

It wasn't enough.

His expenses in Dallas were going to be astronomical because he planned on not working for the first two years while he settled into his new surroundings. To begin with, there were the leases on his house and office in Philadelphia. Both had nearly six more months to go, and he had decided to let them run out to help muddy any trail he might leave on his way south.

Things were expensive in Texas, especially if he wanted to move into the right circles. He would need to find a house in a good neighborhood, and that right there would cost him close to two hundred thousand dollars for an extended lease.

Then there were the usual problems, a car, an office, new clothes, a whole range of expenses necessary to introduce himself to the people he was going to rob later on. He liked stealing from people on a first-name basis.

He needed more money. Not a lot, a hundred thousand might do it. Peterson, the man who sold his goods for him, was coming back from a trip to the Midwest in another day or so, and Grant expected to make up some of that from those receipts even with Peterson's commission. Over the last several months, he had pulled the best pieces he could find and given them to Peterson on a regular basis. So far, the dealer had made seven trips, three to Chicago, one to Detroit, one to Cleveland, and two to Atlanta.

There wasn't much left to sell except Julia's small antique picture and frame, and Grant decided he was going to keep that for himself. A reminder to not let himself get involved like that again. His arm still ached from the other night, the one that brought the hammer down. Or maybe, he thought, it was just a kind of phantom pain, the way that amputees feel limbs that no longer belong to them.

Grant didn't want to think about her anymore. The picture was in his briefcase; he would drop it at his office later.

He put everything back into the deposit box, closed the lid, and signaled for the clerk to take it away. One more errand to do before lunch, a short visit to the library. It was a minor thing, a nagging twitch in the back of his mind.

He remembered that there was something else about Paige, some incident he knew he should remember but couldn't. It seemed important that he should.

His work at the library took him much longer than expected, well past his lunch reservation. It was nearly three when he found what he wanted. He was alone except for an elderly woman who read *The New York Times* with heavy glasses.

PATROLMAN'S WIFE FOUND MURDERED, the headline read, and there was a picture of the house and an identification card photo of Paige with it. The detective seemed so young that as Grant studied the picture, he wondered why the face seemed so strangely familiar. Of course, Grant had seen him recently, that was part of it, but he thought there had to be more to his feelings than just that. He wondered if Paige thought history was now in the process of repeating itself. First his wife, now Julia. Grant found the idea intriguing. He made a copy of the article and looked further. In a new reel, an article said that the murderer had been shot and killed by another cop. Grant made a copy of that as well, rewound the reel, and turned off the machine.

He stopped there. It was already too late for lunch and he was getting hungry. He looked at his reflection in the glass and then held up the copy with the detective's old picture on it. Grant stared hard at it and laughed out loud.

They looked enough alike, they could have been brothers.

Not twins, no, but definitely brothers.

7

The lobby of the Hershey was a canyon of white, flanked by a narrow wedge of an escalator that rose to the second-floor function rooms. Light poured in through the sloping front windows, filling every corner. It was bright and airy and vaguely oppressive, Paige thought. The sun beat down through the greenish colored glass, covering everything with an unnatural and uncomfortable glare. It was like being trapped on the surface of some alien distant moon where night might never come. He pursued his own shadow across the floor toward the reception desk at the rear of the lobby, where he got lucky.

The man he needed to talk to was the assistant manager. His name was Franklin Hughes and he was having a late breakfast in the hotel coffee shop. One of the desk people escorted Paige there and pointed him out. Paige saw him in the back of the room, a black man in a gray three-piece suit. He was talking with one of the waitresses. They were laughing.

Paige waited until they stopped laughing and walked over to the booth. The waitress left them alone.

"Mr. Hughes?" Paige asked.

"That's right," Hughes said. He looked at Paige for a moment and motioned for him to sit down.

"I was going to pay those tickets," he said with a grin. "Honest." Hughes seemed to be enjoying himself, Paige thought, almost as if he knew what was coming next and decided it might be an interesting way to perk up a dull day. He noticed that Hughes wore a large gold Penn State class ring on his finger.

"This isn't about parking tickets," Paige said.

The smile never left the man's face. "Didn't think it was," he said. "They don't usually send detectives around to tell you that your meter expired."

"How'd you know I was a detective?"

"I grew up in Philadelphia," Hughes said. "Besides, somebody from the front desk phoned Winona at the cash register over there. She told Cindy, Cindy told me. That's what we were laughing about when you walked up. That bother you any?"

Paige shook his head. "Not if you can help me."

"I don't know if I can or not. You haven't told me what it is you're after. I'll just assume it isn't me."

Paige put Julia Weinstein's picture on the table, pressing it forward with the tips of his fingers.

"Oh, yeah," Hughes said after a minute. "I wondered when this was going to come around." He didn't sound surprised, only slightly curious.

"You remember her?" Paige asked.

"I remembered her the minute I saw her in the paper this morning." He drank some coffee and lit a cigarette, a menthol. "And here you are. What do you want to know?"

Paige gave him the dates from her notebooks, the ones marked "HH," and Hughes nodded after each except for one back in April. "Vacation," he said. "I wasn't working, so I don't know that one. But the others, she was here."

"Why'd you remember her?" Paige had a small notebook out and began writing in it. "You must get a lot of people in here."

"Because she was something of a regular," Hughes said. "We don't have that many regulars."

"Do you remember the man she was with?"

"Stand up," Hughes said. Paige slid out of the booth and waited while Hughes looked him over. "About your height but

62

a little heavier. Chunky, I'd say. Short hair, light colored, kind of brownish blond."

"Eyes?"

"Don't remember."

"Light or dark."

Hughes thought for a moment. "I'd have to guess dark. If they'd been blue or gray, I'd have remembered that."

"How was he dressed?"

"Casual," Hughes said. "Sport coat, slacks, no tie. Stylish but nothing too radical."

"Accent?"

"If he had one he lost it. That's all I remember."

"Anybody else talk to him?"

"Not that I know about. I can ask. I can also give you the room numbers and let you look through lost and found, see if he left something behind."

"What name did they register with?"

"Smith or Jones," he said. "What did you expect?"

"Did he have a car?"

Hughes shook his head. He seemed disappointed by Paige's questions.

Paige stopped writing. "Why haven't you reported any of this?"

Hughes asked him a question instead. "You from around here?"

The question broke Paige's line of thought. It took him a minute to answer.

"Mount Airy," Paige said. "Long time ago."

Hughes appeared to consider that for a moment, finally deciding that he wasn't that impressed. "North Broad," Hughes said. "Long time ago." He twisted the ring around his finger. The stone was red, so dark that it seemed oblivious to the light. "This makes me a success. Most white folks look at this and they get all relaxed and friendly. I went to college, I'm not going to steal their lunch, I'm safe. You can see it in their faces. It happens." Hughes drank some more coffee. When he spoke again, all traces of amusement were gone. "Except cops. With cops, I'm just a nigger in a suit. You understand what I'm saying?"

Unfortunately, Paige did. He nodded.

"Then I don't have to explain anything to you, do I?"

"No," Paige said.

"You want a cup of coffee?" Hughes asked.

"Sure," Paige said. Hughes caught the eye of the waitress and pointed first to Paige and then to his coffee cup. "How long have you been doing this?" Paige asked.

"Ten years."

The waitress brought the coffee and poured it for Paige. He emptied half a sugar pack into it and stirred.

"It's a funny thing," Hughes said. "Most folks think hotel people are blind. They figure that we just won't look, that it wouldn't be good for business, catching people doing things in hotels. Doesn't matter how smart they are or rich or anything, they really believe it. I've seen people screwing in elevators, trying to hide toilet seats in their bags. One guy tried to bring a sheep into his room, walked it right in through the lobby. Swore up and down it was a poodle and expected me to believe him. Got insulted when I told him we didn't allow poodles in our rooms, either."

Paige listened, keeping his expression neutral.

"But we *see* everything," Hughes continued. His voice lost a little of its polish. "People think they're getting away with something but they ain't getting away with *nothing*, you understand what I'm saying?"

"No," Paige said, just to see what effect it might have. None as far as he could tell.

"Doesn't matter," Hughes said. "You're from Mount Airy, what the hell do you know?" The manager smiled at him, a warm, easy, confident smile, the same one Paige's father wore when he was out talking up the voters before an election day.

"The guy was here before," Hughes said. "About six months ago. He looked different, a little thinner, darker hair." Hughes held up his hand to head off Paige's question. "It was Jones that time, too. How do you like that?"

"Who was he with?"

Hughes stuck a large finger in the middle of Julia Weinstein's face. "Not her," he said.

"You remember what the other woman looked like?" To remember anything accurately and in detail after more than a few weeks was almost impossible for anybody who wasn't trained for it. A few months was hoping for a miracle.

"She was tall, had black hair," Hughes said with a grin. "She was rich and she was married."

"How'd you know she was rich?" Paige said. "Or married?"

"One of the maids got a good look at her ring, said it was so big it put mine to shame." He fluttered his huge hand in the air.

"Might have been fake," Paige said, almost automatically. He was looking for a connection between the two women but couldn't see one.

"Might have been," Hughes said. "But that doesn't explain why she hid in the bathroom when the maid came in to turn down the bed. She said the woman hopped out of the bed like her ass was on fire, ran straight for the john."

"What did he do?"

"She wasn't looking at him," Hughes said. "She was too busy checking out the woman running her ass across the room. She said she dropped the mints on the dresser and got the hell out of there."

"That's when she saw the ring."

Hughes smiled like Paige had just guessed his weight.

"That's right. On the dresser, right next to the TV." The manager cleared his throat. "Now why do you suppose a woman like that would run away from a maid?"

"Because she didn't want anybody to see her face," Paige said.

"Because she was either well known or married," Hughes said. "Maybe she was well known, I don't know. But I do know she was married, definitely married." He leaned back in the booth and spoke judiciously, as if he'd been studying the problem for years. "Married women always take off their rings before they get into bed with a strange guy. Makes them feel like they're somebody else. Cheating doesn't seem so bad if somebody else is doing it."

"Was she like that?" he asked and pointed to Julia's picture.

The manager knew what he was getting at. "You mean, was she trying to hide the fact that she was here?" Hughes asked. "In a different kind of way. She didn't draw attention to herself, didn't hang around the desk making small talk. She was quiet, didn't act nervous at all. He was the same way, quiet, didn't talk a lot. People who don't say much tend to blend into the background. The only reason I remembered *him* was because I remembered *her*, you understand what I'm saying?"

Paige picked up the picture and stared at it until her face became unrecognizable to him. The woman wanted sex without entanglement. Or even without identity. That was another reason she used initials in her notebook.

Why did the burglar choose these women? Was it because he knew they would keep him a secret no matter what happened? That would be very important if he robbed them later. Then why kill Julia? Was it because he was going crazy or was there another reason? Were the other break-ins just a diversion? For what?

Paige had to find the married woman.

Police headquarters was called the Roundhouse because it *was* round. It had been built in the days when police departments were gearing up for full-scale revolution, and it resembled a medieval fortress. Paige thought that it needed a few extra touches—catapults, maybe, vats of burning oil to dump on the peasants—and the resemblance would have been complete. He might have suggested it but was afraid someone would take him seriously.

Tom Ferris wasn't at his desk. When Paige asked where he was, a sergeant told him politely that the detective was taking some personal time. He wondered if Ferris was drinking again.

Of course he was drinking again. Paige tried to remember when he wasn't drinking. Five years ago? Ten? Hell, he'd been drinking before Paige was even around. Ferris was a functional drunk, a lot like his father. That's probably where he learned it, Paige thought.

It was just as well. Paige wanted to be left alone with the business at hand. If Ferris were around, he'd want to know about it, and Paige didn't want to tell him, not just yet. He was going on the assumption that the hotel manager was correct about when the married woman had stayed at the hotel and decided to work forward from there. Six months ago would have put it in November or December, so Paige began with those months, thinking that if the burglar had robbed her, then the robbery would have occurred between that time and Julia's murder. Assuming, of course, that Julia Weinstein was the burglar's most recent acquisition. If he worked more than two women at a time, then Paige's search might turn up nothing at all.

He also assumed that the married woman was wealthy, so he ignored the poor and middle-class sections of the city—which tended to underreport crimes anyway—and concentrated instead on the areas closest to City Line, Chestnut Hill, and the better streets in Germantown. If those didn't pan out, he'd try Rittenhouse Square and Society Hill again. He'd gone through both area reports right after Julia's murder and nothing stuck in his memory. But then he hadn't known what he was looking for earlier. Now he was looking for a robbery within a specific time frame.

Paige kept his own files at home. The one he was looking for was probably filed as a routine burglary, and they happened about every eight and a half minutes, according to the latest FBI stats. That meant his best chance to find the woman would be in the office files.

He began by dividing the various folders into separate piles, the incident reports, neighborhood interview sheets, the crime scene binders with their light blue front pages, making certain to arrange them by month and by area.

It took him until midnight to find her, shuffling through the files until his fingers were black with dust and ink. Her name was Marlene Trombly. The Tromblys had been robbed on a Saturday night in the middle of January. Paige skimmed it quickly. No forced entry, only jewels and cash stolen. The Wissahickon Station had handled it without much follow-up. Paige looked at the signature of the investigating officer and recognized the name of Frank Nolan. He was slow and not terribly thorough, but he wasn't stupid, Paige remembered.

Paige tried to see it through Nolan's eyes. The fact that there was no forced entry made it look like insurance fraud, which is what Nolan would have thought automatically. But no follow-up.

There had to be something else. He looked for it further on in Nolan's report and found it.

There had been a series of smash and grabs in the neighborhood that month, at least six that were reported. The method of entry was simple and quick. The burglar popped the

67

backdoor out of its frame with a crowbar and then booted it open with one hard kick. When the people came home they usually found their backdoor lying in the middle of the kitchen floor.

The Trombly house had been robbed during the same period and it was stuck with the others for convenience's sake. Or out of indifference or the cop's simple prejudice that rich people didn't really have crime problems. For example, the burglar didn't have to boot down the door to the Tromblys' house; presumably he used a key, the same as he had at Julia's. Or had he simply found an unlocked window and gone in that way?

There was the woman's statement. She and her husband had been to an early dinner and then a movie. When asked if they were often away from the house on the weekend, Marlene said yes, they were active socially and that kept them busy. Then Paige found what he was looking for.

When her husband was away, she added, she often went to concerts by herself and spent the night with friends in town. They had no children, she said, and she hated to stay in the house by herself.

He looked carefully at the list of stolen items. In the middle of the list was a diamond ring, nearly six carats and cut as a brilliant.

Paige called the Wissahickon Station to see if Nolan was working. He wasn't. Instead, Paige spoke to a desk officer named Washington, who said he remembered the burglary.

"I remember because of what Nolan said," Washington told him.

"Said about what?"

"The woman," Washington said. "Said she had big tits. Major contenders is what he called them. I remember stuff like that."

It was almost twelve-thirty. Paige didn't want to go home. What could he accomplish there? He took a pair of binoculars from the bottom drawer of his desk.

He wanted to look at the Trombly house.

Paige knew the neighborhood, so it wasn't that difficult to find the house, even in the dark. It was a large house, big enough to be called a mansion, off Wissahickon Drive near the park, set far back from the road behind a stone wall and a row of tall maples.

During the day the yard was probably lost in shade, disturbing patterns of light and dark; at night it was pitch black and difficult to walk through. He kept one hand on the small pair of binoculars in his pocket to keep them from banging into what he couldn't see, the other he held in front of him. He moved carefully, stopping every few feet to stare through the murk at the glow of light coming from the rear of the house. He felt as though he were walking through a dream, each step slower than the one before it.

At the edge of the house, Paige stopped suddenly and listened. He heard faint music. It seemed to be coming from the other side of the house, a steady pulse of drums and distant voices shouting words he couldn't understand. It was past one and the Tromblys were still up.

He stepped away from the corner and looked across the small side yard to a large cluster of bushes. He moved away from the house, keeping well in the shadows. On his right, he could see the light from the upstairs window. It spread like a piece of white lace, marking a pattern across the lawn. The music grew louder, seeming to sweep toward him on the light. He stopped when he got to the bushes.

Mrs. Trombly stood alone on a small balcony on the second floor. The balcony ran across an alcove at the back of the house just over a large patio. She had her back to him, a cigarette in one hand, swaying back and forth, missing the beat despite the fact that the boom box was right next to her on the table. She turned it up. Paige stepped farther back and took out the binoculars. As far as he could tell she had nothing on.

He brought the binoculars to his eyes and adjusted the focus. At that same moment, Mrs. Trombly turned and looked directly at him.

The skin on Paige's neck crawled up the back of his skull. Then her eyes shifted away from his and he realized that she hadn't seen him at all, that it had been an optical illusion. She was staring at nothing, at the darkness, maybe some lost memory that she hoped to revive. She was absolutely stunning, Paige decided. More important, she fit Hughes's description of the woman in the hotel.

Maybe she's waiting for the burglar, Paige thought, maybe she wants him to come back. The notion seemed so correct that he felt like shouting it out loud. She took a drag on her cigarette and dropped it, leaning over the balcony to watch it fall. It landed in a small shower of orange sparks.

She stood up and ran her fingers through her hair, pulling them together at the back of her head and holding them there. The gesture changed her face, made it younger. Paige found himself wondering what she had looked like in that hotel room.

The more he stared at her, the more familiar her face became and he realized that he had seen her picture in the society column of the *Inquirer*, something he read every so often. His normal reaction to the column was the same as if he'd been reading about a tribe of aborigines.

From the room behind her a man's voice called out her name in a dry irritated voice, telling her that he wanted to go to sleep even if she didn't. She looked once over the yard but said nothing. A man walked out and turned off the music. She said something to him, but he ignored her and went back inside. She followed him a few minutes later, leaving the door to the balcony open like an unfulfilled wish.

Paige lowered the binoculars and found that his hands were trembling slightly. He was back in it again, and for the first time in months, he felt alive. It was something that he carried with him, that's what his father would have said.

On his way home he thought that his father was probably right, after a fashion. But so was Nolan, and the two together didn't help much, did they?

8

Mrs. Trombly was not at home when Paige arrived early the next morning, so he bought a cup of coffee and a breakfast sandwich at McDonald's and waited for her to return. While he ate, he studied the house. It looked smaller in the daylight. They always did.

The house must have been easy for the burglar, Paige thought, even if he didn't have a key. The balcony was the simplest way but there were other ways. The Tromblys had iron bars on the windows. People bought that shit, Paige thought, and believed it would protect them. That was the problem right there. They didn't do anything about the windows on the inside. A burglar could pry a window grate loose in about forty seconds and chances are the inside window would be unlocked because people thought that the bars turned their home into a fortress.

There were other problems. There was the alarm system, which was advertised on a little sign out front so any burglar would know exactly what he was dealing with ahead of time. There were also good solid downspouts that could serve as ladders and tree limbs that hung over the roof that were as good as any rope. Of course, if the burglar had a key to the front door none of the rest mattered. Paige wondered if Mrs. Trombly had given it to him. After seeing her last night, it wasn't entirely out of the question. She might have welcomed the invasion.

Half an hour later, Marlene Trombly pulled into the driveway. Paige waited until she was in the house before getting out of the car because he wanted to watch her for a few moments undisturbed, just to see how she moved. He decided she did it very well.

She answered his knock as though she were expecting someone, a glass of orange juice in one hand, the other holding onto the open door. Paige looked past her into the living room of the house. For some reason, it struck him as being empty. Then he realized that it was just the colors he saw. Everything in the room was neutral and opaque, designed to dissolve when exposed to the light.

"Can I help you?" she said and let her hand drop.

Paige held out his shield and ID. She looked at it carefully. He saw a momentary flicker of fear cross her face, a pale triangle of unblemished white skin surrounded by thick dark hair, then it vanished. Once again, her face became as neutral and opaque as her surroundings.

"Is there some kind of trouble?" she said.

"I wanted to ask you some questions about the burglary you had last January," Paige said. "May I come in?"

"Oh, that," she said. "I'd forgotten all about it." Her voice sounded small as if something were about to swallow it up. She stepped aside, taking a drink of juice, then led him into the kitchen. There was a coffee machine on the table tucked away at the end of the room.

"Would you like some coffee?" she said and sat down. "When I opened the door, I thought you might have been my neighbor. We get together sometimes in the morning."

Paige shook his head. He realized suddenly that he was staring at her, remembering what she looked like standing on the balcony. He smiled and tried to put the image out of his mind. Next thing you know I'll be drooling on her arm. He concentrated on her face. That told him everything he wanted to know. She was still beautiful in the daylight but there was a sadness about her, the sharp lines of her mouth, the way she hid her eyes from him as if they might betray her loneliness.

72

She asked Paige again if he wanted a cup of coffee. He said no. She poured herself a cup but left it untouched on the table in front of her. Paige waited for her to speak. He wanted her to get used to talking.

"What would you like to know about it?" she asked. "I thought we went through it all last winter."

"There was never any follow-up," Paige said. "They've asked me to look into it again." He took out a small notebook and pretended to read from it. "There were some discrepancies in your statement."

"You make it sound like I need a lawyer," she said jokingly.

Paige closed the notebook slowly. "Do you want a lawyer, Mrs. Trombly?"

"Of course not," she said. Her hands slipped into her lap. "I haven't done anything."

Paige waited a few seconds. "How did he get the key?"

"What key?" she said too quickly.

"The key to the house. There was no forced entry. The other burglaries in the area had their backdoors kicked in."

"I don't know how he got the key," she said. "I mean, he might not have gotten it. We might have left the door open. I think I mentioned that."

"It's not in the report."

"That's not my fault. My husband did most of the talking. Besides, there wasn't that much taken. I don't understand why you're making such a big deal when he didn't take that much."

"Was there a key missing?"

"I don't really remember," she said. "That's the truth. All I do remember is coming home to find everything"—she searched for the right word—"disturbed," she said. The word caught in her throat. For a moment, she looked as though she might choke on it.

Paige took the report from his pocket and looked down the list of stolen items. "He took your wedding ring?" Paige asked.

"Yes, he did," she answered. She looked down at her coffee.

"You left it here?" he asked. "Why?"

The memory seemed to shake her. "Would you excuse me for a moment," she said and pushed herself away from the table. Paige didn't want to let her go but she slid past him too quickly for him to stop her. He heard a door slam in another part of

73

the house and then the sound of running water. She came back a few minutes later, a scattering of water drops still on her forehead where she had missed them with the towel.

This time Paige didn't wait. She was halfway across the room when he spoke.

"The hotel," he said, and she stopped suddenly as if he'd yelled at her. "I think he got the key from your purse when you were in the hotel room together. He may have made an impression of it and put it back before you knew what he'd done. He probably had time while you were hiding from the maid."

She started to say something, hesitated, and shook her head.

"Yes," she answered quietly. "I always thought so." She pushed her hair back with her hands and Paige could see the red around her eyes, the residue of her tears.

"I need you to tell me about him," Paige said. He moved closer to her because he didn't want her to get away again. Her tears didn't matter.

"I can't tell you anything in detail," she said. "I don't remember anything in detail. I know that sounds convenient but it's true. He was tall, thin. He had a wonderful mouth. I had the feeling when I first met him that he'd done this kind of thing before, picking up married women. He was very good in bed." She smiled at something. "He knew all these little tricks."

"Any scars or unusual markings? Did he say anything about himself, his past, where he was from, where he lived?"

She stepped around him. "Excuse me, I'd like to sit down." She sat down and pushed the coffee cup away from her. "I didn't ask him. Why do you need to know all this? He's only a burglar."

Paige didn't answer her question, only waited.

"He told me nothing," she said finally. "And I did *not* ask. I didn't want to know. It was just fine being strangers."

"Is that why you took off your ring?"

Marlene Trombly blushed. The blood ascended across her cheeks but she did nothing to hide it. "I suppose," she said. She looked at him for a moment. "Do you find it easy to pry into other people's lives like this?"

"Yes." It wasn't quite as simple as that but why tell her the whole truth.

She looked at Paige, holding his eyes with a determined stare. "I don't feel like I did anything wrong," she said. "I don't feel betrayed, not by him. How could I? We both got what we wanted." She managed a neutral smile. "I feel more betrayed by you."

Paige nodded automatically, a reflex action more than anything else. "Did you report everything he took from the house?"

"No," she said. "He took a small gold pin, a coiled snake with an emerald eye. I realized it was gone after the other detective had already left." She spun her finger around in the air. "It was just a silly little piece, not really worth anything, maybe a hundred dollars."

"What about the ring?"

"What about it?" she said. "I don't always wear it when I go out. I don't always wear it around here, for that matter. There's nothing mysterious there." She held out her hand. There was a new one on her finger.

"We have a lot of money. I won't miss anything he took, not even the ring." She held up her hand to admire the ring. "My husband bought me a replacement with the insurance settlement. Nothing is one of a kind anymore, everything is replaceable, that's what my husband says anyway." She looked sadly around the kitchen and then at Paige. "But that's not true, is it?"

Paige had no answer for her and she kept the rest of her thoughts a secret. Or thought she did. Paige had seen that same empty look on her face the night before just when her husband had called out to her.

"Where did you meet him?" he asked.

"At a concert," she said. "I was there alone, so was he. The attraction was mutual."

"When was this?"

"Several months before the burglary. I can't remember exactly."

"Try," Paige said.

"It was October, maybe September. That's the best I can do with it right now."

Paige took the ivory carving from his coat pocket and handed it to her. "Have you ever seen one of these before?"

She examined it carefully. "No, I haven't," she said. Then she smiled. "Is it yours?"

"No."

"That's too bad," she said and gave it back to him. "I can see where it might be interesting, don't you?" She looked at Paige inquisitively.

He didn't know quite how to answer it. He felt like he was entering a dangerous world here and didn't want to trip on the first step, so he produced a bland smile and put the carving away.

"You still haven't told me why you're interested in him," she said. "What did he do?" She watched him carefully, examining his face while he thought about what he was going to tell her. He was on more certain ground here. This time the truth might be enough.

"He killed a woman," he said.

It didn't seem to bother her. "I thought that's what it might be," she said, still watching his face.

"Would you recognize him again?" Paige asked.

"You mean in a lineup, something like that?"

"No," Paige said, "I was thinking more of a concert."

She was surprised. "Would it be dangerous?"

"Maybe," he said. "A little."

"Would you be there?"

"Of course," Paige said.

That was all the encouragement she needed. "Then how could I refuse?"

As he was leaving she said something odd.

"You remind me of him," she told him and touched his face, letting the tips of her fingers run down his skin. He didn't move away and she seemed to appreciate it. "Just a little, around the eyes," she told him. "You both have such wonderfully cold eyes."

9

Peterson was forty minutes late. Grant waited impatiently on a bench in Rittenhouse Square, watching the mothers with their strollers and the young businesswomen in their well-tailored suits as they hurried past. A bag lady, a woman not much older than the ones hurrying home, sat on the next bench and mumbled to herself. A pair of small children splashed in the nearby fountain while their mothers smoked cigarettes and chatted. The noise of the children filled the park.

Grant checked his watch again and tried to keep his irritation from showing. It was nearly quarter to seven. He had to wait because Peterson was bringing his money. So where was he? Grant's briefcase sat next to the bench and he tapped his foot against it, an angry little staccato.

Grant looked toward the corner and saw the dealer hurry across Walnut Street. Peterson was wearing a fawn-colored suit and carrying a blue leather shoulder bag. His hair was brittle and blond from far too many rinses, Grant suspected, and he kept himself trim by running. He also worked out once or twice a week, Grant remembered, although it didn't seem to do him that much good. Peterson's first name was Lindor. The dealer said it was Swedish.

"I'm sorry," Peterson said immediately when he sat down, dropping the shoulder bag between them. "I had a customer who just would not leave. Fortunately he spent some money or I would have been really angry. Have you been waiting all this time?"

Grant looked at him and said evenly, "Don't ever do that to me again." Peterson started to say something but Grant stopped him. "What do you think we're doing here?" Grant said. "Where's the money?"

"It's in here," Peterson said and hesitated before reaching into the bag to get it. Grant did it for him. Peterson looked anxious.

"It's a little short," Peterson said. Grant pulled out a plastic cash bag with the name of Peterson's bank printed on it. The bag was old and the print was worn away. The only thing left that was readable was the word FIRST.

Grant began to count the money in the bag. It was in fifties and hundreds and it took a few minutes for him to count it. Peterson chewed nervously on the cuticle of his thumb. "There's only twenty thousand in here," Grant said when he finished.

"I told you," Peterson said testily. "I said you were wrecking the market with all those things. Nobody in Chicago can take anymore. As it is, I'm going to have to make another trip just to get rid of what I've still got."

Grant took Peterson's thumb, the one he'd been chewing on, and bent it backward. The dealer's eyes widened instantly. He tried to pull Grant's hand away. Grant pressed down harder, bending it back against Peterson's arm. The joints in his thumb began to crack and pop, the sound like tiny tar bubbles bursting on hot pavement.

The blood drained from Peterson's face. Grant found the effect interesting. He could feel the bone getting ready to splinter and he held it there, wondering how long Peterson could stand it.

Peterson's mouth opened in a silent scream and Grant released his hand. The dealer covered the thumb with his open mouth, pouring his breath over it as if the extra warmth might stop the pain. Peterson's eyes filled with tears. They ran down his cheeks, little rivers between the acne scars; he'd tried to cover them with pancake makeup. It was the first time Grant had noticed it.

The dealer put the injured hand between his legs and rocked back and forth. He started to say something.

Grant put a finger to his lips and shushed him. Peterson's reaction was one of fear. Grant liked that. It kept things at a simple level so there would be no misunderstanding. Runyon would have appreciated it; he liked simple things. The simple facts here were that if Grant hadn't let go of Peterson's hand when he did, he might not have stopped. He might have gone all the way and started snapping everything in sight. The idea left him feeling invigorated. It was like a good workout. Peterson could appreciate something like that.

"Does it hurt?" Grant asked. It was the question he'd wanted to ask Julia while he was banging the hammer off her skull. Part of him stood back and watched, and that was the question he wanted to ask most of all. Peterson nodded like a puppy dog, big head bobbing up and down. Yes, it hurt all right.

"Good," Grant said. "Since we know you don't like that very much, we can move the discussion along. I need another seventy thousand and I need it soon. Tell me what you have to have to get it and I'll supply it and we can settle our accounts without any more of this kind of thing."

"I need more time," Peterson croaked.

"Time is money," Grant said. "Time is precious. Time we don't have anymore." He lifted his briefcase to his lap and placed the bag of money inside and snapped it shut. "You can have two weeks."

"I can't do it," Peterson said.

"Never say can't, Lindor," Grant said. "*Can't* just isn't in your vocabulary."

Grant was familiar with Mount Airy but not that familiar. There were a lot of stone houses and after a while they tended to look alike, especially at night. Grant's mind wandered a bit, thinking that the money was now going to be a problem. There were a few personal things he could liquidate that might help. He could make one more pass through what was left in the basement but doubted that would help very much. There was always the possibility of another job, but he had nothing lined up, nothing that would net him real money without an enormous risk so he wasn't thinking very hard in that direction.

He passed the house, drove to the far end of the street, turned around, and pulled over in front of it. Despite the darkness, Grant could see that the house was empty, the first floor boarded up. It surprised him. He assumed there would be people in it and here it was, deserted. Now that he was there, Grant wanted to go inside, just to see what kind of life Paige had lived before. That would be fun, just a peek.

"Is that you, detective?"

The voice came from somewhere behind him. His heartbeat jumped up a notch and for one confusing second, he wasn't certain what he was going to do. Then he turned slowly and looked across the street. A man stepped off the sidewalk and stopped in the middle of the street. He had a small white dog on a leash.

"I'm sorry," the man said. "I thought you were that detective."

"No," Grant said brightly. "I was just driving by and saw the house. I thought it might be for sale. It's a nice-looking house." He put some warmth into his voice and smiled in a friendly, casual way. No sense in drawing any more attention to himself than he already had.

The man shook his head. "I wish it was for sale," he said. "It's not good to have a boarded-up house on the street. People get the wrong idea about the neighborhood."

"Why'd you think I was a detective?"

The dog strained on the leash and moved closer to the car. The man followed and stood a few feet away.

"Because he comes and sits here sometimes, just like this. Sometimes it's three o'clock in the morning and he sits and stares at the damn thing half the night."

The dog sniffed at Grant's front tire, lifted a leg and peed all over it.

"Stop that, Willy," the man said and jerked the leash.

"Why does he do that?"

"Because he's a dog," the man said.

"No," Grant said, "the detective. Why does he sit and watch the house?"

80

"Oh," the man said. "Because his wife was killed in it, I guess," the man said. "I can't think of another reason. It's like visiting her grave. I wish he'd go there instead."

"How long has he been doing it?"

"Before I moved here from what I've been told and that was almost five years ago," the man said.

"And he still does it?"

"Yes, sir. Sometimes we call the cops when he shows up, just to let him know we don't like it. But they don't do anything. His father used to be somebody big in City Hall, I guess that's why they let him keep doing it."

"I don't think there's a law against it," Grant said.

"There should be," the man said. "I just wish he'd sell it. He's wrecking the street."

"What's his name?"

"Paige," the man said. "Patrick Paige. He's got another place in Center City somewhere."

"Maybe I'll give him a call, see if he wants to sell it."

"Good luck," the man said. "He turned down every offer so far. Maybe he'll change his mind."

"Who knows?" Grant said and started up the car. "Maybe I can help him out this time."

10

Paige couldn't pinpoint the exact date when he first told Tom Ferris about his burglar theory but it was a while ago. He knew that Ferris wouldn't understand what he was doing or why, especially the why. Ferris didn't like things that needed extensive explanations. To Tom Ferris, the world was black and white, a philosophy he shared with Paige's father.

Paige had gone to Ferris's house with a stack of cases and laid them out in chronological order on the kitchen table. There were at least two dozen. Paige remembered their conversation exactly.

"What the hell is this?" Ferris asked him. It was eleven o'clock on a Saturday morning and Ferris was drinking a bottle of beer with his eggs and beans, mopping up the brown and yellow mess on his plate with a limp piece of toast. The *Daily News*, open to the sports section, was next to his plate.

"I want you to take a look at these," Paige said. Ferris picked up the first case file. It was from the Delaware state police.

"Where the hell you'd get this?" Ferris asked him.

Paige ignored the question. "Just read them through and let me know when you're done."

"Terrific," Ferris said and pointed to his plate. "Can I finish my fucking breakfast first? Or can this pile of out-of-state crap wait for a few minutes?"

"You can read while you eat," Paige said and picked up the paper. "They're not all from out of town." He closed the paper. It was two days old. "What are you reading Thursday's paper for?"

"Nostalgia," Ferris said and started to skim the reports.

Twenty minutes later, Ferris said, "You think one guy did all these, don't you?" Paige said that he did. "You're going to have a hell of a time proving it." Paige nodded and scooped up the files, careful to keep them in the right order. "You doing this on your own time?"

"After hours mostly," Paige said. "Weekends. What else am I going to do?"

"You could go out, have a few beers, get laid, start acting like the rest of us on the planet," Ferris said.

"I get laid," Paige said.

"I bet you do," Ferris said. He jerked his hand up and down over his plate and rolled his eyes back into his head. "I know how you get laid, the same way I used to get laid." He took a drink of beer and pushed the plate away. "How much more of this have you got at home?"

"A couple file cabinets," Paige said. "Not much."

"And you think there's one guy out there who's been knocking off jobs left and right, big jobs from I can see, and nobody knows what the fuck he's doing?"

"No, I know what he's doing," Paige said. "I just don't know who he is or when he's going to do the next one."

"Maybe it's a she," Ferris said. "Did you think about that?" Paige shrugged.

"There goes your chance to get laid," Ferris said. He pulled the first report off the top and glanced through it again.

"But whoever it is, you think he's that good?"

"He's that good," Paige said.

"And you think he's working out of here?" Ferris said. "That he's doing all these jobs out of Philly?" Paige nodded. "Good luck," Ferris said.

"Look," Paige said. "It's very simple. All of the jobs are big, most of them in the ten- to twenty-thousand-dollar range when you add it up. He never takes cheap stuff, only the best, jewelry, cash, a few antiques. He never goes out the same way he goes in. Sometimes he uses the roof, sometimes a window. There's no time pattern and the locations are all over the place."

"Maybe it's four different guys and you're making something out of nothing that ain't there in the first place," Ferris said.

"No," Paige said. "It's one guy and he's out there right now."

"When you come up with something more than a theory, you let me know. I'll talk to the commissioner." Paige shook his head. "Hey, Pat," Ferris asked, "You been doing this long?"

"A year or so," Paige said.

Ferris looked stunned. "Your old man told me to look after you, now you're starting your own police department. Danny would've fired me for falling down on my job."

"He wouldn't have fired you," Paige said. "You probably had too much on him anyway."

Ferris smiled uncomfortably and changed the subject.

So here he was, how many years later, and where the hell was Ferris? It was early afternoon and he still wasn't around. Paige called his house a couple more times but got no answer. He thought that he might take a drive past his place when Tom Ferris stuck his head around the corner of the file cabinet.

"Nice to see you now and then," Paige said. "You run out of other things to do today?"

"I was busy," Ferris said.

"I called you back."

"I was out."

"I need your help."

"You want me on the Weinstein job," Ferris said. "I figured you would. What is it, your mystery burglar?"

"I knew her, Tom."

That brought him up short, Paige thought. Ferris shook his head. "Oh, Christ, here we go round the mulberry bush again." Paige felt himself freeze. His eyes grew still, like two pieces of milky glass.

"It was a coincidence," Paige said. "I dated her. I date a lot of people. She just happened to be one of them."

"Any others get themselves killed?" Ferris bit down on a chubby finger. "Oh, shit," he said. "I'm sorry. I didn't mean that. I just don't want to see you go crazy again, okay?"

"I won't," Paige said. Ferris was still staring at him. "It's okay. What do you hear about it?"

"They got nothing so far. They're looking at her patients."

"That's a good idea," Paige said.

"You told Sloat you dated her?"

"Sure," Paige said.

"And you think your burglar did it?"

"Yeah."

"And that's why you're going after this yourself?"

"I thought I'd take you with me."

"Right," Ferris said. He didn't sound enthusiastic about it. "What do you want me to do first?"

Paige wanted to tell him to stay sober but didn't. He wanted to tell him this wasn't just for old times' sake, that he wanted to keep an eye on him, but Paige didn't tell him that, either.

"I want you to check out some antiques dealers for me, anyone who might be handling high-priced antiques. See if anybody's been acting funny in the last few months."

Ferris shook his head. "Jesus, Pat, those days are long over, you know that. Fancy burglars, high-priced merchandise, nobody pulls that shit around here anymore. You got the Russians and their little ovens and the only thing they like to cook down is gold chain, and the niggers got that market to themselves because that's all they got the brains for. Every decent burglar I know went south about five years ago. They all got tans now. Half of them dress like Engelbert Humperdinck."

Paige waited for Ferris to finish his complaining. He did it whenever anyone asked him to do anything. As soon as he realized that Paige wasn't going to change his mind, he'd get to work.

"Shit," Ferris said finally. "I'll see what I can do."

After Ferris had gone, Paige took the ivory carving from his pocket and sat it on the desk. Then he called the community relations division and asked for Jimmy Wu.

"Hello, Jimmy," Paige said. "How'd you like to be a real cop again?"

"Not really," Jimmy Wu said. "People don't like real cops."

85

"I need you to look at something, a carving, and tell me what you think it is."

Paige rubbed the carving with his finger. It warmed to his touch. He stroked it some more. No wonder Julia wanted one of these, he thought.

"Bring it down, can't hurt to look at it."

When the Chinese officer held it in his hands, he shook his head. "I wish I could help you, Pat, but I haven't the faintest idea what this is."

"It isn't Chinese?"

"I don't think so, at least nothing Chinese that I've ever seen." He grinned. "It might be Thai, but what do I know, I'm American myself."

"Can you find out for me who might be importing them?"

"Come on, Pat. Do you know how many import firms there are in Chinatown? There must be five hundred at least. Now that the Vietnamese are here, probably more."

Paige ignored the exasperation in his voice. It was a ploy he used when he was bargaining for something. "What do you want?"

Jimmy pretended to think about the situation for a moment. "If I find out something, can I keep it?"

"Sure," Paige said. "Have you got a Polaroid in your department?"

"I guess so. Why?"

"I want to take a couple pictures so you can show them around."

"I thought you said I could keep it?"

"When you find out something."

"Don't you trust me anymore, Pat?"

"No tickee, no washee," Paige said.

11

Paige decided that the hotel manager was perfectly correct in his assessment of the police but that it didn't go far enough. Paige thought about it this way: the city had a black mayor who ordered the predominantly white police department to bomb a black neighborhood, and then the black mayor and the predominantly white fire department and police department let it burn to the ground. Then the black community *reelected* the mayor by a large majority. As far as Paige was concerned, this went into areas that were so far removed from what most people considered normal that they probably didn't register on any scale of reality that he knew about.

Still there were the department stories, the same ones told over and over again. Paige could still hear his voice.

They were eating pot roast in the kitchen. Connie was serving potatoes. "You don't mind a few dirty words, do you?" Danny had said. Connie shook her head. "I didn't think so. Sergeant Grabowski works among our darker brethren, you see, and he likes to take a few recruits out for selective training. They're doing a drive around, seeing the high points, when

Gripp notices a woman come rolling out of one of the bars like a tombstone. The woman sees their car and waves them down.

"Grabowski thinks this will be good for a laugh, so he tells the lads to sit tight and he stops the car. The woman takes her time getting there but when she does, she leans in the window and says that some pin-dicked cocksucker stole her money and she wants it back.

"Grabowski is extremely polite. 'Ah, which pin-dicked cocksucker would that be, ma'am?' The woman smells like a distillery. 'That one' she says and points to half a dozen young bucks across the street. Grabowski gets a twinkle in his eyes and asks the lads if they want to see a magic trick.

"Well, who can turn down magic? So they follow him across the street. 'All right, you assholes,' Grabowski says, 'which one of you stole that woman's money?' There are a few nasty stares all around but not one word.

" 'Fine by me,' Grabowski says and cracks the nearest buck over the head with his stick. The buck drops like a pair of pants. The others take off on the run and don't bother looking back. Grabowski turns to the recruits and says, 'There's your magic trick, boys. Instant suspect.' "

Paige remembered his father laughing, watching Connie for her reaction. She passed him the potatoes as he remembered. Later that night, he asked Paige how he had liked the story.

"Not that much," Paige said.

"What about Connie? You think she liked it?"

"She was raised to be polite."

"That mean she thinks I'm a nigger hater?"

"It means she understands you," Paige said.

"Which is more than you can say," his father countered. Neither one had raised his voice.

"I understand you," Paige said.

"You do, do you?"

"Yeah," Paige said and grinned. "I think you hate everybody."

"Well," Danny said. "No real harm done, either way."

On Thursday night, one day before the concert, Paige went to see Mickey Katz. Mickey was an old fence that Paige had busted

88

for receiving. Mickey did two years in Holmesburg and, after that, they became friends of a sort.

"Listen," Mickey told him, "I don't hold it against you. You did it square and you treated me like a gentleman, which I am, goddammit." Paige went to see him a couple times in prison and brought him some cigarettes, all of which surprised nobody, especially Mickey. Mickey wasn't completely averse to being caught just as long as Paige remembered his manners.

After prison, Mickey talked to Paige on a semiregular basis. He was getting too old to work, and when the heart failure got bad, Paige helped him move into some elderly housing at Logan Square. Mickey shared a room with another man, who suffered from Alzheimer's and seemed to remember only things that happened to him when he was a child. Mickey didn't mind. He said it was nice having kids around.

"How come you're here?" Mickey wanted to know. He pointed a twitching finger at Paige. "You in trouble again?"

"No," Paige said. He brought a handful of paperback books and held them in his lap. Mickey told him to put them on the bed so he could see what kind of trash Paige brought this time. Paige held them up one by one.

Mickey leaned over to look, resting his thin body against the oxygen tank that stood next to his bed. Mickey held the mask in his hand and pressed it over his nose and mouth; he wouldn't use the nose clips, he said they made him look senile. His bathrobe was partially open, and Paige could see his wasted legs, pale white with heavy blue veins running through them like cracks in marble.

"You must be in trouble," he said when he put the mask down. "You haven't been to see me in a couple of months."

"I'm sorry," Paige said. "I've been too busy. I know that's no excuse."

"My sister's been busy, too. She went and died." Mickey laughed. "Cancer. Everybody knew it was coming. She lasted about four weeks." He took another drag on the mask. "Thanks for the books. I can still read. Don't do much else. Read, watch TV, talk on the phone to my sister's husband. The guy don't know what to do with himself now. He lives in Ohio. I told him to move in here with me. He said he'd think about it. How come you don't bring me any girlie magazines?"

"You never asked me for any."

"I'm asking you now. *Playboy, Penthouse*, doesn't matter. I like boobs, always did. I'm a confirmed boob man."

Paige was patient. Their talks always started this way. Mickey liked to take time to warm up.

"So what is it you want?" Mickey asked. He held one of the paperbacks, idly turning it over in his hands. "I don't like this guy," he said and tossed it on the bed. "Take it with you."

"I wanted to talk a little more about Runyon," Paige said. He'd been thinking about the old fence lately, wondering if Mickey might remember something that would bring Paige closer to the burglar. It was a long shot but he didn't have much else at the moment.

"What is there to talk about?" Mickey said angrily. "It was time for him to quit. He tells me no. I say fine. Some spic puts an ice pick in his chest for six bucks worth of gold. What the fuck did he think was going to happen, they were going to give him a prize for being the last white man on the block? He should have done what I told him to do."

"You're right," Paige said.

"Of course I'm right," Mickey answered sharply. He was still angry at Runyon for dying. He took it personally, an attack on his own survival. "He was a stubborn old Jew," Mickey said. "He shouldn't have got careless. I told him that."

"How many did he bring up over the years?"

"You mean before he got himself killed?" Mickey asked. "I don't know. Maybe half a dozen. Half a dozen over twenty some years is a lot. Burglary's a real talent. You don't go to a store and buy a book on it." He held the mask to his face for a long time, studying Paige, his eyes full of suspicion.

"You remember any of them?"

"Not a one," Mickey said. "I was never introduced. That was one of the rules. The other one was I don't like to talk about this, not to anybody. You know that."

"Runyon's dead," Paige reminded him.

"So what? You think it's some kind of mystery? That's why he's dead, he forgot the rules," Mickey said and hid behind the mask again. He pulled it off briefly. "I read more than just those books you bring me," he said. "I know what goes on. I get the papers, too. You're after the one who killed that girl in Society Hill."

"I knew her," Paige said. "She was a friend of mine."

Mickey's eyes widened a little and he leaned forward suddenly, as if this new information had added an extra weight to his already weakened heart. The fact that Paige knew the murdered woman made it a personal request, and that changed the whole process. It was like turning a key somewhere.

"What'd he use on her?" he asked. "They didn't say in the paper."

Even the old man needed a little show business.

"They aren't sure. Maybe a hammer." That was exactly what they thought. Paige had seen the autopsy report. There were cotton fibers embedded in her skull. The guy had wrapped the hammer in a towel.

"You think it was one of Runyon's who did it to her?"

"I don't know," Paige said. "That's what I'm trying to find out." He had other questions but they'd come in time. A bit of nostalgia, then the hard part, that was how it always worked with the old man.

Mickey thought for a minute, breathing in and out through the mask in a slow even rhythm. "None of the ones I knew would've done something like that," he said. "That's way out of their line."

"How many are still around?"

"Nobody. Maybe one or two, but they don't work much. Nobody I know around here works much anymore. All they want is nigger shit now, ripping chains off people's necks, smash and grab, running up and down Chestnut Street, that's all it is. A lot of them moved to Miami. Better money down there. How'd the guy get inside?"

"He used a key," Paige said. "But he had the roof all set up."

"You think he knew her?"

"I think so."

"Maybe she recognized him and he belted her one. That's happened before, you know."

"No," Paige said. "It was deliberate."

Mickey weighed the information in silence.

91

"There was one," Mickey said. "Runyon kept to himself about the guy. He said he was the best he'd ever seen, a real natural talent." He took another whiff of oxygen. "I don't know how much help this is going to be to you. I never knew what happened to him."

"You never saw him?"

"The guy could come up and kiss me on both cheeks and I wouldn't recognize him. I never even knew the guy's name. Runyon didn't talk about him except maybe once that I can remember."

Now it was Paige's turn to lean forward.

"We were having coffee and hard rolls at Annie's," Mickey said. "You remember Annie's? We're in the side booth, the one by the window. He's real quiet and then all of a sudden he blurts it out, like it had been on his mind all the time. He said he was scared of the guy. That was it. I knew who he was talking about, he didn't have to explain that. 'The man frightens me,' he said. I couldn't believe it. Runyon wasn't afraid of anybody."

"Did you ask him what he meant?"

"Sure, I asked him," Mickey said. "But he wouldn't say, not a word. I figured he'd told me enough right there."

"That isn't much," Paige said.

Mickey chewed on his cheek. "There was something else. This was a few years ago. Some dealer got beat up real bad. I heard that he had both his thumbs broke off, couldn't use his hands. The story was that he tried to cheat somebody on a deal. The dealer's long gone now, guy don't stick around with hands like that."

"Is that it?"

"It's all I got. What the hell you want from me? I ain't doing your job, you know." He started to cough and reached for the oxygen mask, pulling it over his mouth. When he did that, he looked very small and very sick. Paige waited until he took the mask away.

"How would he work it?" Paige asked.

"What do you mean, how would he work it? He'd belt her over the skull and get the hell out of there. You know that better than me."

Paige ignored the remark. "No," he said. "I mean, how would he find them in the first place?"

Mickey shook his head. "Easy. Finding people's always the easiest thing. Maybe he sees her car filled with things at one of the malls or something. Maybe he's got a list from some club or something. That's what Runyon used to use sometimes. He had a list of Cadillac owners. Used to call it the gospel. Let me check the gospel, he'd say. Maybe he just sticks pins in the phone book. Hell, it don't take a lot of skill to find rich people."

"But what if he wanted a particular type, rich, married, socially active, somebody who wouldn't want the truth to get around when they got robbed?"

Mickey thought about it. "What's the guy's specialty?"

"Jewels, cash, a few antiques. He's got good taste."

"Then start with the antiques places," Mickey said. "Maybe they gave him the list without knowing it. Maybe they're spottin' for him." Mickey gave Paige a dirty look. "You want me to ask around, that it? You getting tired of the legwork, so you leave it to an old man?"

"You can find out more in two phone calls than I can in a week's worth of walking the street," Paige said.

"You're fucking right about that," Mickey said, pleased with the compliment.

"I think we're looking for somebody new, somebody who won't come up on the usual lists," Paige said.

"Makes sense. I'll see what I can scratch up for you, maybe take a couple days." Mickey looked at Paige. "You okay on this thing?"

"What thing?"

"This murder business." Mickey sounded a little nervous. "You knew her, right?"

"I'm fine. It was a long time ago."

"Seven years," Mickey said. "I always liked her, Pat. Connie was a sweet girl. It was a real tragedy."

Paige looked surprised that he remembered it so well. Then Mickey surprised him again.

"You miss your old man?" Mickey asked.

Paige thought about it. "No," he said. "I don't know. Sometimes."

"I met him," Mickey said. "Once or twice, him and Tommy Ferris."

"Are you serious?"

"Shit," Mickey said. "When did I lie?"

"How come you never told me that before?"

"Never had a reason to," Mickey said.

"Then what's your reason now?"

"Don't have one now either," Mickey said with a grin. "Just making sure you don't get too far ahead of yourself. It can trip you up, little piece of something you never thought about." Paige looked concerned, so Mickey waved him away. "I said I met him, for Christ's sake, I didn't say we were asshole buddies. I shook his hand, he shook mine. He wasn't a complete scumbag, not like Tommy Ferris. Is he working on this thing with you?"

"Yeah."

"Then watch your fucking wallet," Mickey said.

Paige laughed. "I'll call you in a couple days."

"Sure," Mickey said. "Thanks for them books. Bring me some tit magazines next time. You're going to owe me."

On the street, Paige realized that he'd forgotten to show Mickey the picture of the ivory carving. Next time. He stopped and thought about Mickey, an old man full of secrets from the past, alone in his room, nurturing each one. Paige could feel their touch.

How many more did Mickey have?

12

At first he thought it was the heat that drove him from the house. Despite the air-conditioning, it seemed to pour through the windows in his bedroom, squeezing through the glass like beads of sweat, until it sunk into his bones, warming his flesh from the inside out. He hurried to the garage, opened the doors, pushing himself along, climbed into the car and drove into the city, not really seeing anything except the road and the lights of the cars in front of him until he reached Society Hill.

He walked for a while and tried to lose himself along South Street, maneuvering through the crowded sidewalks of teenage punks and summer tourists attracted by the crowds and the lights, the costume clothing stores and nostalgia boutiques.

But he grew tired of the noise and the dirt. He felt constricted and controlled by it all; the heat from the sidewalk seemed to pull him down. He left South Street and walked north. A few blocks away, at Sixth Street, he crossed over to Lombard, directly in front of a small playground and park surrounded by a high chain-link fence. A handful of teenagers played basketball in the near darkness; others sat against the fence, their backs to the street, and watched. Their voices sounded volatile and loud. Grant listened for a moment, then moved away. He turned left down the next street, a narrow lane filled with cars that ran parallel to the park behind a row of neat brownstones, finally ending up in front of a metal fire escape. He looked behind him, saw no one, only the headlights of a passing car on the next block, and jumped.

It was only a short distance from the street. Grant hooked one hand on the bottom rung of the ladder with ease and then spun himself around quickly before it could drop under his weight. Then he was up and free, swinging onto the first platform, scrambling up the metal scaffold to the roof. It was over in a matter of seconds. When he looked down, the alley was still deserted.

Grant moved lightly across the center of the roof toward the park side of the street, hopping over the short brick walls between the buildings until he reached the middle of the block. From there, he could watch the park without being seen.

A pair of mounted police paraded by and stopped to stand guard by the park gate, the horses prancing restlessly in the heat. Crowds of people moved and swirled around the edges of the park, moving toward the lights of South Street. A young couple, each holding a briefcase, he wearing a tie, she a single strand of pearls, passed in front of the park gate, pausing momentarily to work their way through the small nighttime crowd that stood around the police horses.

Grant followed them with his eyes out of curiosity at first, then with growing interest, separating them from the crowd; it was like a hunting exercise, and he did not consider it at all wasted time. They crossed the street directly beneath him and strolled down the block toward the far end of the street. He moved without considering what he would do next, crouching low on the roof as he tracked them.

When they stopped in front of one of the row houses directly beneath him, he held his breath. As if she sensed something she could not see, an unspoken fear, the woman looked up but did not see him, just one more shadow on the roof. Instead, she pointed to something nearby. The man put his arm around her and kissed her. The woman leaned into his shoulder as he opened the door and they stepped inside.

96

Grant whirled around toward the alley side of the building, wondering as he did how long it would take him to find the bedroom and what sort of window locks they used. He leaned over the edge and looked down, studying the side of the row house. There were three sets of double windows with a drain pipe running between them. The drain pipe looked unsafe. Grant shook it gently and the support nails wobbled awkwardly between the bricks. But next to the drain pipe ran a thick set of cables the size of his wrist. Grant pulled on the wires. They seemed solid enough. He could swing down easily. A window went up on his right and he heard the woman's voice.

"It's too hot up here," she said. "Maybe we should sleep downstairs tonight." Her hands dangled out over the window ledge. He could have pulled her out if he wanted and let her dangle over the alley. He wondered what her eyes would look like as she fell, whether she might scream. The temptation was like a voice inside his own head. He heard it for the first time and was shocked by its clarity. It was something pure and without limits.

In a moment of stunned recognition, he looked at his own hands, rubbed one finger across his skin and felt the heat pour through. He thought for a moment that if he looked hard enough, he would see the worm beneath the nail, slowly eating its way out.

Grant pulled back from the edge, farther and farther, shutting out the vision as he went, letting his fingers drag him along. They rasped and scraped along like crabs scuttling over sand. The woman snapped the window shut. Grant closed his eyes and waited, his breath warm on his lips and then headed for the fire escape.

On the street again, Grant discovered that the palm of one hand was caked with dirt and blood. There was a wide brownish smear of it on his pants. He had cut his hand on the roof. It wasn't a bad cut, but he had missed it just the same; like a drunk who wakes up in a different bed and can't remember how he got there. The thought of it shook him, the same way the voice had shaken him; a strange sound filling his mind with its craziness.

But he'd beaten them, hadn't he? He'd been in control all the time, that was the key. You could think all the crazy things you wanted to but as long as you didn't let them get you, you were safe. You were in control and that made you a winner. He hurried along, anxious to get home.

What he needed now was some relaxation, a place where he could sit and not worry about what might happen or even care, an entertainment, a diversion, something to occupy his soul.

A concert.

13

There was little Grant could do except stand quietly while the man behind the box office window examined the line of people. He wasn't the only one being examined. The man did it to all of them, the half a dozen or so people standing in line in front of Grant and even the few behind him. It seemed odd at first, then he realized what the man was doing.

He's looking for someone. The thought was like the shriek of an alarm that Grant could do nothing about. He shut his eyes briefly, forcing himself to remain calm and examined his options while the man behind the glass examined him. After a few seconds, Grant gave up thinking. There was nothing he could do without attracting attention to himself. He couldn't run, couldn't leave the line suddenly, couldn't disengage himself from the reality of the moment.

Were they looking for him? Had the police made a connection between Julia's death and the concert tonight? Was there a note or message he didn't know about? He glanced at the people around him but found nothing that struck him as out of the ordinary, no one who looked awkward or ill at ease, no one who turned away too quickly. He began to relax. There were no police around tonight.

Marlene Trombly crossed in front of the window and looked directly at him. Grant wanted to move out of her line of vision but there was no place for him to go. She stared at him while she lit a cigarette and stepped to one side. The alarm in his head went off again, more urgent this time.

What was she doing here? It was obvious that she wasn't alone, that someone from the police was with her. It had to be Paige. Grant was certain of it. No one else could have managed to find her so quickly. The fact that she was there meant she had already identified Grant or at least given Paige a description. But which one? Grant tried to remember how he had disguised himself when he met her but his memory was vague and uncertain. Were there any others? Was Paige alone?

He looked around the room again and tried to remember what he'd seen when he drove past the building earlier that afternoon in the rain.

The air had been thick with humidity, the gutters filled with thin rivers of concrete-colored water. He had kept the window down and looked carefully at the building as his car went hissing through the wet streets. Unconsciously, he wiped a line of sweat off his cheek. Nothing stood out in his memory and he took one last look around the lobby. There were no other police there. Paige was alone. Then why had she agreed to come with him tonight?

As the thought raced through his mind, Marlene Trombly bent down and stared out through the thick glass window of the box office. Her eyes swept up the row and she looked straight at him. He was close enough now to see the boredom behind her eyes. He remembered her fully now. She was silly and bored and terrified of getting old. She drifted through her life, concerned only with money and her affairs. She had them, one after the other, like little dessert cakes at a party, greedy fingers pushing them into her mouth. Finished with one she would reach immediately for the next one.

She had no willpower at all and he remembered how much she had disgusted him, that fat diamond ring on those greedy little fingers. She was weak and impulsive, filled with her pathetic little needs and wants.

Now he knew why she'd come tonight and why she hadn't identified him yet.

She wanted him again.

Anger flooded through him. She was worse than Julia. Why wouldn't she leave him alone? He wanted to smash her down, to make her stay away. He wanted to feel her flesh in his mouth, to peel it away inch by inch. Does it hurt? Does it hurt now?

Someone pulled the shade back at the other window and Grant saw the outline of Paige's face. The rage turned into a roar, a sound like the grinding of bones.

Stop it. The voice spoke to him severely, like a drunken aunt. Grant was shaken by it, then realized that it was his own voice cautioning him. He eased himself down. Marlene Trombly was gone, vanished into the back of the booth. The only one left was the worried man in the window, staring out as if he expected demons to assault him through the glass.

Grant was in control again. He walked up to the window because there was nobody who could touch him. He was pure and invisible. Let the worried man's eyes roam all over his face, let him crawl around right under his skin, the man would never remember him. Grant's memory returned to him now and he saw himself as he had been.

His hair was different and he had added some color around his temples and at the crown. The glasses he wore distorted the rest of his features; they made him look smaller. He helped that change by keeping his chin down, stooping just a little.

The lights behind him blinked twice, a warning signal for the start of the concert.

Grant stepped up to the window and let the man examine him as he looked inside expecting to meet the woman's gaze. He wanted to see how she looked with Paige.

Marlene Trombly was gone. So was the detective. He slid a twenty-dollar bill underneath the glass.

"Is there anything left in the second tier?" Grant asked. "On the aisle?" The man didn't recognize him. He merely nodded in weary relief and asked how many.

"Just one," Grant said with an apologetic smile and accepted the ticket. The man counted out five dollars and fifty cents in change. Grant put the ticket into his coat pocket and picked up his change. The lights in the lobby flashed again.

As he turned away, he saw Marlene Trombly and Paige as they walked down the hall toward the rear of the auditorium. Paige opened the door and then stopped for one last look at the lobby. Their eyes swept past each other and then Paige was gone.

Grant had to fight his laughter. It was simply too good to ignore.

They were using Julia's tickets.

He took his time, climbing the stairs slowly, a man in no hurry, all the time thinking of Paige and the fleeting glimpse he'd had of the detective's stubborn face.

He took a program from the usher and found his seat. It was next to a young woman in dark slacks and a green blouse who removed a large leather bag from the seat next to her so he could sit down. The first selection was Beethoven's Symphony No. 2 in D Major, a piece that he knew, one filled with high spirits and pure unclouded movements. He watched as the conductor, a small robust-looking man, took the podium. Grant looked over the railing and saw Paige and Marlene Trombly as they sat down. Marlene Trombly sat in Julia's seat, the one away from the aisle that she always enjoyed. Grant thought that, too, was appropriate. He settled into his seat and waited for the first cleansing notes of the music to lift him up.

Paige didn't like symphonies. There was simply too much music as far as he was concerned. He had once seen the movie *Amadeus* and heard the king's criticism of too many notes and wondered why Mozart was astonished. It was like being attacked by gnats.

In the box office, Dickens had held out Julia Weinstein's tickets to Paige. "Here," he said. "You might as well use them." Paige had hesitated before taking them, but Marlene Trombly snatched them up quickly and pulled him from the booth.

Marlene Trombly, he noticed, did a lot of pulling. She pulled him through the lobby, down the aisle, into his seat. He slowed her down momentarily by holding the door for her, taking one last look through the lobby as she started down the aisle without him.

As Paige looked past the crowd, focusing on the heavy glass doors and the rainswept street beyond, he got a weird jolt of energy, a kind of freezing rush that felt like someone was staring down his throat, the same kind of rush he used to get when he was waiting in the dark for a burglar to come dropping in out of the sky. Then Marlene Trombly pulled him away and the rush stopped abruptly. She dragged him down the aisle, her hand warm in his own.

Paige envisioned her pulling on his cock, stretching the thing until it was about eight feet long and snapping him like a whip. When they sat down, she laid her hand on his thigh. Her fingers twitched against his skin. Maybe she was thinking the same thing. He was going to remove her hand, but then the music began and her fingers squeezed out the tempo on his leg and it was too late and Paige started thinking that there were entirely too many goddamn notes going on here.

The little man on the podium increased the tempo of the music, a vigorous allegro con brio, rocking his arms back and forth, snapping out the rhythm. For a moment, Grant was transfixed by the sight. He imagined himself in the conductor's place, whipping at the music as though it were an animal, forcing it to move faster and faster. His hands trembled, and the skin stretched out along his fingers seemed to tingle with sudden sensation. He was in control now, he could do whatever he wanted.

Grant looked down at Marlene Trombly and saw her glance around the auditorium searching for him. Paige doesn't even know what she's doing, he thought. That would change quickly. But this time Grant would leave a message for him, something even Paige would understand, something that would snap him to attention, show who he was up against.

Marlene Trombly rose from her seat and stood for a moment before making her way along the aisle. She wanted Grant to notice her. He was surprised she didn't stand on one of the seats. Was she that desperate to see him again?

He saw Paige turn to watch her go. Maybe if I left you her head this time, Grant thought, dropped it in your lap. Would you get the message then, Paige? He closed his eyes and let the thought take him away. When he opened them again, he rose from his seat and made his way down the stairs to find her, taking his time, not letting himself get too far ahead, knowing that there was no rush.

103

Marlene Trombly would wait for him. He was completely certain of that.

She'd been gone nearly ten minutes when Paige went to look for her. He wasn't worried, it was more caution than anything else. For all he knew, she was out in the lobby trying to pick up somebody else. Or maybe she'd decided that she'd had enough of him for one night and was in a taxi on her way home. If that was the case, Paige would be slightly disappointed. He could still feel the warmth of her hand on his leg. But if it happened, it happened.

She wasn't in the women's lounge. Paige knocked politely, then pushed open the door and called her name. There was no answer. He tried the lobby but found that empty as well.

Paige heard the sound of footsteps and turned to see Dickens and one of the ushers, a small dark-haired woman who moved with an agitated shuffle, like one of those mechanical toys that bounced into the wall and kept on going, walking toward him across the lobby.

"What are you doing out here?" Dickens asked.

"Looking for Mrs. Trombly," Paige said.

"Oh," Dickens said and glanced at the dark-haired usher. "I saw her leave with someone about five minutes ago."

"You what?" Paige said and grabbed Dickens by the front of his coat. "Who did she leave with?"

"A man," Dickens said, a shocked look spreading across his face. "I wasn't paying that much attention." Paige let him go and started for the door.

"She must have known him," Dickens said.

Paige stopped. "Why do you say that?"

"He was one of the last ones in line. When she got up to get a cigarette and looked out the window, she must have seen him. I didn't think anything was wrong. I thought they were friends or something."

"Christ," Paige said and bolted through the door.

Once outside, he made a quick decision and cut across Broad Street toward Society Hill.

Grant walked Marlene Trombly up Pine Street, keeping his hand locked around her elbow.

104

"Where are we going?" she asked. She didn't seem nervous or concerned, just curious, as if they were going out for an afterdinner drink. He was going to enjoy this, he really was.

"Just a little farther," he said.

"I don't think he'll follow us," she said. She smiled at him. He wanted to slap that smile off her face.

"Who's that?"

"Patrick Paige," she said. "The detective who's been looking for you."

Grant moved his hand up to the soft flesh of her bicep and squeezed until the smile vanished from her face and kept right on squeezing until the reality of the pain made her move away from him. She stepped off the sidewalk into the street but he pulled her back quickly.

"Stop," she said. "Please stop."

He loosened his hand and dragged her along, faster now, in a real hurry to get her alone.

It started to rain, a sudden and surprisingly violent downpour that drenched Paige in seconds and forced him into the narrow shelter of a nearby doorway. He was almost to the corner. On one side was a gay bookstore, on the other a pizza place. Paige didn't think they would be in either one. He wasn't even certain if she was in any danger. Maybe Dickens was right. It was just someone she knew and wanted to be with more than she wanted to be with Paige.

What if Dickens was wrong?

Paige looked up and followed the ragged roofline of the row houses across the street. Most still had their original slate roofs; a few were covered with painted metal because it went with the architecture. They were slick and treacherous when they were dry, in the rain they were deadly. His mind suddenly filled with dangerous thoughts. After a few minutes, he gave them up. No, Paige decided, I don't want to go up there tonight. He wanted to find her and soon.

The rain broke slightly and Paige continued up Pine Street, passing first through mixed blocks of antiques stores and row houses. There were just a few people on the street and they hurried past him. I've lost them, Paige thought, and a small seed of panic blossomed in the pit of his stomach. He willed the thought away and hurried up Pine Street, past Seventh and Sixth, deeper into Society Hill.

He took his gun out, carrying it close to his leg and away from the street, careful not to let anyone see it. That would end it all right there, some civilian screaming about a man with a gun on Pine Street. They'd call out the dogs for that one, Paige thought.

The block was solid row houses now, nothing else, three-story red brick façades sheltered by trees erupting out of the sidewalk every few yards. Both sides of the street were lined with cars. The traffic moved up the street in waves.

His hands and face were covered with sweat. It felt thick and greasy on his fingers, like oil oozing from his pores. He stopped next to a high wrought-iron fence and wiped his face with his sleeve.

Suddenly, unexpectedly, he had a clear line of vision all the way down to the corner of Eighth Street, a block and a half away. He saw Marlene Trombly stumble. The man with her grabbed her roughly and they hurried up the street.

Paige broke into a run.

Grant looked once behind him and saw Paige running up Pine Street in the rain. Without hesitating, he shoved Marlene Trombly into the street in front of a BMW. The driver swerved in time and she bounced lightly off the front bumper and fell backward onto the pavement. The BMW skidded to the left, straightened out for a few feet, and then slammed into a parked car on the other side of the street. Two other cars skidded to a halt behind him. One of the drivers got out to look at Marlene Trombly.

Grant raced to the next corner and was gone.

The driver of the BMW wanted everybody to know that it wasn't his fault. Paige knelt down next to Marlene Trombly to see if she was all right and the driver knelt down with him to tell him that she'd jumped right out in front of him. Paige waved the gun in his face and told him to get lost. Marlene Trombly was crying, holding her face in her trembling hands.

If she was crying, she was probably all right. Paige ran for the corner.

106

The man was gone. It couldn't have been more than thirty seconds and the son of a bitch had disappeared. Paige swore out loud and ran to the next street, a narrow slip of street he remembered as Addison, and glanced frantically left and right, looking for anything that moved. Nothing. He looked up at the roofline on either side of him and thought he saw something. It turned out to be only shadows. Not that it mattered. Paige knew where the man had gone.

"Shit," he yelled again, and started to look for a way up.

Grant watched for Paige from the rooftop, moving from one side to the other side, crawling crablike up the slick metal roof and then sliding down slowly and carefully, keeping his hands at his side like suctions to hold him as he descended toward the round cluster of exhaust pipes near the center of the steeply angled roof. From there he could see the parking lots along Addison Street and the gray stone entrance and massive wooden doors of Mother Bethel Church.

There was a large banner proclaiming the church's fiftieth anniversary that hung limply over Seventh Street. A patrol car crept past the church, paused at the corner and then turned down the alley between the church and a small fenced-in parking lot. Grant wedged himself against one of the pipes and felt the cold metal press against his skin through the thin fabric of his shirt. His coat was tied around his waist, rainsoaked and filthy, a seat pad to slow him as he slid down the roof.

Paige was nowhere to be seen. Grant had deceived him again. It was as though the man had been lost at sea, tossed overboard in a sudden squall. Grant closed his eyes and laughed, a sound only he could hear. When that stopped, there was something new, a scraping noise that came from below.

The sound of someone climbing onto the metal fire escape.

Paige hooked both hands onto the bottom rung of the fire escape and swung his legs up as the ladder shook and trembled and slowly began to drop. Paige moved up several rungs. The metal sweated beneath his fingers. Bits of rust and paint fell against his face. He caught the toe of his shoe in the platform grating. The ladder dropped another inch. He let go with one hand and swung hard, his arm curving up to grab the edge of the grating. His hand caught hold. He slipped off the ladder and hung precariously a dozen feet from the ground.

He slammed his free hand into the metal, fingers catching. He laced them into the grate and twisted his other foot between the bars of the platform. For a moment, Paige dangled like a spider. His fingers ached. The metal cut into his hands. Above him, the metal lacework of the fire escape was swallowed by shadows. More dirt fell on his face. Paige closed his eyes and shook it off. Then he climbed slowly onto the platform, the sound of his heart pounding in his ears.

A shadow broke away from the wall and descended on him. Paige saw it seconds before he was slammed back down on the platform, the metal biting hard into his face. A foot pressed into the center of his back and squeezed the air from his lungs. Paige went limp and then pushed up suddenly on his hands, twisting to the right to dislodge the foot. He didn't get far. The man who held him brought his knee down hard over Paige's kidney and slammed him into the grating. Then he jammed a gun into his neck and said very slowly, breaking the words down so Paige would hear each one, "Don't . . . fucking . . . move." Paige froze in place.

The man frisked him carefully, removing his gun and wallet, dropping the wallet on his back so he could look inside. A few seconds later the man spoke again. "Shit," he said angrily and stood up. "Goddammit," he said, a little louder this time. He stamped on the grating and the entire fire escape trembled.

Paige turned his head. The cop leaned against the side of the building and offered Paige a weary smile. Paige recognized him, the black cop who was on the door at Julia Weinstein's. "You were about that close, Batman," the cop said and stuck his hand out. The forefinger and thumb were an inch apart.

Paige didn't bother asking him to what.

"What the fuck are you doing up here?"

"I thought I heard something," Paige said. A patrol car drove down the alley from the far end, pulled underneath the fire escape and stopped.

"You know what I think," the cop said with an irritated grin. "I think you're fibbin'." He tossed the gun and shield back to Paige and sat down on the grating. A spotlight from the patrol car washed over them, stopped.

A head stuck out the window. "You all right up there?"

"We're okay," the cop yelled.

The light died and the patrol car backed slowly out of the alley.

"Sorry about that," Paige said. He stepped onto the ladder and it slid noisily to the ground. The cop watched while Paige climbed down.

"You're sorry," the cop said, sounding defeated. "So's Brenda Lee."

Paige walked up the alley for half a block before cutting over to Pine Street and back to the Academy. The sky had cleared and there were more people on the street. Paige passed through the crowds without seeing them, fighting the urge to return to the alley.

To his surprise, Marlene Trombly was waiting for him in the lobby. Her dress was muddy and wet and she held a paper towel to the palm of one hand. Paige took it away. The heel of her hand was scraped raw.

"You're a mess," he said. She acted as if it were a compliment.

"Did he get away?"

"Yes, he did," Paige said. "What the hell did you think you were doing?"

"I just wanted to see him again," she said. "That's the truth. I can't explain it." She took out a cigarette and lit it. "Look, I'm sorry he got away. I know it's my fault."

"You lied to me," he said. "That was stupid and dangerous." Marlene Trombly stared at him, unaffected by his anger. She didn't believe a word he said.

Paige turned away from her, sick of her carelessness.

"You shouldn't take this so personally," she said to him. "I lie to everybody. I don't seem to be able to do anything about it."

Grant showered at home, taking time to wash all the dirt from his hands and face, getting them as clean as he could. The cut on his hand had had no time to heal. He squeezed the wound and watched as blood oozed from it and ran down his fingers. Afterward, he dried himself on an immaculate white cotton towel and left little pink mouths scattered all over it. He stood before the full-length mirror in his bath and looked at himself.

In the light, his skin seemed dark and mottled. Not like Julia's. Hers was as white as the towel, as clear as ice. He could see through it, right down into the heart of it, the way she moved when he touched her. Or was it that other woman? For a moment he couldn't remember, then he saw Julia's face in his mind and his memory became clear.

Hurt me, she said. That was how it began. Grant moved closer to the mirror and felt himself growing hard. Julia was never that much interested in his cock, he thought, what she liked were his hands. Hurt me, she said. Where? Here, she told him and placed his hand on her breast, fingers close around the nipple.

He squeezed harder and her eyes closed. Beads of sweat caught in the fine hairs on the side of her neck. Grant squeezed harder, twisting the small dark bud. Her mouth fell open but no sound came out, only a rush of air, hot and moist. Grant felt himself quiver and touched himself, a light feathery touch that danced down the length of his cock. In the mirror, his legs bent at the knees.

That first time, Grant pulled down hard and Julia arched her back, opening her legs for him. With one hand, he rubbed between her legs, felt his fingers come away wet. He shoved two inside her suddenly, heard her gasp and felt her tighten around his fingers.

She moved against his hand, a hard fast rhythm. Grant stroked her anus with his thumb and she pressed up against it, forcing penetration. He slipped another finger inside her and pushed hard. When she responded, he started to release his other hand but she screamed at him to keep going. Grant's hands worked her body in a frenzy. He had never felt that kind of power. It seemed to surge through him and spilled over into her. Julia's words ran together, changed into a low throaty howl that she screamed into the mattress, her face buried in the sheets that she pulled around her neck.

Grant couldn't stand anymore. He released her and shoved himself inside of her, pounding and pounding, hands pulling and tearing at the flesh of her back. Julia screamed. Grant came, a blinding shot that snapped his head back, a spasm of pure pleasure, endless release. He ignored the feeling and pounded on her until she went limp and collapsed, sobbing against the bed.

Grant knelt beside her and stared at the flecks of blood on his hands, then glanced over and saw the scratches that covered her back and buttocks. She turned over and sobbed into his chest, licking the blood off his fingers like a small grateful animal.

Grant placed one hand against the mirror and jerked himself to a climax, sudden and sharp. Semen landed on the tile at his feet, a small reckless offering.

The next time, it was more interesting. Julia had wanted him to do more. By then she had bought the masks. And the ivory carving. And the other things. When Grant looked at himself in the mirror again, the memory burned bright in his eyes. He remembered the way her face had looked at the end and wanted to see it again.

That was why he'd gone after Marlene Trombly tonight.

It wasn't the chase that he missed, it was the blood.

14

Paige picked up Ferris at noon on Saturday while he was watching a baseball game on a portable television in the backyard.

"Come on," he said. "You feel like crabs?" Ferris sat there making up his mind. Paige turned off the television and the big man followed him out of the house.

Paige slapped the seat, his hand sticking to the plastic. "Get in, Tom," he said. "We'll sit down at DiNardi's and you can tell me what you've found out."

"Yeah," Ferris said, "and you can tell me all about playing Tarzan on the rooftops." Paige shrugged. "Good attitude," Ferris said and started laughing. "Jesus, Pat, didn't we go through this movie once before? Wasn't that enough for you?" Paige started the car. "I hope you get to grow up before you get yourself killed," Ferris said.

DiNardi's was on Race Street, about three blocks away from the Roundhouse. It was dark and cool inside, the big dining room not too crowded, only a dozen or so people. Ferris stopped first at the bar and spoke to the bartender. He bought a pitcher of beer and headed for the smaller dining room in the back.

The chairs and tables were thick and heavy. They sat down at a long table in the corner and drank glasses of beer.

Ferris drank quietly for a while, emptying one glass, refilling it, and drinking half before he spoke.

"I haven't found anything out yet," he said and took another drink.

"Nothing?"

"Not a damn thing. I told you nobody did that shit anymore. So what were you doing on the rooftops last night?"

Paige told Ferris what had happened and the detective listened impassively. "Who told you about it?"

"A fucking bird," Ferris said and grinned. "I just heard about it, that's all. Did you get a good look at the guy?"

"Enough," Paige said.

"What about the broad?"

What about her? Paige had driven past her house that morning, circled, and then parked a block away. He sat there until he saw Marlene Trombly turn out of her driveway and pull away in the opposite direction. Paige followed her back into Center City where she parked in a garage near Rittenhouse Square. She spent the morning shopping on Walnut Street. Around eleven-thirty she met another woman and they went to lunch at an expensive Chinese restaurant. He left them there and picked up Ferris.

"So where were you this morning?" Ferris asked casually. He held up his glass by the rim and gently swirled the beer around. "I called when I heard and when you weren't at home, I figured you were getting your dick sucked." Paige told him. Ferris shook his head in disbelief. "I don't know how you can let all these opportunities pass you by."

"What do you know about Nolan?"

"At the Wissahickon? Not much. He's all right. Why?"

"She had a burglary last year. He handled it. He thought it looked like an insurance scam." Paige tapped his fingers. "No forced entry, nothing else disturbed, only some jewels and cash taken, a couple antiques, everything insured."

Ferris put down his glass. "And you think it was your boy?"

Paige nodded. The waitress came just then to take their order. Ferris asked for two orders of crabs and extra cole slaw. Paige didn't object. Ferris filled their glasses again. "So this was

113

the same guy you were chasing around the rooftops down on South Street the other night?"

"You bet."

"Then you ain't doing so good then, are you? You plan on doing it some more?"

Paige let the question go unanswered. They drank in silence for a while and then the waitress brought the crabs. They were orange-red and covered with seasoned salt and stacked on big metal serving platters. Ferris pulled one in front of him, turned it over, and smacked it with a small wooden mallet. Paige did the same. Juice poured out onto the newspapers. Paige pulled away the cracked shell and dug through the crab to the pockets of pale white meat. The meat was sharp and tangy with the seasoned salt. Paige sucked some from his fingers and drank more beer.

Ferris picked through the shell of the crab and pulled out more meat.

"How many you think this guy does a year, half a dozen?"

"Maybe a dozen," Paige said. "Maybe more. He might still do some out-of-town work, I don't know."

"I forget," Ferris said, "you been a fan of this guy for years. You think he takes any contract work?"

"No," Paige said. "I don't see him working for Little Nicky."

"There's a couple more might use him. Nicky's looking at some serious time. He's not the only one hiring crooks these days."

"No," Paige said. "He works alone. One of the things he took from Julia's place was a small picture, a pen-and-ink draw-ing, nothing you could move easily. Most galleries wouldn't touch somebody off the street because it's too risky. Everything else is private collections. My guess is he follows the market, watches the auctions, knows who's buying."

"Is that what I'm suppose to be looking for, a fucking painting?"

"I want you to find out who's buying, that's all."

"Why don't you send a flyer out on it?" Ferris asked. "The painting, I mean. I'll take it around to the usual places." The unit had a list of antiques stores that had cooperated with them in the past, letting them know if someone was offering suspect merchandise. It never worked. Ferris wanted to do it because he thought the whole case was a dead end. Paige exploded.

"Jesus Christ," he said. "Can you do the goddamn job or not, Tom?"

Ferris drank his beer in silence, irritation hidden behind his eyes. "Yeah, I can handle it, Pat. Just give me a couple more days."

"Okay," Paige said.

"Hey, maybe he'll go and fuck up on us," Ferris offered sweetly.

"I don't think we can count on that," Paige said. He took a swallow of beer and watched while Ferris pulled another crab in front of him. They ate without talking. Ferris cracked crab after crab with the precision of an assembly line. After a while, Paige sat back and marveled at the man's appetite. Ferris stared up at him from underneath heavy eyebrows.

"I'm hungry," Ferris said.

"I can see that," Paige said. "How's Marion?"

"None of your fucking business," Ferris answered. "At her place, I hope." He loudly sucked a piece of crab from his fork. "She thinks because we screw every now and then she can come and go like her name's on the deed." He ate some more and then changed the subject. "I heard this the other day, this is no joke. They're going to send all the captains to manager training classes at Penn. The commissioner's got everybody fired up about it. He says we're like a major corporation now and we got to know how to prioritize things." He rolled his eyes. "Hey, I'm all for it. When all those assholes are finished, they can go to work for Wa-Wa. Your old man would've shit green."

"I've been thinking about him lately," Paige said.

"I think about him all the time," Ferris said. "At least he knew what worked. I listen to these guys and half the time I can't believe what I'm hearing. Nobody cares what works now, they just care what it looks like. I'm surprised they didn't invite the neighbors over to Osage Avenue and pretend it was a fucking barbecue."

"That's what Danny might've done."

"Only he'd have made them believe it. Now we got Wilson Goode, talks like he ate shit for breakfast and liked it. Ten years

ago we would have dropped a fucking hydrogen bomb on it."
Ferris turned serious. "The point I'm making here, Pat, because
I am making a point here, is that you want to watch what you're
doing. This is the wave of the future and if you start running
around the rooftops again, they're going to whack your nuts
for you."

"Lay off it, Tom," Paige said.

"Okay, you make your own mistakes," Ferris said. "Just
keep it in mind. I'll get on that other thing."

They paid the check and got up to leave.

"I saw Mickey Katz the other day," Paige said on the way
out. "He said to say hello."

Ferris looked straight through him. "Mickey Katz," he said.
"I didn't even think the little fuck was still alive. I haven't seen
him in years. You guys buddies or something?"

"I bring him breakfast now and then. I busted him,
remember."

"I busted a lot of guys. I don't deliver their donuts."

"He said he knew Danny."

They were out on the street, trying to talk over the sound
of passing cars and the stench of exhaust fumes.

"Did he?" Ferris said. A cloud passed briefly over his face,
then he was all smiles again. "Isn't that something."

"Come on, Tom, why didn't you tell me he knew Danny?"

"Hey, maybe he did, how the hell should I know? Your old
man knew everybody, from the cardinal on down. Maybe he
knew Mickey Katz. It's no big deal if he did."

"I didn't say it was. I just thought it was strange that I never
heard about it before."

"That your old man didn't tell you that he met Mickey Katz
once in a blue moon? Come on, Pat, this isn't a serious issue as
far as I can see." He started walking up the street.

"Where are you going?" Paige asked.

"I'm going for a walk," he said. "I need the exercise."

"You never exercised in your whole life."

"So I'll start today. Do me good." He stopped for a moment
and laughed. "Hey, Pat," he said, "this Trombly broad, I heard
she's got great tits. Too bad you didn't get a shot at 'em."

Paige started to say something but Ferris was already walking away, laughing like crazy, one hand pounding out a nervous rhythm on the side of his leg.

When Paige got home, he tried to get in touch with Jimmy Wu to find out what he'd learned about the carving, but he was gone for the weekend on a management study retreat.

15

The house smelled. It had been closed up for so long that the odors had worked their way into the walls. Dirt, mildew, blood, in the dark Grant could smell each one. In the kitchen there was a trace of something burned on the stove; upstairs, the blood smell was still there, tinged with the scent of disinfectant. They'd tried to clean it up and botched the job.

Grant was in Paige's old house, trying to imagine what it must have been like to come home and find your wife waiting for you in the bedroom with her head busted open.

Did you have a rough day, dear?

The newspaper articles didn't elaborate on her exact location in the room, so Grant used his imagination.

He picked the bed.

Maybe tied up. Arms and legs strapped down. Mouth taped shut. Maybe the guy got cute and stuffed a couple surprises inside of her just for fun. Cheap theatrics, Grant thought. He leaned against the row of windows and looked up. There was an exposed beam running across the ceiling.

Better yet, maybe he hung her up there, so that when Paige

stepped into the room she was spinning like a top, round and round.

Want to dance, honey?

Grant breathed deeply in the darkness, trying to suck it into his lungs. The place definitely had potential.

Hell, his whole life had potential at the moment, nothing but.

He ran down the list in his mind.

Money. That was potential number one. He had a lot but wanted more. It was like Runyon's rule, know what you want. He definitely wanted more. Once he cleared that up, his life would definitely run much smoother. Peterson. The dealer had some potential, too, and if he didn't come through on it, Grant was going to stick his fist down his throat.

Marlene Trombly. That was an interesting potential, Grant thought, and wondered what it would be like to leave her hanging from a ceiling hook in the living room. By August she might get a little ripe but it would be fun for Paige to have to explain what the pile of goo with hair was doing in the front room of his old house. I'd pay to see that, Grant thought.

Paige. That was dangerous potential. Everything else was just bits of matter to be manipulated, none of it with any real power to harm him. Paige was different. Paige was in his way and Grant was going to have to figure out a way to stop him.

If the detective somehow found out what Grant was doing or where he was going, there was nothing to stop him from destroying those plans. He could just leave now, take the money and run. That was something he'd thought a great deal about.

But there was something unsatisfactory about that solution. It had the air of retreat to it. Who the hell was Paige to get in his way? He'd never been caught, never been arrested for anything, and now he was thinking about running out because of one man, one fucking cop! Grant slapped the beam, his fingers scraping across the rough surface.

No potential there. None.

Running was definitely out.

16

Paige brought Mickey his breakfast on Sunday morning, bagels, a smooth white chunk of cream cheese, whitefish, sliced onions, and tomatoes, always the same. One time he bought nova lox because the deli was out of whitefish and Mickey dumped them in the wastebasket. "What the hell you bring me this Presbyterian fish for?" Mickey said and looked insulted. "A Jew can't eat this."

He was sitting up reading the *News*, rustling the pages nervously. "You took your sweet time," he said. "I thought maybe you were going to forget."

Paige laid out the food and watched the old man smear a poppy seed bagel with cream cheese and take a bite before covering the rest of it with chunks of whitefish, onion, and tomato. When he bit into it, his hand shook. He saw Paige staring at him.

"What's the matter with you? I'm old. You never seen an old man eat breakfast before?" He held out his hand. It still shook. "It's a new one. Hell if I know what it is." He took another bite. "Don't worry, this shit happens to everybody. You'll get your turn." When he finished the first bagel, he wiped his mouth with a napkin. "You bring me those tit books?"

"I forgot," Paige said. "Next time."

"Yeah, right, next time," Mickey grumbled. "That's all I keep hearing from you." He pointed at the bag. "Cut me another half a bagel there, Mr. Next Time, put some fish on it." Paige did that and then cut an onion bagel for himself and ate it plain.

When he was finished eating, Mickey reached in the drawer of the nightstand and fished out a plastic jar of toothpicks. He selected one and began to probe his teeth for poppy seeds.

"Stuff's in the top drawer of the dresser," Mickey said. "You give it to me first before you start putting your fingers all over it." Paige opened the drawer and found the pad of paper and handed it across the bed. Mickey reached in the nightstand again and took out a pair of reading glasses. He propped them on the bridge of his nose and began to read. After a few minutes, he tossed the pad on the bed. "Go ahead," he said. "You probably know them already."

There were seven names on the list and Paige had heard of only four of them. Three were new. He wanted Mickey to explain it, but the old man was breathing comfortably through the air mask. Paige thought he did that when he wanted to be courted. Finally, Mickey lowered the mask.

"All of them done business one time or another," he said. "I don't know if they done any recently. The first two, Anderson and Rothman, they act as sales sheets only, maybe they take a piece of the business when it goes through but maybe not. They don't need the money, that's for sure."

A sales sheet was a legitimate dealer who sometimes made "special sales" arrangements for their best customers. The risk was minimal. "What about a list of transactions?" Paige said.

"Please," Mickey said scornfully.

"I had to ask," Paige said. "What about the last three?"

"Nobody knows too much about them except that they're new and doing a good business. Maybe somebody thinks that business is too good, who knows? No guarantees."

"When did you ever give me a guarantee?"

Mickey picked some crumbs off the bed. "You start bringing me magazines like you promised, you might get a few."

121

"Why don't you ask Archie to get them for you?" Archie was Mickey's private nurse. He came in three days a week, no weekends.

Mickey laughed. "Archie's a goddamn Baptist. He's too busy praying for my soul. You imagine what he'd start praying for if I asked him for a couple tit books? He likes Jews. Now that we got Israel, he thinks the Messiah's coming back." He started to cough, grabbed the mask and took several deep breaths. "I tell you, I ain't interested unless he brings a *Penthouse* or two with him."

Paige stood up. "Tom Ferris says hello."

Mickey eyed him suspiciously. "He does, does he? He remembered me after all."

"He was surprised you were still around."

"Yeah, well fuck him, too," Mickey said. "That's all he said?"

"That's it. Why's this so important?"

"Who said it was important? A man does some favors, he likes to be remembered, appreciated, that's all. Shitheads like Ferris don't think like that."

Paige sat down on the bed. "What kind of favors did you do for Tom Ferris?"

"Nothing," Mickey said but then he saw that Paige wasn't going to let it go. "Okay, okay," he said. "Same stuff I do for you, checking up on things, asking around, nothing."

"You're pretty upset for it to be nothing," Paige said.

"I'm an old man, I can do what I goddamn well please," Mickey shot back. "What did Tom Ferris ever do for you that you couldn't do yourself? What's he doing for you now?" Mickey pointed to the papers in Paige's hand. "Ferris could've given you those. He knows about those places as good as anybody."

"What do you mean?"

"I mean, if he wasn't such a prick, he would've given you the names of those places and maybe a couple more. What do you think he spent all those years with your old man playing chauffeur without learning something about how things work around here? His trouble is, he lives in the past too much." Mickey stuck a finger in his mouth, searching around for something.

"Like you. You live alone. You still keep the old house.

You get caught up in this new business. You worry too much. You need a girlfriend, take her out to dinner, go to the zoo. You got a girlfriend?"

Paige shook his head.

"Nobody since Connie," Mickey said. "That's a real shame. Just this one who got stiffed, right? I hope you find this guy, maybe your luck'll change." Mickey seemed to grow tired suddenly. His eyelids fluttered and he leaned his head back against the wall and closed them for a moment. Paige cleaned up the bed and put what was left back in the bag. He'd take it with him, have it for lunch.

Mickey opened his eyes. "Margate," he said. "That's where I met your old man for the first time. Tommy Ferris, too. We used to drive down there together." His eyelids fluttered once more. He spoke again before he dozed off. "Man does a few favors, he likes to be remembered."

Paige's father had the use of a house in Margate, an expensive two-story brick house with a long sloping roof and a big front porch and a nice front lawn that was kept mysteriously trimmed all summer long but Paige never saw who did it. The house was a block from the ocean and you could hear the waves all the time. In the morning, his father drank his coffee standing on the front porch, watching the street.

When Connie died, Paige stopped going to Margate but that wasn't what bothered him now.

What bothered him now was that if Ferris knew all the dealers, why hadn't he told Paige about them? And if Mickey Katz had been in Margate with him, why hadn't Paige ever seen them together?

There was a message from Marlene Trombly on his answering machine at home. She refused to have a patrol unit parked outside her house so he made a point of asking for some additional patrols of her neighborhood. It might help, it might not. Unless he wanted to sit on her front steps, there wasn't much else he could do for her. He decided to drive out and talk to her in person.

When she opened the front door, Paige could see that she was a little drunk.

123

"I got your message," Paige said.

The sound of her voice felt like something warm on his skin.

She smiled. "Yes," she said. "Well, I called to apologize for the other night. I'm not sure that really covers it but I wanted to say it. I don't know what got into me." She smiled again. It seemed an automatic thing. "You came over here to check on me?"

"I wanted to make sure you were all right."

"I'm just fine," she said. "Can't you tell?" Then she retreated into the house. Paige followed her inside.

"Is your husband here?" Paige asked.

"Of course not. He's playing racquetball or something like that," she said. "I don't try to compete with him anymore. Do you play at anything?"

Paige shook his head.

"Aren't you wonderful," she said. She made herself another drink at the small bar in the living room but didn't offer him one. She hesitated, then took a deep breath. "There's something else," she said. "I remembered it after I got home. Maybe it'll help, I don't know, but I did want to tell you about it. A little peace offering."

There was another pause as though she was going to ask him a question first, then she continued. "It was something the burglar mentioned, I don't remember why. We were talking about art and he said that he liked the Art Museum."

She stirred her drink with her finger, then sucked it clean. "We talked some more and then I said that I never went there anymore except to the Patrons' Ball. He said that was nice, too, and we went on to something else." She stopped to make certain Paige understood. "That's what I wanted to tell you, about the Patrons' Ball."

Paige had been half listening, now his mind clicked into focus.

"Did he say anything else," he asked. "That he was going to attend?"

"No," she said. "That was it."

"Did he mention it after that?"

"I told you, that was the only time. It was such a small thing."

"Who goes to the Patrons' Ball?"

"Anybody who wants to, I suppose. It's not really for members only. You buy a ticket and go. They're very expensive. I think they start at five hundred dollars or something like that. I don't plan on going this year, so I don't know how much they are now."

"When is it?"

"A few weeks, I guess. I don't remember."

"Did he say he was a member of the Art Museum?"

"No. I don't think he'd do something like that, do you?"

Paige thought about it. No, he doubted if the man had his real name on anything important.

"Will that help you find him?"

"I don't know," Paige said.

"Well, I hope it helps." Another deep breath. "I'd like to see you again. I mean away from work. Do you understand?" When he didn't answer right away, she said, "Now who's being a shit?"

"I don't think that's a good idea," Paige said.

"Why? Are you married?"

"No," Paige said. "But it isn't a good idea anyway."

"You don't approve of me, do you?"

"Look," Paige said suddenly, "I think you should leave town for a while."

"Why? Because you don't want to sleep with me?" She laughed and took a long drink.

Paige wanted to shake her out of her foolishness. "He might come back, he might not. Whatever he does, I don't think you ought to be here."

"I'm not going to run away from him," she said. There was some defiance in her voice now.

"Did you have the locks changed from the last time?"

"My husband did. The insurance company recommended it. The agent came out and did a survey afterward. Made us promise to do all sorts of things."

"Like what?

"Change the locks, put in the security system, that sort of thing. Frank said he took care of it." She put her drink down. "You're just trying to scare me."

"He threw you in front of a car," Paige said.

125

"I fell," she said. "Don't you tell me what happened the other night. I was there. You were a block away. Some hero. At least he still wants me." She laughed at her own joke.

"Jesus," Paige said. He couldn't tell whether she was excited or terrified of the idea of the burglar coming back for her. She seemed quite capable of both. Once again, he felt the need to get away from her and her urge to self-destruct. He couldn't help her; she wouldn't let him.

Paige turned to go. She hurried after him, nearly falling as the heel of her shoe caught on the edge of the rug. Paige caught her and then gently pushed her away.

"Oh, for God's sakes," she said. "Frank's got a better sense of humor than you do and he doesn't have any at all. Just tell me what you want me to do and I'll do it. There, is that what you wanted to hear?"

"Just go somewhere for a few weeks," he said.

"Where?"

"I don't know what you like," he said.

"Why don't you come with me and find out? Frank won't mind. He never has."

"Maybe he just never bothered to look."

She smiled again, the full force of her sadness coming through. "All he does is look," Marlene Trombly said. "That's all he likes to do these days."

That night Paige ate dinner at McDonald's and went home. He drank one Rolling Rock and then another and watched the beginning of an old Paul Newman movie where Newman played Billy the Kid. The color was bad but the movie was all right. He hadn't seen a decent western in years, and he had forgotten how much he liked them. Paul Newman was awfully young in this one, though. He closed his eyes for a minute and let himself drift into sleep. It was like opening the door to a fun house somewhere in his brain. People kept popping out at him in no particular order.

First there was Marlene Trombly, who kept asking if Paige wanted to go with her, and when Paige said sure, why not, she disappeared into another room and the room turned into the house at Margate and his father kept asking him to turn it up, turn it up, goddammit, and Ferris came out and said he was

126

sorry that things had turned out the way they did. Paige couldn't hear him anymore because the screaming was too loud, and then the dream started again.

In the dream, it was always the same.

Connie stood in the kitchen, her back turned toward him. She wore a filmy pink nightgown that hung awkwardly from one shoulder, as though she had been forced to dress in a hurry and was now too preoccupied with something else to straighten it. The nightgown bunched and covered her feet. It reminded him of waves rolling onto a beach.

Paige could not reach her, he could only watch her through the window from the backyard where he stood with his fingers pressed lightly against the glass. The glass seemed to warm to his touch, a living creature responding to a caress. He tapped lightly, trying to catch her attention. She stood with her back to him on the other side of the kitchen and did not hear his tapping. Paige grew frightened, a horrifying fear that felt like ice along the back of his neck. He began to pound on the glass harder and harder, trying to break it, to warn her to get away. But the glass merely bent to his blows. Paige screamed out her name.

The door opened and let in the darkness. Then the darkness took shape. Arms reached out to cover her, lifted her gown and rushed like the wind through her hair. Paige screamed her name again and swung at the glass. It gave way with a shattering roar.

Connie turned around.

The first sprinkles of blood fell like wet snow, splashing here and there around her feet. Paige could not look at her at first; then, he could not take his eyes away. Blood ran from her head in long rivulets. It poured down her arms and dropped from her fingers like water from a sluice. It would not stop. The darkness rolled out across the floor toward him.

Connie looked directly at Paige and said, "Help me." But the darkness was in the way and Paige could not reach her to make the blood stop falling.

Paige woke up.

He was still in the chair. The movie was over and the news was on. He stayed there for a few minutes and then went to the refrigerator for another beer. It foamed over his lips and

127

ran down his chin. Paige moved from the kitchen to the back-door, swinging it open with one hand, tipping the bottle of beer to his mouth with the other. Paige stood in the doorway and breathed in the smell of the city.

The thought struck him that in the years since his wife's murder, only one woman had spent the night in the house he lived in now. The idea of it amazed him.

He could not remember her name. All he remembered was that she was a grad student from Temple who said she had a thing for cops. She didn't talk much after that, and then scared the hell out of him when she started screaming while they were in bed together.

She screamed so loud, he was afraid that the neighbors would call the police. Then she looped her legs around his neck and pulled him in close, and Paige didn't care if they called the National Guard. He was suddenly blinded by this enormous lust, and she sensed it, urging him on with her tongue and her hands, and Paige slammed himself into her and didn't care about anything at all.

Paige drank more of the beer and wished for a little of that blindness now. The dream did that to him. When Connie was killed, he spent the nights after her death searching the streets for her killer. During the day he was on the phone to homicide, demanding to know what they'd found, what suspects had been questioned, what leads looked good. His father was like a ghost. Paige was never certain whether he was there or not.

He barely ate, seemed incapable of speech and appeared to walk past people without seeing them. The funeral was at Ivy Hill near the house. He refused to stand by the grave when they lowered the coffin and went straight back to work from the cemetery. His actions seemed simple and clear. Until he found her killer, he would not accept the fact of her death. The dream would not let him.

He told Ferris about the dream and Ferris told him that if he didn't lighten up, he was going to end up out at Philadelphia State Hospital counting Ju-Ju-Bees. They didn't have psychologists and stress seminars for cops then. They didn't need them. Cops were tough. Everybody went crazy all by themselves.

And then it was over. Ferris killed the burglar and his father spit on him in his coffin and the dream stopped. So did everything else for a long time.

Paige finished the beer and sat down on the doorstep. The bottle rested at his feet, balanced on one of the battered bricks that passed for his patio. This was how far he'd come in those seven years. He no longer wept or went crazy or became something he could no longer put a name to, he drank beer instead.

A light passed through the bottle, warming the green glass. Paige looked up to see where it came from and saw a woman's shadow pass in front of the shade on a third-floor window in the building directly behind his. She paused for a moment as if she could feel him watching her and then faded from view. The light went out. Maybe she's watching me now, he thought, wondering how far you had to go before you escaped completely from some stranger's eyes.

Then it struck him. He saw the woman on the third floor and then Connie standing alone in the kitchen and then the Trombly woman lying in the street and thought that there was another way to catch the man he was after.

He couldn't use Marlene Trombly again. That would be too obvious, and besides, she might decide to run off with the guy again.

He would need somebody else. Like Mickey said, maybe you just hung around someplace until you found somebody you thought looked good.

17

Paige tried to find Ferris Monday morning, but he wasn't in the office or at home. He thought about calling his girlfriend but said to hell with it and spent the day going through the list of dealers Mickey had given him.

The Hazen Gallery was the last one on the list. The others, as Ferris had predicted, turned out to be dead ends. The address for the gallery was on Locust a block or so west of Rittenhouse Square.

But it wasn't there. In its place was an oriental rug shop. The owner, a well-dressed Iranian, told him that yes, the Hazen Gallery had been there, but had moved out over a year before and no, he did not know where. Had Paige looked in the phone book? The man made no effort to help until Paige said he was with the police and the man was suddenly eager to accommodate. There was no new listing for the Hazen Gallery in the phone book, either.

"Who did the moving?" Paige asked.

"I beg your pardon?" the Iranian said.

"Do you remember the name of the movers?"

The Iranian thought for a moment, disappeared into his

office, and came out with a dirty business card. "They did," he said. "I remember I asked them for a card. I thought perhaps it would be good to have one."

Paige read the card: WARREN MOVERS in Chester.

"Please," the Iranian said and graciously offered his office and his phone.

It took a few minutes but in the end they gave Paige the information. The move wasn't a big one. Just to Society Hill, they said.

On his way out, Paige showed the ivory carving to the Iranian for the hell of it. He'd taken to carrying it around for good luck. The fact that it hadn't produced anything like that was beside the point.

"I have seen something like this," the Iranian said.

"Where?"

"In a movie, I think," the Iranian said. He had begun to sweat just thinking about it. "Do you think you can get it for me?"

The name was no longer the Hazen Gallery but Peterson's Antiques. The blond man at the front door of Peterson's Antiques shook his head.

"We're closed," he said, and Paige heard the words from behind the glass as though they were whispered into a bottle. Paige flopped his shield out and the man looked perturbed. But he opened the door and let him inside.

"I hope there isn't a problem," the man said as Paige strolled across the showroom. The room was small but the high ceiling made it seem much larger. Some larger pieces, a dark wood armoire and an elaborately inlaid desk, dominated one side. The other was composed of smaller pieces, a group of rosewood nesting tables, several small paintings, and some glass pieces.

"Are you looking to buy something?" the man asked. He stood behind an Empire desk, the light blond legs curved down to delicately clawed feet. Paige noticed that the color was nearly the same as the man's hair.

"No," Paige said. He took out a list of stolen items that he'd made up from several recent robberies including what had been taken from the Trombly house. "Has anyone tried to sell you any of these items in the last few months?"

131

"We have quite a bit of street traffic," the man said. "And I don't keep as good a track of things as I should." He looked at Paige curiously. "May I see your badge again, please?"

Paige held out his shield and ID. When he was satisfied, the man handed him a business card from a little rack on the desk.

"My name is Peterson," he said. "It's on the card." Paige looked at it. It said his first name was Lindor. The dealer turned his attention to Paige's list and after reading it, sighed. "These are mostly American pieces and we don't have a lot of Americana these days. There's not a lot of it around."

"Sure," Paige said. "This being America, I can understand that."

Peterson looked at him even more curiously than before and handed back the list. "I see," he said. "Is that it? Do you want to look around?"

"Sure," Paige said. There was something odd about Peterson, Paige thought, he didn't quite fit together. He wanted to look at him some more, so he handed the list back to Peterson. "Why don't you check through this one more time and I'll take a look around. We can meet back here at the desk when we're through."

Peterson took the list without comment. That was it, Paige thought. He figured Peterson to be about his age, maybe a year or two younger, which would have made him just shy of forty and his face showed it. But the rest of him didn't. The rest of him looked like a twenty-two-year-old.

"You work out?" Paige asked.

"And run," Peterson said. "At a certain point, it's required, isn't it?" He read through the list again, shaking his head.

"I could never find the time," Paige said.

"You have to make time," Peterson said without looking up. That was the other thing about guys who exercised a lot, Paige thought. They were arrogant pricks.

Paige walked around the shop, halfheartedly looking at what was displayed. There were a few nice items, pieces of English silverwork, a pair of matching mother-of-pearl inlaid picture frames, things only a thief who knew what he was doing would steal. Peterson was watching him. Maybe the dealer thought Paige was going to steal something.

132

Paige looked at the other wall and picked out one of the paintings at random. He looked back at Peterson. The dealer held up the list.

"There's nothing here I recognize, I'm afraid. I'm sorry."

Paige moved toward the picture and took it down from the wall.

"This is a nice one," he said. "Where'd you get it?"

Peterson stayed behind the desk.

"I can't tell from here," he said. "Let me see it."

Paige handed the picture to him. Peterson seemed annoyed.

"I bought this in Atlanta last month," Peterson said.

"Do you remember who you bought it from?"

"Cusslor Antiques," Peterson said smugly. "Do you want to see a receipt?"

Paige hung the picture back up. He reached in his pocket and took out the ivory carving. "What about this? Have you ever seen anything like this? Somebody said it looked South American."

Peterson looked at it, then handed it back. Most people liked to look at it. They enjoyed touching it. Peterson acted like he couldn't wait to get rid of the thing. "They don't know what they're talking about. It's obviously Asian."

"But you've never seen one before?"

"No," Peterson said.

"Then how do you know it's Asian?"

"Do you know anything about art history?" Peterson asked.

"No," Paige said.

"If you did, you'd know. They have a tradition of erotic carvings. South America doesn't."

"What do they have?" Paige asked. "South America, I mean."

"Dictators," Peterson said. "Why don't you try Chinatown?"

"I might do that," Paige said.

There was a newspaper clipping on his desk. Paige ignored it at first, then the headline caught his eye: THE OPEN WOUND. It was a column by Dave Loomis. Loomis wrote a lot of tough talk with great side helpings of revved-up pathos. Usually Paige never bothered reading him. When he saw his name in the first paragraph, he groaned out loud and read it standing up.

"It says something about a man the way he goes about his work," Loomis wrote. "Sometimes the work is dangerous. Sometimes it's even painful. The best ones do it quietly. They keep the pain inside. These are the ones you'd like for your friend.

"Patrick Paige is a cop, a good cop. He's had more arrests in the burglary squad than anybody else in the department. He's the kind of cop you'd like to see on your street and in your neighborhood, the kind you'd like to see talking to your kids. He's the kind of cop, the kind of man, they don't make anymore.

"Seven years ago, Patrick Paige's wife was killed by a burglar. You wouldn't know that unless you read about it in the newspaper because he doesn't talk about it. He keeps the pain to himself and does his job and doesn't ask for special favors the way a lot of professionals do these days, from athletes to airline pilots."

Paige couldn't read anymore. The words had the ring of something unpleasant; at any moment he expected them to turn and bite him. He put the clipping down and went to get himself a cup of coffee. He didn't know whether to laugh or throw up.

He wasn't surprised when he came back to find Ferris at his desk reading the article. "You want to tell me about that?" Paige asked mildly.

"A story on one of our local heroes?" Ferris said. He did it with just the trace of a smile on his face. "I thought you could use it," he said.

"You thought I could use it?" Paige said. His voice had grown rough, a slight burr that rasped around the edges of his words. "Do I look that lonesome? Do I look like I need the publicity?"

"I didn't write it," Ferris said.

"The hell you didn't," Paige answered.

"All this just so you could turn down a favor?"

Paige grabbed the article and threw it in the metal wastebasket near the side of the desk. "This isn't a favor," Paige said. "This is bullshit. I don't want to be a story. I was one once before and I didn't like it. My life is my own. I want to keep it that way."

Ferris nodded. He seemed calm and remote. Paige wondered if he had even heard what he had said. "I did it to help

134

you," Ferris said. "I did it because you deserve it. The story's true and you know it."

"It isn't true," Paige said. "It's not even me, it's somebody else."

Ferris pulled the article from the wastebasket and smoothed out the pages. "You may think it's a piece of shit but the public won't. They like heroes. They'll think it's the truth." He folded the paper and stuck it in his pocket.

"I don't want to be a hero, Tom," Paige said. "Don't do this anymore." He saw a look of betrayal in Ferris's eyes. I should have seen it coming, he thought. It had always been easier to agree with Danny than fight him, and Ferris had turned out the same way. His father would have been beside himself.

"You got anything else planned?" Paige asked.

Ferris shook his head. "How about you?"

Paige hesitated, then told him about the Patrons' Ball and the other thing, the thing that woke him up after the dream and then kept him up while he thought about how to do it. When he finished, Ferris rubbed a hand across his eyes as if he were wiping away tears.

"You know this is crazy, don't you?"

"It'll work fine if we find the right person."

"And get lucky as hell," Ferris said. "I should have got you in the fucking Sunday magazine."

"Have you got anything better?"

"How about we both get drunk as hell and forget the whole thing."

"After we get it done," Paige said.

Ferris shook his head. He played with a paper clip from the desk. "I started checking some places for you today. I didn't get anything."

"Did you check on Peterson's Antiques?"

"No," Ferris said.

"It used to be Hazen Gallery. That ring any bells?"

Ferris shrugged. Paige was too tired to argue with him. "I want you to keep an eye on them for me. Nothing special. Just for a few days, see if you get anything."

"You want anybody from the unit on it?"

"No," Paige said. "Keep the Art Museum to yourself, too. I don't want to see it in another one of Loomis's columns."

Ferris glanced down at his crotch and grinned. "Gee," he said, "I think I'm getting excited already. Who have you got in mind for the museum?"

"I thought I'd start with Kate Evans at the DA's," Paige said.

"Sweet Katie? Since when did you start banging the DA's little helpers? I hear she's starting to get ambitious over there."

"She can help and she won't talk about it."

"Why the hell is that?"

"Because she hasn't done it before," Paige said.

Ferris appeared mildly surprised, as if he'd just discovered something about Paige he hadn't known before.

"When did you get to be such a secretive prick?"

Paige pointed to Ferris's shirt pocket, the one with the article inside. "When did you?" he asked.

18

The DA's office was at 13th and Chestnut, the former Blum Building, which had been a clothing store for women. There were still stores on the first floor, a discount shoe store and a stereo place that kept its front door open during the summer and blasted rap music out onto the sidewalk. The DA's offices occupied the rest of the floors, two through ten.

The story on the building was that the city rented it from ex-Congressman Frank Dodd, who not only owed substantial back taxes on the building but also kept a large pornography collection as well. The city forgave him the taxes and he let the city use the building and nobody bothered him when he added to his collection, which was said to contain a lot of funny stuff, young boys doing cuddly things with house pets and weight lifters.

Chestnut Street crossed Broad Street one block south of City Hall. During the day, it was closed to all traffic except the SEPTA buses, which roamed up and down, spewing black exhaust at the shoppers. Like the rest of that stretch of Chestnut

Street, the DA's building was grungy. One window of the shoe store was boarded up and covered with unreadable graffiti.

When Paige phoned Kate Evans, she told him to come to her office anytime after eight o'clock that night. "All the assholes will be in bed by then," she said without laughing. "But I'll still be here."

Paige thought she looked older than the last time he'd seen her, which was almost a year ago. She still smoked and there was a gray pallor to her complexion, as if someone had rubbed cigarette ash into her skin. Only her eyes remained alive and alert. She sat in her open cubicle on the fourth floor wearing a beige skirt and blouse, her shoes were off, her legs bare. Her shoes had been tossed in a corner by her desk. A pair of panty hose stuck out of one of them. He noticed she'd put on weight; her calves were plump with fat.

"My mother says the same thing," Kate said to him before he could open his mouth. In the small cubicle there was one other chair, but it was covered with paper, so he sat down on two boxes of files stacked beside the desk. She lit a cigarette and blew the smoke straight up in the air. It hung over them in the white fluorescent light.

"She says I need to take better care of myself. I tell her I'll take care of myself when she moves the hell out of Atlantic City. How are you, Pat?"

"I'm fine," he said. "You look all right to me."

"Aren't you sweet when you want something," she answered. "I look like my job." She smiled at him then or what he thought was a smile. Her mouth was a straight line across her face. "On the other hand, you look like somebody who just got his name in the paper." She picked up Loomis's column off her desk and held it delicately between two fingers. "Morrissey says you suck hard cheese."

Morrissey was her supervisor, an ex-Marine who had been in the career criminal unit for over a dozen years. He told everybody who would listen that he wanted to die there. Morrissey was a prick and would probably get his wish.

"It's junk and you know it," Paige said.

"It's news," she said. "And everybody loves the news." Paige took the column from her and deposited it back on the desk. Kate shrugged and took another long drag on the cigarette, sucking the smoke deep into her lungs and blowing it out through her nostrils. Her hair was pulled back and tied at the back of her head, giving her face a strained look.

"So," she said, "what do you want with little old me?"

"I want a look at the Cherry Sheet," he said. "No big deal." The Cherry Sheet was a clandestine list of people who hadn't been popped yet; or at most, popped only once. No other proof existed but everyone suspected them of doing bad things. Illegal surveillance was conducted on them occasionally.

Kate frowned at him, a momentary glance of disapproval.

"The assholes like to talk about it in front of me. They think it's cute. I told Hank Greider he ought to keep his brains in a condom where they belong. He accused me of being a lesbian. I told him to try a smaller size. He didn't get it." More smoke. "What do you want with the Cherry Sheet, Pat? And don't tell me any more lies."

"I'm thinking about setting up a sting," he said.

"Now that's something I haven't heard before," she said and waited for him to say something else, thought better of it, and pointed in the direction of what appeared to be his crotch. Paige looked down, wondering if this was another one of her jokes.

"You're sitting on them," she said. Then she stood up herself, picked up her shoes, tossed the panty hose in the wastebasket, and slipped the shoes on her feet.

"You're a nice boy, Pat, but there are some things I don't want to know about," she said. "When a local hero comes asking for favors, I'm willing to take his word that some sort of reward will come in time. At least I'll take his word that no shit will come flying my way if he screws up. You tell me you're setting up a sting and I say you suck hard cheese." She ground her cigarette out in an ashtray already filled to overflowing and stepped past him.

"I'm going out for a sandwich. I'll be gone maybe forty-five minutes. Make sure you get finished by then. Everything goes back to pumpkins and mice after that. Nobody else'll be around. There's a baseball game tonight."

"Can I buy you a drink later?" Paige said. It was only a gesture but he felt obligated to make it.

"You are crazy," Kate said, and left.

Paige knelt on the floor and went through the files, sorting out the women quickly. There weren't that many, only four. One was an arsonist who appeared to be quite good at what she did; there was a list of at least a dozen suspicious fires that had been linked to her but no arrests.

This is what feminism is all about, Paige thought, equal opportunity for everybody. The trouble was her age. She was in her early fifties and too old for what he wanted.

The next one had a dead husband and an apartment near Rittenhouse Square, although she was currently living in Key West, according to the file. The husband fell down in the bathtub and broke his head. He might have lived but nobody bothered to call an ambulance for him for what the medical examiner figured was close to seven hours, more than enough time for him to die of a brain hemorrhage. The wife said she was a heavy sleeper. The Monroe County sheriff had been notified in case another boyfriend turned up KO'd down south.

The third woman stole cars. She was seventeen years old and had been doing it since she was fifteen. Arrested once and released with six months probation and counseling. She liked Corvettes. They estimated she had stolen an even hundred so far.

The fourth was a burglar. She was twenty-nine years old and lived in Society Hill. Her name was Caroline King. Paige studied her photograph and decided she was damn near perfect.

On the second page, he found a bad copy of an old arrest report. Paige looked at the signature on the old report and laughed out loud.

It was his.

19

The same night that he found her file, Paige used the key he'd gotten from the landlord to enter a vacant third-floor apartment that was across the street from Caroline King's row house on Manning Street near Washington Square. It was a little after nine-thirty when he went inside.

Paige carried an imitation-leather flight bag. In it was a pair of binoculars, a small penlight, an Italian hoagie double wrapped in wax paper and put in a brown paper bag so it wouldn't leak all over the flight bag, a six-pack of Rolling Rock, a thermos of coffee, several sets of keys, and a calendar. If anyone stopped him, he could tell them he had just flown in for the night and wanted to surprise an old girlfriend who used to live on the third floor. He had used the excuse before and it always worked. Whenever they told him the apartment was vacant, he had always managed to look heartbroken.

The apartment was small, a little box of a place, and smelled of disinfectant and dust. He walked past the bedroom, the kitchen, and the bathroom and ended in the living room. He dropped his bag and went back to examine each room carefully.

Once he'd been on a stakeout in a vacant apartment near University City in West Philly and he hadn't bothered to search the place first. A derelict couple had been using one of the bedrooms as a place to sleep. When one of them woke up in the middle of the night to take a leak, Paige almost killed him. It scared the hell out of everybody, Paige most of all. He had to give them the last of his beer to calm them down.

The apartment was empty, but it had been shown recently. There was a paper ashtray on the kitchen counter with two different cigarette butts in it, one with lipstick traces, and a realtor's card next to it. He put the card in his pocket. He could call about the place, see when they were going to show it again. For now, Paige figured he was safe until at least five in the morning. Until he found out more about the place, he didn't want to risk staying too long.

The shades were down in the three front windows. Paige took off his jacket, folded it, and made a cushion for himself on the floor in front of the center window. From there he could see Caroline King's row house and both ends of the block.

Paige lifted the shade. He saw no movement but there were lights on the second floor. Everything seemed normal. After setting up, he cracked one of the beers. He drank the beer, glancing at the house through the binoculars every few minutes, a rough scan of the building, up the street to Washington Square. A Cadillac raced the short block and slid through the stop sign as it disappeared around the corner.

Paige scanned the house again, going from window to window, looking for signs of movement behind ornate lace curtains. The intricate patterns changed from window to window. Some were woven in a fleur-de-lis pattern, others in paisley, still others were delicate snowflakes. Paige wondered if she'd stolen them.

No. Only stupid thieves kept what they'd stolen and she didn't strike him as stupid. For one, she was too successful. Besides, he'd known stupid thieves. For some reason, they'd all been men.

He remembered a couple things about her arrest. Ferris had been with him at the time. She was very young. Ferris thought she was hot. Now Paige was after her again. So where was she?

Something moved on the second floor, the window on the

right. Was that a bedroom or something else, maybe a study? Or would she leave that for the third floor. He had no way of knowing, not even a guess. So he moved back and forth, searching for something that might give him an answer.

More movement, a pale shadow wavering in the background. The lace fractured motion. It was like watching blood pushing through a wall of cells, each cell filled and then drained, rising and falling. The light passed through each new pattern of the lace as the shadow shifted to and fro.

What was she doing? Was she with someone? He wanted to see into the room, to be there. He wanted to part the curtain and plunge into her life. The thought was so real that he felt himself rising up to meet it. Paige dropped his eye from the binoculars and fought the feeling, forcing it away. When it had receded far enough, he took out the calendar, another enemy.

He held it up so that the light from the window illuminated it and marked off the days. Today was Monday. The Patrons' Ball was Saturday. He had five days to get her to do what he wanted and no time to finesse it. He wanted to catch her at something bad and use that to twist her around.

When he looked again the shadow was gone. There was nothing but the light and the lace and the uncertain knowledge that she was no longer there.

For the first time in years, he had come up with something he could not predict and once again he felt himself rising toward it. He wanted to circle all around it and hold it close to keep it from getting away from him.

And since he had no illusions about his ability to do that, he went back to watching with the binoculars and tried to imagine what she was doing.

20

The only time Caro had ever been arrested it had rained. That was one of the things she remembered about that night, the way the air had turned silver with mist and hung in billows around her head. Although she did not consider herself superstitious, she had never been out on a job since then while it was raining. It was nine years ago. She had been twenty years old and had had a real urge to steal; she'd been doing it for about six months, learning on the job.

It had been strictly a spur-of-the-moment thing. She had been walking down Delancey, a narrow street filled with expensively restored row houses near Rittenhouse Square, when she saw a black leather key purse on the sidewalk. There was no one else on the street. Without stopping, she picked it up and hurried away. No one called after her. When she got to the Square, she sat on one of the wooden benches and examined it. Inside were seven different keys, three of which she recognized as house keys, the other four she didn't care about. Except for a large letter *H* monogrammed on the inside of the flap, there was no identification.

It was a minor problem. Caro knew the block and the initial.

In a nearby office lobby, she sat in a phone booth and searched through the *H* section of the phone book until she found the right name. Donald Harvey, Esquire, 2003 Delancey. Below that was his business address. Mr. Harvey was a lawyer. It was perfect, Caro remembered.

From there, she went to a locksmith she knew and had duplicates of the house keys made, returned to her apartment to change her clothes, and put on a scarf to cover her hair and heels to add to her height, and then walked back to Delancey to return the keys.

Mrs. Harvey had no idea that her keys were missing and was overjoyed to have them back. She offered Caro a reward, but she refused and asked for a glass of water instead. Mrs. Harvey disappeared into the kitchen and Caro looked quickly around the living room. It was large for a row house. They had probably combined the two old parlors into one. She looked at her watch. It was after three and there was no sign of any children. On the floor was an expensive oriental carpet, an antique, not a reproduction, Caro noted. On the far wall was a wood and glass étagère filled with Hummel figurines.

There must have been twenty-five of them. Caro did some quick calculations. Twenty-five figurines at approximately five hundred dollars apiece, give or take a few hundred. She didn't have enough time to do a careful examination to see if the woman had any real classics in her collection, although one or two looked very much like prewar designs. If the woman had one of the "Green Bonnet" series, it would be worth maybe three times that much. But even without it, she was still looking at nearly thirteen thousand dollars at current market prices.

Caro had dealt with the figurines before and she kept in close contact with a number of collectors through the Hummel Society. Their newsletter listed what collectors were buying and what they were willing to pay and provided her with an established list of clients. Nobody asked where she got her figurines. It was a cash-and-carry business. The figurines in front of her presented an unexpected opportunity that she couldn't pass up. She decided to go in as soon as she could, that night, if possible.

Mrs. Harvey brought her the glass of water and thanked her again. Caro told her it was her pleasure. Afterward, she went back to her apartment, changed her clothes for a third time that day, this time into something more comfortable, slacks, deck shoes, a beret, and a dark raincoat. The late April sky had clouded up and the weather had taken on an unexpected chill. It grew worse during the afternoon until by five that afternoon the wind picked up and it began to rain.

Caro watched the house off and on from several different locations until nearly eight-thirty that evening, when a well-dressed man she decided had to be Mr. Harvey came home. She was right. A few minutes later, the Harveys left the house together. They were going out to dinner, she was certain of it, but she followed them to the front door of the restaurant just to be sure.

Then she returned to her apartment to pick up the large legal trial bag and tissue paper for wrapping the figurines. She could be in and out of the place in less than ten minutes. If anyone noticed, they would see a young woman bringing some work to her boss's house after work. No one reported that sort of thing to the police.

As she walked down the street, Caro felt like she was hallucinating. The rain had slowed to a heavy drizzle while the wind blew it across her face and swept it up into the air. Buildings more than half a block away were nearly invisible, the streetlights lost in the mist. Cars glided past her on the street; even the noise of their engines seemed muffled by the rain. She walked through pools of diffuse light on the sidewalk in front of her. When she came to the door, she slipped the first key into the lock, met resistance, tried another, turned it, and stepped inside.

The house was empty. The lights had been left on in the living room, a single row of track lights that illuminated the fireplace and two small bookcases. Caro found a rheostat on the wall and dimmed them further, enough so that in case anyone happened to look closely through the window, she wouldn't be visible. The weather would take care of the rest.

Caro sat the trial bag on the floor in front of the étagère and picked up the first figure, a small shepherd boy with a green bonnet. She wrapped it quickly and placed it carefully in the bottom of the bag.

As she reached for the next figure, someone stuck the barrel of a gun in the back of her neck at the point just above her spine and pressed down until she thought her bones would snap from the pressure. A man's voice told her not to move. Then the man turned her away from the étagère and kicked her feet out from underneath her.

What she remembered after that came very quickly. She was facedown on the floor, the gun still jammed against her neck, the man's hand frisking her quickly and efficiently. It was a cop, she knew it, but she couldn't quite believe it. What was a cop doing guarding a bunch of ceramic dolls? There was no connection that made any sense.

The cop turned her over on the floor, pointed the gun at her face, tore off her beret, and swore. She could barely see him but he looked quite young. Then the lights went on around her and she saw another man standing by the switch, laughing.

"Who's that?" she heard him ask. The man standing over her said nothing. The large man across the room was still laughing. "Is that our bad guy?" he said. "Jesus, are we going to get reamed." Then to her. "What are you, honey, the fucking knick-knack bandit?"

She looked up at the one next to her, but all she really remembered now were his eyes and the way they dismissed her. They were filled with a kind of cold intensity one moment, staring at her, memorizing her features, and then it was as if she had ceased to exist. He pulled her hands behind her back, put cuffs on her so tight that her wrists hurt and dragged her to her feet.

He still kept the gun pointed at her. "I'm going back on the roof," he said.

"Hey, Paige," the other man said wistfully as the other went past him. "You sure you want to leave me alone with Barbie here?" She heard his hurried footsteps on the stairs.

The other man walked over to her and smiled. "I'm Tom Ferris," he said. "Let's be friends."

Caro remembered it all now, scenes and images that flashed brightly and then died, like the light in Paige's eyes.

Ferris frisked her. He took his time. He was intrusive but gentle. Kind of gently intrusive, she thought, moving his hands over her breasts and then down between her legs. He seemed a little bit drunk and smelled like beer and cinnamon gum. Then Ferris shifted the cuffs Paige had put on her. He moved her hands around in front and kept them loose on her wrists. When Paige returned, he noticed it right away. She could tell he didn't like it but he didn't say anything.

She thought they were going to take her to the Roundhouse but Paige drove the car to the district building in Fishtown instead. Ferris talked to her all the way there. She couldn't remember anything he said because she was concentrating on what was going to happen to her when they got there. For a while, it was just confusion. They didn't book her. Instead, they stuck her in one of the interrogation rooms.

Soon Paige came in to talk to her. He wanted to know if she had seen anyone else near the house or heard anything while she was inside. She said she hadn't and he seemed to believe her. She was alone in the dirty little interrogation room for half an hour after that. There was a battered metal desk and a chair that was bolted to the floor. In a box on the desk were some interrogation forms.

Ferris was next. He spent twenty minutes with her, asking about her background, where she was from, her age, questions that had nothing to do with what she was doing in the house. He stayed close to and touched her every now and then. She pulled back every time, afraid to offend him but still angered by his familiarity. After a little bit, he seemed to sense her anger and stopped. Then he told her she was free to go. There was a problem with the bust was all he said. He asked her if she needed a ride home. She told him no.

Since that night, she had learned and prospered. She never pulled jobs on the spur of the moment and she stopped going after Hummel figurines. She changed apartments and took some investment courses and, until recently, had done reasonably well in the market, okay in bonds, and better than expected with the few pieces of real estate she owned.

Her life was in order and so was her work. She did approximately one job a month and she never hit the same neighborhood more than twice in the same year, although that wasn't always possible. She averaged $7,500 a job; her income from burglary last year minus expenses was close to $76,000, a record.

She had one fence, a jeweler on Sansom Street named Leopold who took her merchandise without question, even though he knew it was stolen, because he was half in love with her. He

148

joked that he wanted to leave his wife and two kids and run off to Southern California with her, but there was serious intent unspoken behind the joke. She surprised herself by feeling flattered by it.

The things she sold him were always the best and always safe. She had her own small workshop in her basement where she melted down the gold and silver and reset the stones into innocuous settings. What Leopold did to them after that was his business. They settled up in cash.

As a cover, she also bought gems legitimately as part of her investment portfolio. Occasionally, she did some jewelry designs of her own and even managed to sell some to a few shops. If she ever had to explain the smelter and the jewelry equipment, she could show the IRS the receipts.

She spent a great deal of her time gathering information. Some of it came through Leopold, who picked up information from the jewelry salesman or other jewelers or even insurance agents who came in to confirm an appraisal and liked to brag about the size of the premiums they were getting. She would shop at the better stores and gossip with the saleswomen. From them she might learn who was on a trip, who had a new diamond necklace, who had been on a spending spree. She read the newspapers and watched the society columns and joined the right health clubs and fed all of this, along with more information and some specific financial figures from her previous jobs, into an IBM PC, which provided her with a seventeen-point profile of the ideal victim.

If a prospective job touched on twelve or more, it was a go. If not, she abandoned it immediately. Planning was time consuming and expensive, and she didn't like to waste her efforts. She was in the closing stages of a new job, one that had hit a miraculous fourteen points on the scale. There was also the money. Her investments needed pumping up, one or two rather desperately. The market drop had nearly wiped her out. She felt hemmed in and pressured, but there was nothing she could do about it. Another year, she thought, and maybe she could get out. If she wanted to get out. And she was never very certain of that. She liked it too much.

Caro cleared away the dishes from dinner, put them in the sink, and decided against another glass of wine. Instead, she went upstairs to change her clothes and then retreated to the patio in back of her house, a ten-by-twelve-foot square, covered with brick red flagstones and surrounded by a high wooden privacy fence. In the center was a glass-topped table and two wire chairs with spongy nylon cushions. She sat in the one nearest the door and stared up at the sky. It was almost dusk, the sky a watercolor wash of violet and blue.

She hadn't thought about that night in a long time. The column about Paige had brought it back. When she thought about Tom Ferris, she remembered the way he stayed close to her in the interrogation room. He seemed to radiate heat, his body just churned it out. The small room was heavy with it, and when she left, her clothes were damp with sweat.

There was no warmth in Paige, she thought, but something else, heat of another kind, dangerous and perversely attractive. The notion struck her as something new, surprising, and out of place. All the time he'd spent with her on that night nine years ago, she'd thought what she felt was fear. Looking back now, she realized it might not have been fear at all.

She climbed the stairs to her office, a small room on the third floor, to go over the plans laid out across the drawing board. The room was narrow and dark with only one window facing the street. There had been another window in the rear, but for some reason it had been bricked up before she bought the house.

The room was quiet, the narrow high walls giving it the feel of a cloister. To heighten that, she had had the walls painted a light gray and the floorboards bleached almost white. A single line of track lighting produced two circles of light, one inside the entrance, the other over the desk and drawing board. The computer was on the desk, maps and various drawings of the target house pinned to the drawing board. The drawings were of several hues: blueprints of the house and the most recent addition, stolen from the contractor's office in Paoli; the bright white schematic drawings of the wiring and plumbing systems from the same source; a detailed rendering of the front and rear elevations from the Chestnut Hill Historical Society, in cream and chocolate brown; several close-up color photographs of the windows and doors. The papers and colors overlapped across the drawing board like leftover Christmas wrapping.

Caro examined each item carefully, calmly going over the plan in her mind. She began with the addition. The Wolks were Austrian Jews who had fled before the Anschluss and thought of themselves as serious collectors. Their collection consisted primarily of expensive trinkets from their old country, some furniture, lamps, and decorative sculpture, and a great deal of jewelry and antique gold and silver pieces. The addition created a small museum space in their home. They liked to show it off. Caro had seen it on a walking tour of the neighborhood sponsored by the historical society.

What struck her as interesting was the fact that Mrs. Wolk wore several expensive pieces of jewelry while she led them through her collection. Someone commented on her necklace and pin. She confessed that she liked to wear what she owned and did so quite often. Which meant that not everything she owned was on display. The husband, Caro learned later, was a retired trader who now liked to play the gold market for fun.

As for security, they did what everybody did who had too much money: they bought the latest and most expensive system for the new addition. It was now wired like a mint. Pressure plates circled each display, light-sensitive reflectors were built into each window, and acoustic refraction devices surrounded the room like a spider's web. Because they spent so much on the addition, the rest of the house was left with the old security system, one that came in off a buried cable in the side yard and could be quickly and easily disabled from the outside with little chance of mistake.

Caro didn't care about the collection. She wanted what Mr. and Mrs. Wolk had hidden in the rest of the house.

There was a side door next to the kitchen, near to where the old security system cable emerged. It was the old servants' entrance and was still used by a cleaning company that came twice a week. It was also used for deliveries. Unlike the steel doors in the rest of the house, this one was heavy oak, almost three inches thick with only a single dead bolt.

She would use it to get inside.

Caro turned from the drawings to the calendar on her desk.

The Wolks were hosting a reception on Wednesday afternoon for the Israeli ambassador to the United Nations, then attending a benefit performance of *Cats* at the Forrest Theater with friends later that same evening. She had confirmed all this by pretending to be from the Fox Run Institute on the Main Line to see if they were available to attend a fund-raising dinner.

Mrs. Wolk said that unfortunately they couldn't be there and, because she wanted Caro to know she wasn't stingy when it came to charity, just busy, she spent several minutes explaining precisely what she planned to do for the needy for the next several months, including the night that Caro was interested in hearing about.

She held a small unmarked calendar in her hands and pressed her thumb over the date. Two days, she thought. Two days, and if things went well, she could take the next week off, maybe go to the Jersey Shore, more out of nostalgia than anything else. She hadn't been to the shore for years and decided it would be nice to go back, maybe to Ocean City.

Ocean City was a family place, its wide beach crowded with children and teenagers in the summer, somewhere she wouldn't even think about stealing because there was nothing there worth stealing, just a few unhappy childhood memories. If this job went well, she could rest up and relax before she had to be ready for the next one.

What she didn't want to do right now was remain in the house. Thinking about the past had made her moody and restless. If she stayed home, it would only get worse. It was still early, only nine o'clock. She had nothing to do the next day and she owed herself a good time. She could go down to South Street, drink a few beers, and listen to some rock and roll. That would straighten everything right out.

Paige almost missed her. He stepped away from the window for a few seconds and when he returned, he saw her as she rounded the corner and disappeared.

"Shit," Paige said and hurried downstairs. He couldn't find her at first, then he saw her as she cut through a small crowd at the end of the block and turned right toward South Street. On South Street, she walked two more blocks to Dobb's, near the corner of Second, and went inside. For a moment, Paige couldn't make up his mind whether to go in after her or stand around outside and look like an idiot. He went in after her. The noise hit him before he walked through the door.

The band was at the far end of the short narrow room, the music loud and enthusiastic. He couldn't find Caroline King anywhere, and there was no way he could move forward through the crowd of people jammed against the bar, so he listened to the band. After a few minutes, Paige decided that they knew only three chords but knew them so well that they actually sounded pretty good. He found an opening in the crowd and moved ahead, looking for Caroline King.

The crowd moved back and Paige was forced up against someone at the bar.

"Excuse me," he said loud enough for the person to hear. Caroline King turned around and stared up at him in stunned surprise.

His first thought was that she was shorter than he remembered and a lot better-looking than her photograph. His second thought was to get the hell out of there as quickly as he could. The crowd pushed him into her again. He couldn't get away from her now. Not unless he really wanted to look like an idiot.

"Do I know you?" Paige yelled over the noise.

"I know you," she shouted back and shook her head as though she found the whole thing quite astonishing.

"I busted you, didn't I?"

"Yes, you did."

A space opened up next to her and Paige slid into it.

"Nice seeing you again," Paige said. He knew he sounded like a jerk but he couldn't think of anything else. He knew what Ferris would have said: hey, nice to see you, do any time? He caught the bartender's attention and yelled for a beer.

"You want one?" he asked.

She shrugged.

Paige held up two fingers and the bartender sat two Molson's on the counter. He handed one to her.

The lead singer announced that the band was going to take a twenty-minute break. The music went on for a few more minutes, then dribbled out. The crowd responded with scattered applause and a few spirited yells.

The sudden silence made Paige feel like he'd been sucked

into a vacuum. Now they only had to listen to each other. He drank his beer and smiled at Caroline King. "It's tough starting a conversation after all these years, isn't it?" he said.

"I think this is our first. We didn't have much to say the last time."

"I was busy."

"So was I." She took a drink. "I saw the story about you in the paper."

Paige waved his hand back and forth, a vain attempt to make the whole subject go away. "I had nothing to do with it."

"I thought it was a nice article."

Paige wondered what she meant by that. He took another drink. There was a rhythm going here, he thought, drink a little, talk a little. He started to relax; he could keep this up all night if he had to.

"Thanks," he said. "You like the band?"

"I wanted to hear some music."

"And not talk to a cop," Paige said.

She drank more of her beer and set the bottle down.

"I'm going to look for a table," she said. "Thanks for the beer." There was no invitation in her voice.

"Sure, no problem," he said.

"Nice seeing you," she said and slipped into the crowd. A few minutes later, he saw her at a table in front talking with the lead singer of the band. Paige ordered another beer. He drank that until they started playing again and Caroline began to dance by herself near the edge of the small stage. Paige watched her for a while, then he ordered another beer.

He didn't want to go home and he didn't want to go back to the apartment. He wanted to stay and listen to the band and watch her dance.

From where he sat, Grant could see them both. He didn't completely understand Paige's interest in the girl beyond the fact that he definitely had one. He thought it might be something sexual but that didn't make any sense. You didn't move into a vacant apartment to watch somebody's house just because you were interested in screwing them.

Grant smiled to himself. Occasionally you did. But he seriously doubted that Paige would do it even if he had the opportunity. He'd followed the detective for most of the day and this was the most interesting thing he'd done so far. What did he want her for? Why was he following her? Their meeting was clearly a surprise—for both of them. So who was she?

Grant had the rest of the night to find out.

21

Grant used the door on the roof and was inside Paige's house in Queen Village in less than fifteen seconds.

Like most people who knew anything about burglary, Paige had no fancy locks, no burglar alarms, no dogs. Grant did more or less the same thing, preferring to keep his real valuables in his safety-deposit boxes. The detective used a brace bar, but Grant popped the hinges and the door opened up for him with no trouble at all. If he had to, he could put the whole thing back together in less than a minute without leaving any visible trace.

The house was at the end of the block, isolated by the vacant lot next door. Grant glanced at the rabbit cages and the pile of beer cans and descended the stairs into the house. He started on the third floor and worked his way from there. He moved quickly but thoroughly, using a small flashlight to illuminate his steps. There was nothing of interest on the top floor, only unfinished rooms and stacks of moving boxes covered with dust.

The second floor was a disappointment as well. The house was a cipher; for all that it contained, it might have belonged

156

to a plumber. There were no pictures on the walls or anything else to identify the owner. Paige had succeeded in turning his new house into a motel. Maybe that's what he wanted. Maybe he wouldn't risk another home; he'd already had one taken from him in his life. Grant examined the bedroom. It was functional, nothing more. The first floor was no more revealing than the others.

That left only the basement, Grant thought as he descended the stairs.

He found what he was looking for there. Paige's files were neatly stored in four large file cabinets, two on either side of an old wooden desk. There were copies of reports, clippings, photographs, all arranged chronologically and then cross-referenced with their location in another file, with method of entry and anything else that seemed unusual about the job in a fourth box. It was a simple and effective system. Grant was impressed.

He found most of his own jobs in the files, all of them unsolved and marked with a red tab. The red tabs were scattered throughout all four boxes, little flags to mark the progress of Grant's work in the city, even a few of his out-of-town jobs. Judging from the extent of the files, Paige had been working on it for some time. Grant's intuition about him had been correct.

He found Julia Weinstein's notebook stuck in the back of one of the files, and after reading through it knew how Paige had found Marlene Trombly and why he'd been at the concert. Julia had written it all down. His first impulse was to take the notebook with him but it was too late now and he slipped it back in its place and, doing so, found something else hidden away, a report on a woman named Caroline King.

Caroline King was a burglar.

There was a grainy black-and-white blowup of her in the file. She was coming out of a shop on Walnut Street near Rittenhouse. She wore a dark-colored sleeveless dress and carried her shopping bag high on her arm. He looked closely at her face.

It was the woman from the bar.

He read through the report carefully. It wasn't an arrest file, although there was a copy of an earlier arrest report that

Grant could barely read. It was more like some raw FBI files he had seen once, mostly gossip and rumor, and a lot of speculation. The picture must have been a chance thing, probably a routine surveillance that she mistakenly stumbled through. Grant studied the picture again.

He found her very attractive.

Grant hesitated, then pulled the picture from the file and slipped it into his pocket.

He made one more sweep through the house, rechecking everything in case he'd overlooked something. As it turned out, he had—a closet in one of the unfinished third-floor rooms. In the back, still in its dry-cleaning bag, was Paige's old police uniform. Grant took it out and held it to see if it might fit him.

It looked good. Without another thought, he tried it on. The shirt was a little tight in the sleeves, but the rest of it fit quite well. He stood in front of the full-length mirror in the bathroom and modeled it, turning from one side to the other, to see how it looked.

It looked perfect.

He held up Caroline King's picture and felt his imagination begin to soar. He had no idea what Paige had planned for her but it was nothing compared to what he had in mind.

22

Paige slept in the abandoned apartment that night and woke up at six-thirty the next morning to the sound of a garbage truck. The air in the apartment was stagnant and warm and Paige sweated in the early morning sunlight. He could taste a thin residue of beer each time he ran his tongue over his lips, and his stomach felt sour. The coffee he'd brought with him was cold. He drank it anyway and picked at what was left of the hoagie.

There had been only one bit of excitement after he'd returned from the bar. Around midnight a car had stopped at the far end of the block, a Chevy station wagon, silver blue with Jersey plates, the guy in the front seat reading the *Asbury Park Press* and eating donuts. He looked like an older guy, close-cropped dark hair, fat arms, and a face as white as an egg. He finished the donuts and the paper and left. Paige waited up until twelve-thirty when Caroline King returned alone and fell asleep soon after that.

Paige went home, showered, and ate breakfast and was back within an hour with a fresh thermos of coffee, two more hoagies, a pry bar, and some tools. I should have a Walkman to listen to while I'm waiting for Caroline King to make up her mind to rob somebody, he thought, maybe try some of that reggae music just for a change.

He didn't have that much time to wait for her, and if something didn't happen soon, he was going to have to push it along.

She went out shopping at two o'clock in the afternoon. Paige followed her to Wanamaker's and hung around while she picked out a new dress and a small fan. She seemed to know exactly what she wanted and didn't spend a lot of time browsing.

At six o'clock a man in a white linen suit and driving a Mercedes 190 showed up. He doubled-parked the Mercedes out front, put on the flashers, and knocked on the door. Paige priced the car and realized that it cost more than he made in a year, even with overtime. Caro opened the door wearing her new dress, took his arm, and let him inside.

And who the hell are you? Paige thought. How come you rate a new dress? They emerged a few minutes later. She had her arm through his and he led her around to the passenger side. He was taller than Caro by half a foot or better. And older. Paige thought he noticed a touch of gray at his temples.

The man said something to Caro just before she got into the car and she laughed. He tells jokes, too, Paige thought. Then she stood on her toes and kissed him on the cheek and climbed into the seat.

The whole thing reminded Paige of a wine commercial except that now he knew one of the players and she was a burglar. Paige waited until it was dark and picked up the tools and the pry bar.

He thought he'd go in through the roof, that seemed the most sensible way.

The roof door was old, the wood cracked and weather-beaten, so Paige was careful taking it down. He popped the hinges slowly, moving the pins up a half inch at a time, collecting the bits of rust and dirt in an envelope. When he had the hinges off, he pried the door open, reached in, and turned the lock. He pulled the door off, set it down on the roof, and put his foot down on the darkened stairway.

And stepped into thin air.

Paige fell forward, his right leg buckling beneath him. He had one hand on the doorjamb and he held on tight and swung out over open space. He pushed off the stairway wall with his free hand and then pulled himself back onto the roof. He took out his flashlight and pointed it into the darkness.

Caroline King had taken out the stairs. There was nothing left except a single rafter running down the center. Several feet below that he could see the old slat-and-plaster ceiling. Paige tested the rafter with his foot. It seemed solid enough, so he tried his weight on it. The rafter held. He moved back to the roof.

It certainly was effective, Paige thought. He had this picture in his mind of smacking face first into the rafter and then falling through the ceiling. He'd be lucky to get away with a broken neck.

Paige had underestimated her. She was a lot meaner than she looked.

He inched his way down the rafter, using the walls for balance and reached the door. It was locked. It took him a few minutes to work the bolt free.

The door was chained. Jesus, Paige thought, and dug in his pocket for a short length of wire. He fished the wire around the door and pulled the chain loose. Finally the door opened.

Paige sat down next to the door. He was sweating. This was like the Flying Wallendas, he thought. He wouldn't have bothered with it if she had just gone off and robbed somebody the other night. No, that would have been too easy. Or if she hadn't gone out with the guy in the Mercedes. It was the car that really pissed him off. If the guy had driven up in a Subaru, he wouldn't have cared.

"What the hell has gotten into you?" he whispered to himself.

Paige stood and scanned the sparsely furnished room, the computer on the desk, the drawing table covered with the pictures and the maps. It was a professional room, he thought. I am dealing with a professional woman.

He divided the room into quadrants and began to search it systematically. He didn't want to lose anything valuable by rushing right to the drawing table. Which was how he found the bookcase and, because of that, her workshop in the basement. The bookcase was in the back of a closet, behind a pair of louvered doors.

The books on the top two shelves were devoted to antiques, mostly American, French, and English, although there were half a dozen volumes on Russian and Japanese antiques. The next shelf dealt in coins, the one below contained several volumes of the Pennsylvania criminal law as well as some standard reference guides to locks as well as electrical, heating, and plumbing systems.

On the last shelf was the Philadelphia City building code along with a guidebook and set of instructions for a Mickelson Portable Gold Smelter.

Paige skimmed the instructions. The smelter could handle up to a maximum of twenty-four ounces at a time, but it needed a direct 220-volt line on a separate circuit breaker. It also weighed nearly one hundred pounds, not including a heat-proof hood-shield and base, which had to be purchased separately.

Since there was no evidence of any of that on the third floor, it had to be somewhere else. She either kept a separate studio or it was in the basement. He could look for it later.

He found nothing else of interest until he got to the drawing board and realized immediately that he was looking at her next job. Her planning was solid and systematic. Paige went through it, sheet by sheet, down to the computer printouts of several newspaper articles about Mr. Wolk's gold-trading business that were written when he sold the business to a private Chicago brokerage firm.

If you had to rob somebody, Paige thought, the Wolks were the ones to rob. He flipped through more printouts, what seemed to be a seventeen-point checklist that included age, income, location, and health status among others, that she apparently used to decide whether or not she would do the job. The Wolks, he saw, registered positive on fourteen. Everything was so precise, he thought, all except for a single exclamation point that stood out at the bottom of the printout. As if she let her enthusiasm get out of hand for one brief moment, then quickly smothered it again.

He went through her plans one more time. There was

nothing more that he needed except the time and date and he found that in a terse notation in her careful and deliberate hand that the Wolks would be out of the house most of the day and all evening on Wednesday. That was the day after tomorrow.

Paige went to take a look at the basement.

The door to the basement was at the bottom of a short flight of steps. There was a long workbench against the far wall. The stubby little smelter sat at one end like a black ceramic mushroom. Beside the bench was an auto mechanic's big red metal tool chest on casters. Above it was a pegboard covered with pieces of gold and silver filament and several plastic cases filled with inexpensive gemstones. The air smelled of burned metal and propane.

He went through the tool chest first. It was spotless, the tools divided by drawers, the point hammers in one, the cutting chisels in another, pliers and threaders in still another, each tool wrapped in a thin white cotton bag to keep any discoloration from reaching the metal.

A small saddle vise on the workbench held a jewelry piece, a piece of pale yellow topaz surrounded by bits of gold and silver spun around each other. She had crossed the gem with flattened bands of gold. There was a magnifying lens attached to the vise and he brought it down for a closer look at the design.

It was an insect, a wasp.

I should have known, he thought.

An artist, he thought, I'm dealing with an artist who steals from rich people and goes out with stockbrokers and sets traps for people to break their necks.

He went through the third floor carefully to make certain everything was in its place and then worked his way back up the rafter. He set the door back in place and cleaned up the debris so there would be no trace of the break-in. When he finished, it looked as if the door hadn't been moved in years. I would have made a hell of a thief, he thought.

After that Paige was too restless to sit and watch the empty house. He thought he might go visit Mickey for a few hours, to see what he knew about Lindor Peterson.

23

Paige could smell the beer from the hallway. He heard Tom Ferris's voice and stopped just before the door, leaning forward so he could look into the room without being seen. Ferris was sitting in the big Naugahyde chair. He'd turned it around so it faced away from the door, and the only thing Paige could see was the back of his head and the six-pack of beer on the floor next to the chair.

"I ought to call the desk, tell them to throw your ass out," Mickey said.

"Wouldn't work. I told them we were old friends." Ferris was drunk. Paige could hear it in his voice. He tossed an empty beer can in the wastebasket and pulled another from the six-pack.

"Since when?"

"You want one?" he asked Mickey.

"I don't want any of your beer," Mickey said.

Ferris laughed. "Since when did you turn down anything free?" Ferris tossed a beer on the bed. "Go on," Ferris said. "It's not going to kill you."

"I can't open it by myself," Mickey said. "My hands."

Ferris popped the beer open for the old man and handed it to him.

"Pat didn't tell me you were sick," he said.

"You were probably too drunk to listen," Mickey said and took a careful sip.

"Yeah," Ferris said, "but I'll be sober tomorrow."

"I doubt it," Mickey said.

Ferris leaned forward in the chair. His voice sounded tired.

"What'd you want to tell Pat all those things?" he said. "He doesn't need to hear any of that now. All that stuff about Danny. What good's it going to do him after all these years?"

"After all these years, why don't we let Pat decide what's good for him," Mickey said. "He's a big boy."

Ferris shook his head. "I thought you had more brains than that," he said sadly.

"What the hell would you know about brains? You're still kissing his old man's ass and that son of a bitch has been dead for six years."

Ferris stood up suddenly, weaving back and forth in front of the bed.

"What are you going to do?" Mickey's voice was filled with fear.

"Me?" Ferris said. "Not a goddamn thing. What do you think about that? I'm going to go on being a cop like I always was and you and Pat can go fuck yourselves."

"You were never a cop," Mickey said. "You were a crook like the rest of us."

Ferris waved a finger at him. "I was better than you," he said. "I was better than all of you."

"You're a crook," Mickey said.

Paige stepped into the room.

"This looks like fun," he said. "You guys selling tickets?"

Mickey pointed a bony finger at Tom Ferris. "Ask him," Mickey said. "He's the one come barging in here."

Ferris turned around and grinned stupidly. "Hey, Pat," he said, "I didn't hear you come in."

"That's because you're a goddamn drunk," Mickey said.

"Why don't you shut the fuck up, you little Jew," Ferris said. The words were casual things, tossed off like a piece of paper from a passing car.

165

"Hey," Paige said loudly, and the sound of it seemed to open Ferris's eyes. "That's enough."

"Yeah, I guess it is," Ferris said. He looked at Mickey and then at Paige. There was a flicker of hate in his eyes. Paige didn't know who it was directed at, Mickey or himself.

Ferris picked up the rest of the six-pack and cradled it in his arms. Paige stepped out of his way. Ferris shoved the cans into Paige's hands as if he were pushing something painful away.

"Have a drink, Pat," he said. "The way you're going, you're going to need one."

"Go home, Tom."

Ferris stuck his hands in his pockets. The hate was still there in his eyes, only now it mingled with something close to despair. "I don't even know where that is anymore," he said and walked out of the room.

Paige turned to Mickey.

"You want to tell me what that was all about?"

Mickey sat up in bed. "What, you coming in here, giving me orders, too? You ain't your old man, you remember that."

"I know that," Paige said.

"You want to know about me and him, is that what you come around for? Okay, I'll tell you. I did some work for him, found out who was doing things they shouldn't, who liked hookers or dope or little boys. That's what he wanted. He knew everybody and knew what needed to get done and that's how things worked. We all made money and things got done. What the hell else you want to know?"

"Why didn't you just tell me that," he said. "It doesn't make any difference now."

Mickey waved a shaky finger at him. "Because it was none of your goddamn business, that's why. I don't have to tell you everything. I don't owe you a goddamn thing." Mickey grabbed the mask and breathed deep and stared at Paige with hard little eyes over the top of the clear green plastic.

"Then why is Tom so interested?"

Mickey ripped the mask away. "Because he's an ass kisser, that's why. If it ain't your old man, it's you. He don't know what else to do."

"Come on, Mickey," Paige said. "There's more to it than that."

166

"Then ask him, I'm tired of all this. Why don't you get the hell out of here. The little Jew wants to be by himself for a while."

Paige started to say something else, to tell Mickey that Ferris didn't really mean it but suddenly he wasn't sure of that.

"Go home, Pat," Mickey said.

Paige went to see Tom Ferris instead.

They sat around his kitchen table and drank like they'd done so many times that Paige had lost count. Ferris was working his way through two more six-packs, trying to drink himself sober. Paige had seen him do that, too. Ferris put his hands on the kitchen table to get up, changed his mind, and slumped back down.

"That looks like a bad idea," Paige said.

"So Mickey told you he worked for Danny," Ferris said. "Well, fuck him."

Paige's mouth felt dry. He took a drink that he could barely taste. It was just something to take the dryness away.

"What did he do for him?"

"Do? He broke into places, what the fuck you think he did?" Ferris shook his head. "What do you need this for, anyway?"

"I just want to know," Paige said.

"So now you know."

"What did you do for him?" Paige asked. Except drive him around and provide the laughs when he needed it.

The flicker of hate came back. Ferris leaned forward in the chair so that his elbows rested on the table and his head hung down between his arms. He looked like a worn-out bulldog.

"I greased the little fuck who murdered your wife," he said. "That's what I did for him."

Paige felt like his past had just been torn loose from him. It floated free with nothing to hold it down. Paige struggled to keep himself from drifting away with it.

"Don't look at me like that, Pat," Ferris said. "Hell, if you didn't suspect it, you're dumber than I think you are. Half the department wanted that little shithead dead and I'm talking about the top half of the fucking department. They were all afraid you were going to do it. They wanted the whole thing to go away. It was just a matter of time."

"Was he carrying? I don't remember," Paige said. It was as

167

if one whole section of his brain had emptied and now he was waiting for it to fill up again.

"He had a four-inch jackknife with a white plastic handle," Ferris said. "It was in his pocket." Ferris finished one bottle and opened another. "You know what I remember most? The little fucker bled all over the stairs. It was everywhere."

"So Danny told you to kill him and you did it."

"I didn't do it just for him," Ferris said. He held out his bottle, waiting for Paige to touch it with his, a toast to put an end to what he'd done, to help shoulder some of the guilt. Paige dragged himself backward and tried to reconstruct his feelings at the time. What came back to him was a scream of rage that he'd kept inside and never let out. It was still there, buried so deep that no one would ever hear it.

That's why Danny spit in the coffin, Paige thought. He was pissed he didn't get to pull the trigger himself. Maybe I've been looking for the same thing all these years.

Tom Ferris was smiling at him.

He thinks I still owe him for it, Paige thought. He tapped his bottle against Ferris's and took a long drink.

There, he decided, debt paid.

24

From the road, the Wolks's house looked splendid. The ivy had overgrown the chimney and most of the brick in front. The rest of it was painted white and it shimmered through the front hedge and the dark green wall of pine trees that filled the yard.

Paige left his car six blocks away on a side street and stuck a parks and recreation department parking permit on the dash; he also had permits from both the fire and welfare departments.

Caro was already inside. Earlier on Wednesday, Paige had watched her park her car at the lot near the train station and then take her bike off the roof rack. She was dressed in shorts and a black leotard top. From the trunk, she removed a tan canvas knapsack and slipped it around her shoulders. She drank once from a small plastic bottle, tilting her head back and squeezing water into her mouth, then clipped the bottle to the frame of the bike and peddled away.

She had been inside the house for nearly half an hour. The job would take an hour, maybe a little less, he thought. Her timetable would have a certain amount of built-in flexibility in case of something unexpected. He could imagine her movements, clean and economical, nothing wasted, nothing extraneous. She would probably start on the top floor and work her way down. That would bring her closer to the way out as she neared the end.

There was an empty corner lot fifty yards from the house, not much more than an oversized grove of trees with a white wooden fence surrounding it. Paige swung over the fence in a single motion and crouched down to watch the house.

Paige knew how she'd planned to get inside. So he planned on doing it the same way—if she did it the way he thought she would, shimming the locks with a plate, then another one to hold the mechanism in place. While she was still in the house, he could pull the second plate, pop the dead bolts, and walk right inside. Caro had already done most of the work for him. All he had to do was play connect the dots. He heard a car engine and moved back from the fence.

A patrol car stopped at the corner. Paige threw himself down low and pressed the side of his face into the carpet of pine needles and dirt. He could see through the fence but only the road and the side of the car. The cop revved the engine twice, sending a plume of smoke billowing from the exhaust. Paige began to relax. The car moved ahead a few feet and stopped. Paige heard the door on the driver's side open and froze in place. The cop poured what was left of a cup of coffee on the road. Paige watched the liquid stream across the asphalt into the gutter. The door closed. Paige waited a full five minutes after the car had gone before getting up.

The road was clear when he crossed into the backyard. There was a two-car garage and a small woodshed to his left. The driveway curved past the garage to the front of the house, where it ended in a short cul-de-sac. Paige looked in the garage. Caro had hidden her bike behind a blue Cadillac Cimarron that was parked on the right side. It made sense. If they came home unexpectedly, they would miss the bike; if someone else happened to see it, the bike wouldn't appear suspicious left in the garage.

The door was as easy as he thought it would be. He entered into the kitchen, a narrow room sunk several steps below ground level. From there, Paige went through the dining room. A brass chandelier hung over a long oak table. On one wall was a som-

170

ber-looking portrait of a Colonial family, the children dressed like stuffed dolls, the wife's face grim and humorless.

Off the dining room was a small foyer and a slate floor leading to the front door. Beyond the foyer was the living room. Immediately to his left was the stairs and to the right of the stairs, the entrance to the new wing of the house.

Paige stopped when he heard the car roll up the gravel drive. He stepped across the foyer to the living room and watched the patrol car make a lazy turn around the cul-de-sac and come to a halt. Nothing happened for several seconds. Then the driver's door opened and the cop stepped out. His cap was off and he ran his fingers through his hair. He tried the front door first, then started walking toward the rear of the house.

Paige had forgotten to lock the backdoor.

In the next few seconds, Paige moved on instinct and adrenaline. He kept low and scurried through the dining room and the kitchen, stumbled once on the polished tile but caught himself before he fell. From there, he crawled to the door on his hands and knees. He pressed his shoulder against the door, reached up, and gently turned the bolt. The cop was at the door ten seconds later. Paige tucked his knees up close to his chest and waited.

A few minutes later, he heard the sound of the patrol car, faint at first, then louder as it pulled around the driveway. Paige waited several more minutes, then looked out the kitchen window to make certain it was finally gone.

He was sure that Caro had heard the car, probably the cop as well. Now he had to find her. She had to be somewhere on the second floor. He took the stairs gently, one step at a time, the noise muffled by the thick carpeting.

The upstairs hall was lined on both sides with half a dozen doors, all closed. One window faced him from the far end where the hall turned sharply to the right. Paige moved silently toward the window and stopped at the first door. He pressed his head against it and listened.

He didn't hear her right away and was almost ready to move to the next door when he heard a gentle click. Then a single cough, closer to the door. Paige stepped to the side and reached for his gun. He changed his mind. There wasn't any need for it.

She opened the door and took a step into the hall. Paige pressed a hand over her mouth and spun her around so that her back was toward him and propelled her toward the bed.

She struggled at first, fighting against the shock of it, then gave up. Paige shoved her ahead of him and forced her to kneel in front of the bed, one hand pressing her face into the mattress, the other holding her wrists together. He let go of her neck, took out his handcuffs, and snapped them on her wrists.

"How do those feel?" he asked. She didn't answer. Paige turned her over on the bed and sat her up in front of him. For the first few seconds, her memory seemed to fail her and then she recognized Paige. Anger and surprise fought a battle across her face; anger finally won. She was even better looking than he remembered from the other night.

She was off-balance. Paige hadn't arrested her, hadn't read her rights to her, hadn't done much of anything except stare at her. He didn't touch her, made no move to get closer. He crouched in front of her, arms on each knee, hands hanging casually between them. He smiled at her and forced one in return.

Caro tried to kick him in the balls. Her foot struck him on the leg, high up on his thigh, knocking him over. He grabbed her as he fell and she toppled over on him, swinging her knees up to hit him again. Paige rolled her over and held her legs down while she fought against him.

"You through?" he asked. She glared at him but stopped struggling.

Paige stood up and picked her knapsack off the floor. He sorted through it quickly.

"You've got good taste," he said and put the bag aside. "How'd you know the cop was going to be here?" he asked, tilting his head toward the front of the house.

Caro shrugged. "It's a new routine," she said finally, keeping whatever anxiety she felt out of her voice. Just the facts, he thought, two professionals swapping shoptalk. The unreality was getting interesting.

"They stop every two days," she said. "They walk around, check the doors and windows and leave. It keeps the neighborhood happy."

"How'd you find that out?"

"It was in the paper," she said. "A new Burglary Watch policy." It was her turn to smile. "They were going to make a different stop each time, change the days and the routine, keep the crooks off guard. But you know cops, they like routine. After a week of it, they started to work the same ones in a row."

Paige shook his head in surprise. "I'll have to tell them how well it's working." He stood up and pulled the knapsack over one shoulder.

"What do we do now?" she asked.

"First, we're going to put this stuff back and then we're going to wait."

"For what?"

He finally realized how fearful she really was. "For it to get dark so we can leave here without getting caught."

When it was almost dark, Paige took her to the kitchen. He attached one of her handcuffs to his own wrist. They sat on chairs in front of a wide counter near a large restaurant stove with six burners and a raised griddle. The pilot flame beneath each burner grew brighter as the outside light faded. She sat closest to the stove. It cast a pale blue light over her face and shimmered in her eyes. Paige liked the effect. He was happy sitting quietly in the dark. They weren't going anywhere.

She broke the silence with an unexpected question. "You're the only one who ever busted me, did you know that?"

"Sure," Paige said. "But they let you walk."

"They always do the first time. You weren't paying that much attention."

"I was preoccupied," he said. Paige looked at her closely, seeing her face through the darkness, staring at the light as it caught the edge of her cheek.

"Your partner paid attention," she said.

"What did he do?" Paige asked, interested in what Ferris might have done. Everything about Tom Ferris interested him now.

"He said he wanted to be my friend," she said. "I didn't believe him."

Caro shifted on the stool and their hands touched. Her skin was warm and dry.

"You don't want to be my friend, do you?" she asked. Paige kept silent.

"I didn't think so," Caro said. "You don't seem the type."

Outside, the daylight had vanished. Darkness enveloped the house except for the glow of the streetlight.

"Time to go," he said.

They retrieved her bike and walked to his car, handcuffed together. Paige kept his arm tight around her waist while she pushed the bike along with her one free hand. After all the time in the kitchen, it felt like an outing. They went several streets out of their way to get to his car, a circular tour of the neighborhood. Once or twice they nodded to other couples who were out walking as well.

"We fit right in," she said.

When they got to his car, he helped her to put the bike in the backseat.

"What about my car?" she asked.

"We'll pick it up tomorrow."

"We?" she asked, but Paige didn't answer. He handcuffed her to the door handle and got behind the wheel.

"I hope nobody steals it," she said.

"I don't know," Paige told her. "There're a lot of thieves around here."

"Not anymore," she said.

They rode in silence until they were on the West River Drive. Paige felt pretty good. He gave her the key and let her take the handcuffs off and that seemed to relax her. At least she hadn't tried to jump out when they stopped at the traffic lights along the way.

"You do this a lot?" she asked.

"Only when I've the time."

"You remind me of somebody I know," she said. "One part."

"What's his name?"

"How do you know it's a he?" she said. "I could be a dyke." She watched a car pull in front of them and make a quick right turn just before Logan Circle. "His name is Jack."

"He the one with the Mercedes?"

"Yeah," she said and stared at him with sudden intensity.

"Which part do I remind you of?"

"The part where I tell him I don't screw on the first date," she said and looked out the window again.

174

Paige went around the Circle and took the Parkway to 17th and turned right. Four blocks later, at the corner of Market, she jumped.

"Oh, hell," Paige said and swung the car against the traffic on Market and drove it up on the curb. Caro was already a block away on the other side of the street, running toward 30th Street Station. What the hell did she think she was going to do, catch a train? She ran at a steady pace. Paige closed the gap until he was only half a block behind her. He wanted to see how far she'd go.

Market Street rose gradually as it arched over the river but Caro had begun to slow down a block before that, finally stopping in front of a brick building with a two-story tall mural of Ben Franklin painted on one wall. Caro paced around in a circle, her hands on her hips, breathing hard. When Paige got close, she took a swing at him and missed. Paige stood back.

"You son of a bitch," she said, working the circle tighter and tighter until it stopped. "Is that what you do? Peek in my windows, watch me while I get undressed? Is that how you get off? Is that what this is all about?"

"No," Paige said. He was very close to her now, a little surprised that she had given up this soon. Sometimes it was the stronger ones who reached the wall first.

Caro wrapped her arms across her chest as if she wanted to pull her fears close to her and smother them. "Then what is it?" she screamed at him. "What the hell do you want from me?"

Paige waited until the scream faded away.

"I need your help," he said.

25

On Thursday, Grant met Lindor Peterson for lunch. He tried to get out of it but Peterson was insistent. They met for lunch in Bucks County. Peterson had a house there, so Grant drove out.

Peterson had made reservations at a restaurant that was on the canal. Grant was purposefully late. Peterson was at an outside table underneath a wide striped awning. He had already started on a bottle of rosé, sipping carefully from his glass, trying hard not to look nervous and failing. Everything the dealer did seemed prearranged. He was wearing a light tan sweater without a shirt. The muscles of his arms swelled against the material.

They ordered lunch. Grant asked for poached chicken breasts with a mint-tarragon dressing while Peterson had a warm seafood pasta. Grant watched while Peterson plucked the shrimps and scallops out from among the strings of angel hair with careful deliberation. Grant didn't like the man personally but until recently had few complaints about him. Now he thought Peterson was getting to be a real problem.

He just hoped he wouldn't have to kill him, at least not

today. Grant was too involved with Paige to have to take out Lindor, too.

Since it was the middle of the week, the restaurant wasn't crowded, a dozen customers at the most. Peterson pushed the plate of pasta away and raised his hand to get the waiter's attention.

"Two coffees," Peterson told the waiter. "Do you have brewed decaffeinated? Fine, make mine decaf." He picked up his wine glass, fingers bent like spider's legs, and swirled the pale salmon-colored liquid around, then finished it in a single gulp.

The waiter brought the coffee. "Isn't this the place where that television woman died?" Peterson asked.

"You mean Jessica Savitch?"

"That's the one."

"No," the waiter answered bluntly. "That was another place." He was probably asked it all the time and sick of explaining it by now. "Interesting," Peterson said and stirred his cup. The waiter left them alone. "I'm being investigated," he said to Grant.

Grant took a sip of his coffee, allowing only a moment's hesitation as he raised the cup to his lips.

"You took that well," Peterson said.

"What makes you think you're being investigated?" Grant asked the question quietly and without force.

Peterson kept stirring his cup as though it might help him think better. "A detective named Paige came to see me the other day," he said. "Then I saw another one yesterday. I thought I remembered him from a few years back."

Grant allowed his irritation to show.

"Did he say what he was looking for?" he asked.

"He showed me an ivory carving and asked if I'd seen it before."

"Did you?"

"Of course," Peterson said. "It was one of the ones I sold to Julia."

Grant wasn't certain he'd heard Peterson right. "Which one are you talking about?"

"I sold her a second one. She said she wanted something

177

for herself," Peterson smiled. "But don't worry, I did it through the import company, not the gallery."

Grant wanted to tear Peterson's face apart. It was such a stupid thing for him to do, play little games behind his back. But at least he knew about it now.

"What else did Paige want?"

"He showed me a list of some stolen antiques. I didn't recognize any of them." Peterson started to say something else but Grant told him to be quiet.

"Have you seen anyone new in the shop?," Grant asked. "Any construction work going on nearby, power company trucks, phone company, anything like that?"

Peterson thought a moment and shook his head. "There's still the IRS. I have an audit coming up but I told you all about that."

"Yes, you did," Grant said. But how did Paige find Peterson so fast? Grant looked at the dealer and forced a smile. There was an answer to the question, one that he didn't like.

"I know what you're thinking," Peterson said. "But I haven't done anything like that. I'm not stupid or crazy. You have to believe me. It works both ways, you know."

Grant was beginning to think that the easiest thing to do would be to wait a few hours, slit the idiot's throat, and dump him in the canal.

Peterson drew closer and Grant could see the tiny network of broken veins that climbed across one cheekbone and clung to the corner of his eye. Peterson's face was older than the rest of him, an incongruity that Grant found strange and distasteful.

"I know you're leaving the business here," Peterson said. His voice rose in pitch, filled with barely controlled excitement. Grant forced himself to remain still. He tried to imagine Peterson with his head on a stick, eyelids all aflutter, mouth gagging open; the image made him smile. "I figured it out," Peterson continued. "All the things you're selling. It had to be that."

"What is it you want?" Grant asked. "Money?"

"No, no," Peterson said in alarm. "I don't want money." The dealer cleared his throat. "I'd like to go with you on your next job," he said. "To see how you do it." He pointed at Grant. "You're the best. I want to learn how."

Grant drank some wine to hide his reaction. Is that all he

wanted, to see how it's done? It was so pure and wonderful that it was beyond description. Maybe I could give him a little demonstration right here at the table, Grant thought. What would Peterson's reaction be if I cut out his tongue and fed it to him, one small bloody bite at a time, just crammed it down his throat like some fat French goose.

He glanced at Peterson's face and saw the hunger there and realized that Peterson was ready to walk into his own grave.

"I see that I've underestimated you, Lindor," Grant said. "Are things at the shop getting a little boring?" He smiled to reassure him.

"A little."

"Then maybe we can put a little excitement in your life. I could have something in the next week or two. You might be able to help."

"Really?"

Grant caught Peterson's thumb and gave it a gentle twist. It was the one he'd nearly broken a few days before. Peterson choked down the pain.

"Really. But next time, don't forget my money. We're living in a material world, Lindor, and we all have deadlines to meet. Remember that." He released Peterson's thumb. The dealer clutched it in his lap.

"Now," Grant said, "let's talk a little bit more about this cop problem that's developed."

Peterson explained Paige's visit once more.

"What about the other one?"

"He looked like the same one who used to visit Randy when he had the shop." Peterson glanced down at his hand.

Grant had broken Randy Hazen's thumbs when the dealer had tried to cheat him out of some money. Except he didn't stop at the thumb. He smashed the man's hands so badly that the doctors couldn't put them back together again.

"If it's the same one Randy used to pay off," Peterson said, "maybe he's just looking for more money."

"Maybe," Grant said. "Just don't give him any. They might be looking for an excuse to search, so let's not provide them with one."

"And the other thing, going with you?"

"Don't worry about it," Grant said. "I think we'll be able to

179

fix you right up on that." Grant reached suddenly for Peterson's neck. The dealer tried to pull away but Grant caught his tie and dragged him back. With a short tug, Grant straightened the tie, pushing the knot tight against Peterson's throat, and let him go. "Remember," Grant said. "Neatness counts." Peterson held his thumb and grinned through the pain.

The waiter brought the check. Peterson glanced at it and dropped some money on the plate. Grant followed him outside to the parking lot and then down a worn dirt path that ran beside the canal.

"Let me know if Paige stops by again," Grant said. "If you have to call, don't leave your name. Just say there's a problem. I know your voice."

"After four years, I hope so," Peterson said. The dealer pointed to the brown muddy water in the canal. It moved sluggishly, the current barely visible. "Imagine drowning in that," he said. "What an ugly way to die."

"There are worse," Grant said.

26

She knows what you're doing?"
Ferris asked. Over the phone, his voice sounded unsteady as if
somebody were pulling the words out of him with a string one
at a time.

"You don't think she's smart enough to figure it out?" Paige
asked.

"I don't know her," Ferris said. "I hope to Christ not." Ferris
went into a fit of coughing. Paige pulled his ear away from the
phone. "If I was that smart," he said when he stopped, "I'd be
on my way to Miami Beach and screw the costume party. She
could make more money there in a week than she makes in a
month here and get a tan on top of that. Instead, she's going
to play along. What's your secret?"

"I told her she'd be safe," Paige said. "I meant it."

"I'm sure you did," Ferris said. "I'm sure she believed you.
You screw her yet?"

"Please."

"Hey," Ferris said, "this is a crazy idea and I'm just trying
to make sure there isn't more to it than what you tell me. Maybe

she thinks she's taking you for a walk, how the hell do I know? Maybe she wants to see your dick in a blender."

"You want to ask her?"

"No thank you," Ferris said. "The point is, does she have other plans?"

"I can handle it if she does."

"That wasn't what I asked. Do you want to handle it?"

"I'll handle whatever comes up," Paige said. "You can cover my ass if anything else goes bad. That make you happy?"

Ferris laughed. "This kind of thing I do standing on my head. She there with you?"

"Not yet," Paige said. He was waiting for her in a hotel room at the Hershey and not entirely certain she would show up. The last week had not been easy for either one of them. Paige had tried to keep close in case she decided to run, but so far she'd done exactly what he'd told her to do.

He asked her why she was being so cooperative.

"I like to think of it as damage control," Caro told him.

Very little else had happened. Ferris said he'd been watching Peterson, but the dealer had done nothing out of the ordinary except spend one or two nights at a transvestite bar on Walnut. Ferris also brought a young cop named O'Neal to help watch Caro. A friend of the family, Ferris called him, whatever that meant. O'Neal was pleasant and relatively competent and Paige decided he needed the help.

Paige set up the room at the Hershey and the surveillance at the Art Museum. The only thing left was the waiting.

"So when do I get to meet her?" Ferris asked. He seemed to have dropped in from another conversation.

"You don't remember her?"

"Should I?" Ferris said blandly. Paige shrugged and said nothing. It was such an obvious lie that Paige wondered why Ferris even bothered. He did it without much thought or effort; he'd been doing it all his life and saw no reason to change. A small lie but it was the kind of thing Paige noticed.

"We busted her about nine years ago," Paige said. "She was after some Hummel figurines."

"I remember her. Keep your dick in your pants." Ferris hung up.

Paige sat on the bed and waited for Caro to arrive.

* * *

It was a simple plan with only a single fallback, which Paige didn't think would be necessary. Ferris could approve the equipment and sign it out under a separate voucher.

He told Caro what he had in mind and she listened carefully, raising objections only when they were important.

"There are two main areas of the ball," he said, "the courtyard in front and the inside lobby. The courtyard will be roped off and the orchestra will be there. Unless it rains. The forecast says it won't. Ferris will be with you. I'm going to stay out of the way."

Caro stopped pacing. "I want you to be there."

"I'm going to be there. I'm just not going to be wearing a sign that says 'cop' around my neck. The man we're looking for knows me. I told you that."

"I know what you told me."

"Then what's the problem?"

"You're the one who got me into this," she said. "If something goes wrong, I want you close to me."

"Tom Ferris can handle it," Paige said. He hoped he was right. Since their talk the other night, Ferris had begun to act like a cop again.

"I trust you more than I trust him," Caro said. "It won't be that big a problem." She laughed, bright and sharp with a touch of mockery to it. "You can do it, I've seen your work, remember. Cut your hair, dress like a waiter, and no one will recognize you." She looked at him curiously. "Have you ever been a waiter?"

"I was never anything but a cop."

"I've never been anything but a thief," Caro said. Her back was to the front window and the afternoon sunlight cut through the oversized white shirt she wore over her jeans. Paige saw the outline of her waist and the curve of one breast, the nipple dark against the white material. He had the urge to touch her and thought that if he did it would seem the most natural thing in the world. She stood there as though she was waiting for him to do it, but he didn't and held out for the feeling to pass.

Caro moved away from the window, sorting absently through a pile of magazines on an end table. "You're a pretty good burglar," she said.

183

"I do it for the job," Paige said. That was true as far as it went. When he added up the hours of his life, he'd probably spent more of his time with burglars and thieves than with anyone else and that included Connie.

Caro seemed to look right through him. "Is that the only reason?" she asked.

"Let me tell you about the wire," he said, and she stopped staring at him and listened instead. It was one of the things he liked about her.

"It's a standard techpack," he said. "Single-filament condenser mike with a three-battery pack. The pack is new. It hooks around your waist so there's nothing showing. It's not supposed to leak. We can run the wire up a seam and either tape it to you directly or sew it into your bra. As long as it won't rub too much against your dress."

"I don't wear a bra," she said.

Paige shrugged. "So buy one," he said. "It won't kill you once."

"What happens if he finds me?"

"Then we'll take him in the parking lot. If that doesn't work, then we can do it here. He's been to the same hotel, so I don't think he'll object. You already have a room, so you can tell him you've used it before for the same thing."

"What do I say?"

"We don't have any code words or prearranged signals because they're too easy to screw up. You just tell us what you want, only don't make it too obvious."

"What's so obvious about me standing around talking to my tits?" she asked.

Paige burst out laughing. "Only if they talk back," he said and it was her turn to laugh.

"Who's going to hook me up?" she asked.

"Your choice."

"I don't want Tom Ferris to touch me," she said, and before he had a chance to react, she moved next to him until she was close enough that he could feel the heat coming off her skin. Her arm brushed against his as she walked across the room toward the small refrigerator. Inside it was a six-pack of soda, some beer, and a few small boxes of apple juice.

Caro took out one of the boxes, inserted the straw, and drank. "You want some?" she asked.

"No, thanks," he said.

"Do you miss your wife?"

The question took him by surprise. They had never talked about him before. He didn't see the need.

Paige tried to sort out his answer. Did he miss her? Yes. What did he miss most? The simple fact that she had been there.

"Sometimes," he said.

"What happens when we're done?" she asked. Paige looked up at her and shrugged.

"We go on with our lives," he said. "This isn't a cruise. I don't have anything else lined up. I don't live that way."

Caro finished the juice and tossed the empty box in the wastebasket.

"What about my career?" she asked.

"I don't know," Paige said. "Maybe you should think about changing jobs." He looked at his watch. "You want to get something to eat?"

It was a little after four o'clock. "Not right now," she said.

"I didn't mean now," he said. "I meant later. Dinner. Do you want to get some dinner later?"

"Sure," she said.

"I'll come by around eight," Paige said.

"Like a date?"

Paige shook his head as though she'd told him a bad joke that he'd already heard for the second or third time. "I'll see you at eight," he said. "We'll eat near my house."

"I'll pay for mine," she said.

"You can pay for the whole thing if it makes you feel any better," Paige said.

It was like watching pigeons fuck, Grant thought, watching Paige and Caroline King for the last week. Nothing but mindless bobbing and weaving that didn't make any sense to him and was driving him crazy with frustration. They went nowhere and did nothing. First it was just Paige. He'd stop at her house and they'd go out to dinner. Sometimes he'd eat there. Sometimes they ate at the hotel.

When Paige wasn't around, he had this young cop park on her doorstep. Sometimes the young cop stayed at Paige's house. Occasionally, an older cop would come by and talk to the young one. Grant knew him from his days with Randy Hazen but couldn't remember his name. It was all so haphazard that Grant couldn't make any plans. He tried following Paige around once or twice but the detective drove to the Roundhouse and back to his apartment or the hotel so goddamn often Grant nearly ran him over out of sheer frustration.

So, Grant was mildly surprised to see Paige pull up in front of the house in Queen Village with Caroline King in his car. There didn't seem to be anybody else around. That bothered him. It was the kind of surprise that he didn't like. It could make you start to believe in things that weren't real.

After Paige parked his car, he and the woman went inside. Twenty minutes later, he emerged wearing a light jacket with his hair combed. Date night, Grant thought. They left the car and started walking toward South Philadelphia. Grant watched the street for a few more minutes, then followed along.

Half a dozen blocks from the house, they entered a small restaurant with a sign that had a picture of Mount Vesuvius on it hanging over the door. Grant turned around and went back to the house. There was still nobody around, but just to be safe, he took Paige's uniform from the trunk of his car. He could wear it inside, in case one of Paige's friends came around. Besides, he was starting to like the way it made him feel, like his dick was a yard long.

Paige's house was a mess. He needed a cleaning service, Grant thought, looking at the pizza box sitting open on the table, half a pizza still in it. Grant went to check the sheets on the bed, just to see if Paige was taking advantage of Little Miss Muffet. He doubted it. He was right.

As Grant roamed through the house, he felt as if he were staring at something important and not really seeing it. He had to control himself to keep from tearing the place apart to find what he was sure the detective had hidden from him. The basement was the same way. Paige hadn't touched his desk. Files were stacked in the same place, nothing had been moved. It was like Paige knew he was going to look there and deliberately set out to frustrate him.

The phone rang. Grant stopped at the sound and looked for a way out. The phone rang again. Grant didn't move. This had to be a joke, he thought.

The ringing stopped and he heard Paige's voice.

"This is 555-9422," Paige said. "Please leave your name and message and I'll get back to you as soon as possible."

The beep sounded and then Marlene Trombly's voice filled the room.

"Hello." A pause. Grant moved closer to the desk. "Are you there? Hello?" Another pause. "I know I'm supposed to be out of town somewhere but I'm not. But I did change the locks. Or at least I told Frank to change them. Why don't you come by when you're through with your little adventure at the Art Museum this weekend? Just to talk. I'll be good, I promise. Please come by."

After she hung up, Grant listened to the tape once more, then searched through Paige's desk until he found a replacement for it and slid it into the answering machine. Paige had a small desk calendar and Grant picked it up to check the date. He looked at it for several minutes, just to make sure he was right.

By the time he reached his car, Grant was moving so fast that he felt like he was flying. A few blocks from Paige's house, he pulled the car over to the side and got out. He couldn't sit still. He wanted to keep moving, keep up the speed. Two black children, a girl around five years old and a younger boy, sat together on a narrow concrete stoop and watched him as he walked down the street in the police uniform.

"Hey," the girl said to him. "You forget your gun?"

"Yeah," the boy said. "What'd you do, lose it?"

Grant walked a few feet past the stoop and whirled around. The children jumped back in surprise. Grant dropped his head down so they were eye to eye. The girl stared at him.

"I don't need a gun," Grant said. "You know why?" The boy shook his head. "Because I scare them to death, that's why." The boy giggled, and then the girl started, and Grant laughed with them.

I do more than scare them, Grant thought. I suck the life right out of them.

27

It rained Saturday morning, but by late afternoon the wind had carried the clouds away and the sky was clear. Paige watched while they brought out the tables and spread them around the courtyard of the Art Museum. A tall man dressed in a white shirt and white pants directed the placement of a dozen large ornamental vases filled with flowers around the main entrance to the museum. On either side, tall pastel banners in green and gray hung down from the roof and were anchored to the courtyard by more flowers. To the right of the main entrance, there was a small raised platform for the band. Over the entrance hung another banner with *Patrons' Ball* spelled out in a delicate white script. Some maintenance men set up extra lights, focusing them on the banners.

Afterward, Paige went back to the hotel and helped Caro with the wire. She bought a bra and he taped the microphone to it near her armpit and ran the wire down into her panties. He slid the battery pack around her waist and hooked it in back.

"I don't like the way it feels," she said.

"It's only for a couple hours," he said. "Don't worry about it, keep your mind on what you're doing."

"I know what I'm doing," she said.

Paige spun her around. "This isn't another job," he said. "I don't want to lose this guy and I don't want you to get hurt, so don't screw around tonight."

She opened her purse and took from it what looked like a flat metal square a little smaller than a cigarette pack. When she pressed the center of the square, a three-inch triangular blade popped out. "I can use this if I have to," she said, and held it up so he could see it.

"I'll make sure you don't have to," he said.

"Do you want me to take it or not?"

"Take it," he said. "But don't get cocky. It's not all that easy to cut somebody."

"Probably easier than you make it sound," she said, and pushed the point of the blade against the wall and slid it back in its case.

Paige closed his hand around hers. "I mean it."

"Don't worry about it."

On the way to the Art Museum he had a single moment of regret that he had picked her for this. But it passed and he let it go without a fight.

Ferris opened the car door for her and watched her legs as she slid into the front seat. He was parked in one of the lots behind the museum. "You look nice," he said.

"Thanks," she said.

"You pissed at something?"

"Let's just get this over with."

"Jesus Christ," Ferris said wearily. He took a thin pair of earphones off the seat between them and hung them around his neck. The receiver was in the trunk and the wires ran along the floor under the seats. Ferris remembered when the stuff used to take up half of a van and weigh a ton. Now everything was made in Taiwan and didn't weigh shit.

He reached across the seat to open the door because he wanted her to stand away from the car and talk. What he wanted to do was hit her, just a quick one to snap her head into place.

It wouldn't be worth it, he decided. When they were finished, he was glad to be rid of her.

Paige stood at the side of the room near the stairs and watched her. When she moved too far away, he followed her, trailing behind at a close distance, scanning the crowd. She would catch his eye every few minutes, just to gauge his reaction, and then she'd move on as if she no longer cared.

Men gathered around her, and when she moved, they moved with her. They came and went, drawn back to their wives or dates or just to themselves.

None of the men who approached her looked remotely like the burglar. They were too old or too young or too good-looking, pretty men with sculptured chins and devious eyes. Paige had never seen so many jerks in one place in his life. If I was the guy, he thought, I'd be ashamed to show up here. His gun was uncomfortable beneath his jacket. It pinched the skin of his back and chafed against his spine whenever he leaned against the pale marble walls. It was like suddenly being allergic to someone you've lived with all your life.

After forty-five minutes inside, Caro moved to the court-yard, stepping away with an older man who wore half-glasses on his nose and carried a cane. Outside, she helped him down the wide stairs. The band, a small quartet, stuck on a raised platform to the right of the main entrance, played "The Girl from Ipanema" in a smooth dance-along beat. The sax man sweated out the melody line.

There were too many people outside. Paige realized it the moment he stepped into the courtyard and tried to follow her to the bar, a long table on the other side. She was there for a moment and then he lost her and the old man. He pushed his way through the crowd until he found her again and moved next to her. He watched while the old man took a drink from the bartender with hands that quivered the same way Mickey's had done only not quite so bad. "Don't get too far ahead of me," Paige told her. "Who the hell is he?"

"His name is Alexander," she said. "He wants to adopt me. He's very sweet."

"Keep out of the crowds," Paige said. "It's too easy to lose you out there."

190

"Where am I supposed to go?"

"Stay close to the edge," Paige told her. He saw Alexander approaching with a drink in each hand. The old man handed one to Caro and then turned to Paige.

"Young man," he said. "Could you find us some hors d'oeuvres? We're both starved, aren't we, dear?"

"Starved," Caro echoed.

"I'll see what I can do," Paige said and moved off a few feet. He had his back to her for just a few seconds but when he turned, he saw the old man leading her into the center of the crowd and suddenly they were gone. Paige plunged in after them. He could see the back of the old man's head but not Caro, and then he was surrounded by people and couldn't see anything at all.

He pushed his way through the crowd, trying to catch a glimpse of her somewhere ahead of him. He saw her, just a quick glance, and he began to move people out of the way. The crowd swirled back to block his way. Someone fell against him and he pushed her away. Behind him, somebody yelled and a hand grabbed his shoulder, spinning him halfway around. Paige shrugged it off. He saw Caro again. She wasn't with Alexander this time but another man. She looked back at him, her eyes wide.

Then he fell. His feet were suddenly knocked out from under him and he crumpled into the man in front of him. It set off a chain reaction; several other people collapsed with him. Paige pushed hard on the man's arm and stood up for a few seconds, then stumbled again. He heard a woman scream and a glass fell and shattered somewhere in the crowd. There was laughter and another scream. Paige got to his feet and broke away.

Paige pushed through the crowd, ignoring the cries of protest, unable to find Caro anywhere. He was close to the band and the music had grown loud. He went a few yards more and he saw Alexander standing by himself.

"Where is she?" he yelled at the old man. Alexander looked confused at first, then smiled.

"Gone off," he yelled back. "Can't keep a pretty girl around long these days."

"Where'd she go?" Paige demanded.

191

"Off that way," he said, waving toward the entrance. "With somebody younger, I'm afraid. Tall, rather good-looking, don't blame her, really. Lovely girl. They always go for a man in a uniform."

"What do you mean?"

"A policeman, that's what I mean. She went off with one of our boys in blue."

Paige saw Caro and a tall, thin man in a police uniform going through the entrance. The man looked back once, a narrow profile, and there was a sick feeling in the pit of Paige's stomach, and the man saw that Paige was watching them and he smiled, a winner's smile, Paige thought, and then they went back into the building and disappeared.

Paige fought his way up the steps, sweeping people past him with his arms until he reached the top. The crowd thinned and he ran into the main ballroom but Caro wasn't there.

Paige rushed toward the center of the room, one hand automatically reaching for his gun. Then he saw Tom Ferris coming at him from the other side of the room with an angry expression on his face and Paige's brain did a jerky little side step and he thought that something had happened to Connie and then he remembered that Connie was dead a long time ago.

"I lost her," Ferris said. "Something happened to the transmitter. One second she was there, then she was gone, just like that. Where is she?"

"I don't know," Paige said. "Did you see her on your way in?" All the time he spoke, he kept looking around, one part of his brain willing her to appear.

Ferris shook his head and wiped his mouth with his hand, covering half his face with his fist, breathing hard.

"I think she found him," Paige said. "He's in a cop's uniform." He grabbed Ferris by the elbow. "The parking lot."

The crowd turned toward them as they ran, two big men tearing across the marble floor, one of them reaching behind his back as he ran, pulling out a gun from underneath his coat and carrying it low, close to his leg, elbow tucked against his side so that if he had to use it, all he had to do was raise his arm a few inches and brace himself and fire.

They searched the parking lot first. The attendants remembered no one matching Caro's description leaving the lot, either alone or with a man. Still, they checked each car until Paige decided that it was pointless. They finished the lot and then split up to check the rest of the grounds. Paige took the side by the river.

He crossed the drive behind the museum and worked his way down to the Waterworks, a small cluster of buildings constructed to look like scaled-down versions of Greek and Roman temples along the river.

They were being restored now and surrounded by scaffolding and wooden barricades. Spotlights on the riverside tossed white wings of light upward through the empty rooms. Through a window, Paige heard someone whisper and then the whisper was cut short.

He stepped over one of the barricades and listened hard, but all he could hear was the music from the museum. He looked behind him, north along the river to Boathouse Row. The small squat buildings, so ordinary during the day, were outlined in lights, their reflections glimmering on the water. Paige heard the whisper again. He took two steps and pressed himself against the cool concrete of the nearest building, closed his eyes, and focused on the sounds closest to him.

He heard the shuttle of something scraping the ground. Paige moved swiftly along the wall, ducking under the carefully framed portico, racing past the Doric columns that lined the front of the building.

His feet kicked up the dust as he ran, roiling it into small clouds that coated his hands and face and the slick metal of the gun. For a moment, he thought he might sneeze. He pressed the back of his hand to his nose and held it. At the corner of the building, a tiny piece of plaster fell off at the touch of his shoulder. Through an open window, he heard voices coming from inside the building and saw the flicker of a flame.

Paige pushed off the building and threw himself through the open window, coming down hard on his shoulder, ducked and rolled into a kneeling position, the gun pointed in the direction of the flame.

Two kids dropped their crack pipe and ran toward the door. Out of pure instinct, Paige followed them with the gun. He kept the barrel sighted on the middle of the slower one's back, high

193

up between his shoulder blades. His finger edged down on the trigger, then he snapped the gun up and they vanished through a doorway.

Paige's hand trembled for a few seconds and then he was up and running himself, through the maze of buildings to the museum to find Ferris.

"Where are we going?" Caro asked.

Grant maneuvered her through the parking lot quickly, avoiding the attendants.

"They said there was a problem and told me to take you back to the hotel," he said and shrugged. "I didn't wait for details."

"Is Paige going to be there?"

"I guess so," Grant said. He wanted her to stop asking questions until they were in the car. If she started something in the car, he could deal with it. But in the middle of the parking lot, it might become a problem. He tightened his grip on Caro's elbow and moved her along.

"I feel like I ought to be on roller skates," Caro said.

Rolling right along, Grant thought, and saw the car a few yards away, parked away from the lights. He could feel her hesitate as they got closer, so he pushed her forward ever so carefully. No need to make her feel frightened. There would be enough time for all of that later. Grant was going to put some real fear into her life; he planned to take her back to the house and show her the basement, haul her down there and hold her face in the dirt for a while.

At the car, he held the door for her.

"Where's your gun?" Caro asked. "You're not wearing one."

"They asked us not to wear them inside the Art Museum," he said. "Don't want to frighten the guests." Caro got into the car. "Mine's in the trunk. I'm going to get it right now."

In the trunk he found the paper bag with the roll of tape and the bailing wire. Grant slammed the trunk closed. He was zooming now and nobody could touch him. He slid into the seat and dropped the bag between his feet.

"You forgot your gun," she said. There was just the slightest hint of suspicion in her voice. Grant started the car and backed out of the space.

194

"I figured what the hell," he said. "Live dangerously."

"What's in the bag?"

"My lunch," he said. "Want some?"

"No thank you."

Grant drove around the lot to the East River Drive exit and waited for the traffic to clear. "We'll be on our way in no time," he said. He leaned forward to see the road.

Caro gasped and stared at the back of his neck. Grant reached up and touched his shirt and then his hair. His fingers came away sticky. Grant thought he was clean before arriving at the museum but obviously he'd missed a spot or two. All the excitement had made him sloppy. He wasn't worried about it.

"There's blood on your neck," she said. There was nothing but fear in her voice this time. He let his hand drop to the seat.

"I must have cut myself shaving," Grant said mildly.

Caro looked at him as if he'd lost his mind. She grabbed her purse and shoved her hand inside, searching frantically for something.

"Maybe not," he said and swung his fist around hard into the side of her face. Her head bounced off the window and fell back. Grant hit her once more before she dropped to the seat, the top of her head resting against his leg. He shoved her away from him and pushed her down until she was trapped between the dash and the front of the seat. She couldn't reach him now even if she tried.

Grant pulled out and drove a quarter of a mile to the parking lot near Boathouse Row. The lot was nearly full but he found a place near the end and parked. He sat for a few minutes to collect himself and then went to work.

He pushed her seat back as far as it would go and Caro slid all the way onto the floor, her head next to the accelerator. The side of her face was bruised and one eye was swollen shut. He slapped her hard on the cheek. She didn't respond.

He turned her head and looked at the bruise again. "What a mess you are," he said, and grabbed her purse from the floor, resting it on his lap so he could see what she was trying so hard to find. There was nothing there. Some keys, a pen, her wallet. He checked the wallet. She had a hundred dollars in cash. Grant put it in his shirt pocket.

"Every little bit helps," he said to her. He reached for the bag between his feet. The tape was first, in case she decided to get vocal on the drive home. He tore off a piece and covered her mouth with it, pressing down hard to make sure it was secure.

The bailing wire was next. He looped one end around her left wrist and twisted it so hard that it cut into her skin. "That should work," he said, and reached for her right hand.

Caro hid the knife she'd taken from her purse in that hand. When he grabbed her wrist, she brought the knife up blindly, swinging it toward what she thought must have been his face. She could only see from one eye, and the pain in her head made her sick and weak. The knife connected and she felt something tear. She dug the blade in deeper.

The blade cut an uneven pattern down the sleeve of Grant's shirt, ripping into his arm. He felt nothing for a minute, then the shock roared through him. Caro raised the knife again and he tried to pull back but the tip of the knife caught the edge of his cheekbone and cut a shallow line along the edge of the bone out to his ear.

Grant screamed and clutched at his face.

Caro slammed the door handle down and rolled out of the car onto the ground. She was confused for a moment by the lights and the traffic but then she saw the Art Museum in the distance and began to run toward it, keeping her one eye focused on it and nothing else. There were things she could see on the periphery of her sight, bright rainbows of color, movement and sound, but she ignored everything and stumbled through the parking lot toward the Drive. She tore the tape from her mouth and threw it away. A hand reached out to grab her but she slashed at it with the knife and the hand went away.

The next thing she knew, she was walking down the side of the Drive and the cars were coming up behind her, first fast, then slow. Somebody yelled at her to get off the road. She stayed where she was and moved a little faster. She didn't want to look back. If she looked back, he was going to catch her.

Someone called her name. Caro ignored it. What she wanted to do was get to the Art Museum and the crowds of people. Nothing could happen to her once she got there. Someone called her name again, closer this time. She kept moving.

They grabbed for the knife. Caro swung her arm up. She

196

knew she had cut him before, she just wasn't sure where. So she tried again. A pair of arms circled her waist and lifted her off the road and threw her on the grass. She dropped the knife and searched frantically for it, tearing up patches of wet grass to find it. Another hand found hers and held it down.

"It's okay," Paige said. "You can stop now." Caro continued to struggle. "Caro," he said again, louder this time, "stop it, you're all right."

She stopped then and collapsed in his arms. Paige held her like that for a few minutes and then lifted her head up. He winced when he saw the bruises and touched the one on her cheek lightly.

"It's going to be all right," he said.

Caro jerked her head back.

"Liar," she told him.

Paige was completely worn out. He'd spent over an hour searching the parking lot and interviewing several witnesses. All of them had seen Caro staggering toward the East River Drive. None of them remembered the car she arrived in or the man who was with her.

They were at the hotel now and Caro was asleep. The hotel had a physician service on call. There was no concussion and no broken bones, so he gave her a prescription for Darvon and suggested she have an X ray in the morning just to be safe. Ferris sent O'Neal out to fill the prescription. When O'Neal returned, he sent him out for coffee.

"No hits, no runs, we struck out," Ferris said. "So go home." They were sitting on chairs in the hall outside her room.

Paige leaned his chair against the wall and shut his eyes. "I'll stay here," he said.

"What'll that prove?"

"I said I'll stay here. I don't want to argue about it."

"So you'll stay here. How about I get O'Neal to stay with you? Will that piss you off, too?"

"Do whatever you want, Tom," Paige said and kept his eyes closed.

Ferris grunted as he leaned back in his seat. "That's exactly what your old man used to say."

Ferris shook his arm. Paige came awake with a sudden jolt, a sick feeling that he'd missed something again.

"Is Caro all right?" he asked.

Ferris stood there looking edgy and grim.

"Fuck her," he said. "We got real problems."

Paige glanced at his watch. He'd been asleep for approximately fifty-eight minutes, but it felt like he'd already been gone half the night.

28

The Tromblys' backyard was staked out with lights. They formed a ragged circle around the big maple and the small garden that surrounded it. From a distance, it looked like a plane crash site, all bright lights and wreckage. Shadows moved among the lights searching for traces of the victims.

There were a few neighbors in the streets. They gestured at the house while two uniformed cops stood behind the barricades talking to each other. One of them recognized Paige and Ferris and let them both through. Paige kept looking for Marlene Trombly, thinking that maybe she'd survived but he knew it was pure folly to hold out that kind of hope. One of the cops confirmed it.

"Two in the back," he said and passed a quick finger across his throat. One woman in the crowd gasped and started to cry and Paige wanted to take the cop's head off.

There was another cop at the front door. "Come to see the show?" he asked. Another clown, Paige thought. It was like an infestation of them had broken out somewhere nearby.

Paige saw Sloat talking to Nolan on the other side of the

living room. When Sloat noticed Paige, he pursed his lips and nodded.

Paige looked to his right and saw a pool of blood on the white rug. It had begun to cake up around the edges, but in the center it was wet and darker than the rest of the pool. The police had rolled out a trail of brown butcher paper on either side so you could walk around it without disturbing the scene. Ferris went on ahead of him.

Paige noticed something on the stairs, a smudge of color that seemed out of place. He moved closer.

There was blood on the fifth step from the top, not very much, but no one else had seen it. "The bodies are out back," Ferris said to him. Paige ignored him and climbed the stairs. He wanted to see Marlene Trombly's bedroom.

A single cop was watching television in her room. When Paige entered, the cop hardly looked up. There was a pile of tapes next to him, most of them prerecorded movies and a handful of blank cassettes. Behind him, the tops of the trees showed through the open French doors. Paige stepped around the edge of the bed.

Marlene Trombly was making love with someone on the screen.

"Do you believe this," the cop said. "She and her husband took movies."

Paige looked at the screen. Marlene Trombly had her husband's cock in her mouth and a mad frantic look in her eyes as she moved up and down on him. The angle of the camera cut him off just below the chin. She moved faster and faster, and when he came, she caught the first spray in her hand and smeared it up and down on the shaft, the movement of her hand nearly a blur. She began to lick her hand, then his glistening cock.

"Jesus," the cop said. Paige turned around. Where was the camera? From the angle, it should have been at the end of the bed. There were two sets of closets on the other side of the room and a full-length mirror between them. The camera was behind the mirror. Paige found the door in the left-hand closet and stepped inside. He could see the cop watching the television through the two-way mirror.

The cop was ready to leave. "I can't take any more of this,"

200

he said. Paige glanced at the set. Her husband's face came into view briefly, a quick flash and then it was gone. Paige found the remote control, stopped the tape, rewound it, and watched it again, this time frame by frame.

It was her husband. He let the tape continue. Marlene Trombly stood up. When she returned, he saw an ivory carving in her hand. Paige stopped the tape.

"What are you doing?" Ferris asked.

"She took some pictures of her and her husband in bed," Paige said. Ferris looked at the screen and shook his head.

Ferris turned to go downstairs and Paige left the tape on the bed. Sloat was still talking to Nolan when he got to the bottom of the stairs.

"I want to talk to you," Sloat said.

"No problem," Paige said. What they were doing down in the yard caught his eye and blotted out everything else. He held his breath, just a second or two, then let it out.

The bodies of Marlene Trombly and her husband hung from a limb of the big backyard maple. Even from there it was clear that their throats had been cut. The medical people were having trouble getting them down.

Paige left the terrace and walked toward the bodies. They had brought in the Mole, Paige noticed, a certain sign that somebody was taking the murders seriously. It would be serious enough as it was, two white people found hanging from a tree in their own backyard, but the Mole raised it to another level.

The Mole was Harvey Moel, the chief medical examiner, and he didn't bother coming out unless the case warranted headlines. The last one he attended was a butcher shop of a basement in North Philadelphia where he spent several days digging up the bodies of half a dozen black women chopped and buried in the dirt like so many dog bones.

Everybody said that the basement was perfect for the Mole, he finally got to play in the dirt. They also said it was the first time he'd ever been close to black people and that he sort of liked them that way. The Mole liked people, they said, but he liked them mostly when they were down.

He had a fuzzy dome, enormous hands, and weary little eyes that always seemed to be watching you from under permanently heavy lids. He wore a yellow happyface pin on his coat. The Mole knew Paige through his father. The Mole had worked on Connie. Now he was here, working on Marlene. The Mole was almost family.

Paige watched them load one of the bodies onto a portable gurney. The numbness began to leach out of him. The Mole peeled off surgeon's plastic gloves the color of sea water and carried them in one hand as he walked over to Paige. He seemed pleased to see him.

"Everybody comes out for these things," the Mole said. He shook Paige's hand but made it seem an unsanitary exercise. "I expect to see the mayor and city council any minute."

"What happened to her?" Paige asked.

"Is that a rhetorical question?" the Mole asked. For a second, his face resembled the one on his lapel.

"Your best guess."

"My best guess," the Mole repeated, then spoke very quickly. "He got it first. Probably a blow to the head, then a short slice through the carotid. He was probably dead within sixty seconds, maybe less."

"Why do you think he was first?" Paige asked.

The Mole loved to explain things. "Because she was tied up. But I don't know the exact sequence yet. Maybe the killer got to her first and then killed the husband, maybe he killed the husband first and then went after her. I just don't know yet."

But Paige knew what he was thinking. "You think the killer made her watch it in the living room?"

"I didn't say it was done in the living room, although that's the obvious place. Whoever did this has been reading too many Charlie Manson books." The Mole sucked in his breath in appreciation; an interesting death was a thing of beauty. "This one is very methodical, very gruesome. He cut off her ring finger." The Mole smiled knowingly. "But that shouldn't concern you or should it? I understand you knew the woman who was killed in Society Hill. Is that right?" Paige nodded. "And what about this one?"

"A little," Paige suggested.

"Then you're taking it personally?" the Mole asked and brushed a dead leaf from his sleeve. Paige was sure the Mole was thinking about Connie and checking his mental pulse, making certain that Paige wasn't going to lose it right here on the lawn. Paige shook his head.

"Was she awake when she died?" Paige asked suddenly.

The Mole considered the possibilities. "Probably. There's what looks like tape residue around her mouth. My best guess is yes, she was awake to the end. He seems to like them that way." The Mole looked at Paige to see if the answer satisfied him. "Do you know if she wore a ring?"

"A brand-new one," Paige said and walked away toward the other side of the yard.

He took his time down the long grassy slope to the rear of the garage. He glanced inside. The front door of the garage was open and her car was missing. That was what he had seen earlier driving up to the house, a quick observation that had gotten lost until somehow it worked its way back to the surface of his mind. He walked past the garage toward the house.

Ferris caught him before he went inside and steered him away.

"Sloat wants to know about the guy at the Art Museum," he said. "What do you want me to tell him?"

"Tell him what you know," Paige said.

Ferris looked strickened. "I'll make something up."

"Whatever," Paige said and started down the front steps.

"Wait a minute, where are you going?"

"I need to talk to Jimmy Wu," Paige said. The Chinese officer was the only one who might be able to locate the source of the ivory carvings. The source might lead him to the killer. It would certainly bring him closer than he was right now.

"Why don't you get some sleep, Pat," Ferris said. "Let me handle it for a while." He wore a pleading look that surprised Paige. "I'm only trying to help you," Ferris said.

"Not this time, Tom," Paige said.

O'Neal was sitting outside Caro's room when Paige got back to the hotel. It was nearly three in the morning and the energy that had carried him from the Trombly house had vanished completely.

"Why don't you get some sleep?" the young cop told him. "I'll be here until the morning. Tom said he'd be back by then."

Paige opened the door to Caro's room and went inside. She

slept on her back with her arms wrapped tightly around her chest as though even in sleep she was still trying to protect herself.

"Nice-looking girl," O'Neal said.

Paige closed the door.

"Where'd you come from, O'Neal?" he asked.

"I work at the warehouse," he said. The warehouse was where they kept the city voting machines. There were several officers permanently attached to it; it was everybody's dream job.

"Tom get you the job?"

"Yes, sir," O'Neal said.

"Don't let anybody try to take her out of here," Paige said. "If they do, shoot them."

O'Neal grinned. "Is that an order?" he asked.

Paige walked down to the hotel garage and got into his car. His eyes felt like the insides were covered with tar. He leaned back in the seat. First he just wanted to rest for a minute or two. When he got home, he could take a quick shower, eat something, and by then it would be time to call Jimmy Wu at home and shake him out of bed.

He was asleep in seconds.

For the first time in his life, Grant felt like a fugitive. The pain was bad; the fear was worse. Blood poured from his arm and down the side of his face and when he glanced into the mirror it looked like he was wearing a red mask. His arm lay useless at his side.

Grant glanced at the blood on the seat as he drove, scared that it was his, scared that there seemed to be so much of it. He was quickly losing track of time and direction, turning off the Wissahickon and suddenly finding himself in a maze of streets that seemed both familiar and strange.

The fabric of his shirt rubbed against his wound and he pulled the car over to the curb and held the arm tightly, willing the pain to go away. The throbbing accelerated, like the steadily rising pulse of an engine. Grant breathed through his teeth and forced himself to calm down. He concentrated, pushed the pain toward the back of his mind until the throbbing became a slow

204

solitary pulse. When it became tolerable, he started the car again and drove home.

He felt so weak that he had trouble closing the garage door and setting the lock. Then he staggered across the yard to the side door and into the kitchen. When he turned on the light, yellow and white clouds blossomed in front of his eyes and seemed to heighten the pain. He moved slowly and carefully, filling a pan full of hot water and pulling a stack of clean dish towels from the drawer near the stove.

There was a large first aid kit in the downstairs bathroom. He got that next. On the table, he set out a bottle of hydrogen peroxide, some gauze, a tin box of bandages, and a roll of adhesive tape. The wound on his arm was the deepest and the most difficult to clean. It kept bleeding through his fingers. He knew he needed stitches, but that was out of the question. He closed the wound with the bandages, pulling the open flaps of skin together as tightly as he could, and then he wrapped it with gauze and wound adhesive tape around that.

As for the cut on his face, Grant wanted to see what it looked like in a mirror.

It wasn't as bad as he thought, more blood than any real damage. It would still be difficult to hide but not impossible. He wiped it clean and covered the worst part of it with a bandage. He was still a mess. The rest of his face was covered with dried blood, as were his shirt and pants. His hair was soaked with it and matted to his head. He stripped off the uniform and dropped it in the washer.

From the medicine chest, Grant removed several vials, reading each one carefully as he poured the contents on the counter. It was clear what he needed. He took two Percodan tablets for the pain and poured the rest back in the bottle. If he waited too long, the drug would knock him out and he wanted to be awake. In another vial he found some fifteen-milligram Desoxyn and chewed three of the little yellow tablets.

He kept moving. In the kitchen, he found a plastic bag and wrapped his arm so he could shower. The drugs kicked in while he was under the water, letting the warm spray pound on the back of his neck, feeling the rush as it sped up the back of his skull and tingled along his jaw.

By the time he threw back the curtain the pain had subsided. He could feel his heart beat hard and fast in his chest. From his bedroom window, he could see lines of color in the sky. It was already morning. He was flying now, soaring right through it.

Before the day was out, he was going to find Caroline King and teach her how to fly, too.

29

A car started in the garage and jolted Paige awake. His face was pressed against the window and he stared out at a wall of concrete. For a second he had no idea where he was. Then he remembered and peeled his face off the glass and sat up.

His neck hurt. He opened the door and stretched out his legs, leaning back and rubbing the back of his neck. He remembered falling asleep a little after three o'clock. It was almost seven-thirty now. If he hurried, he could get Jimmy Wu at his house. Paige used the phone in the hotel lobby.

As it turned out, Paige woke him up.

"Why are you calling me?" Jimmy Wu told him. "I gave what I had to Tom Ferris."

"When did you do that?"

"I don't remember. A few days ago. He said he'd turn it over to you."

Paige hung up and called Ferris at home. Marion answered.

"He's not here," she said angrily.

"Where did he go?"

"How should I know where he is? I haven't seen him since

Friday. He didn't come home last night, either. Why don't you tell me where he is, Pat? You spend more time with him than I do." Marion hung up.

Paige rode the elevator to Caro's floor. O'Neal was in his chair next to the door, reading a book.

"Has Tom been here?"

"Here and gone," O'Neal said. He fought back a yawn. "You going to stay?"

"I need to find him. Do you know where he went?"

"He said he had to see somebody this morning. He told me who it was but I don't remember."

"Mickey Katz."

"That's it," O'Neal said.

Paige went straight up to the room. Archie, the black man Mickey hired to take care of him, was packing up Mickey's things in his suitcase. Archie looked up at him and shook his head.

"He's gone," Archie said and jerked his thumb over his shoulder. "They took him to intensive care." Archie looked down at the empty bed. "It don't look good," he said.

"When'd it happen?"

"Late last night," Archie said. "They didn't call me until six this morning. One of the nurses said he was up late, talking to himself, and that's when it happened." Archie folded up what few remaining clothes Mickey kept, a pair of gray gabardine trousers that were too big for him, a flannel shirt that he liked to wear in winter, a pair of worn leather slip-ons. "The swelling was getting worse and then he started coughing up blood. She said the blood was the worst part of it. Like something broke inside of him."

"You bring him breakfast again?"

Paige shook his head.

"That's too bad," Archie said with a weak smile. "I always liked bagels. Liked lox, too, the salty kind. Mickey thought I was a crazy old black man." He closed the suitcase. "You can go see him if you like. He's on the fourth floor, way in the back. They got him hooked up to the oxygen permanently now. He can't talk too much but he's awake. He'll be glad to see you, I know."

"Was Tom Ferris here?"

Archie shook his head.

"What about last night?"

"Don't know much about last night. The nurses didn't say anything to me." He touched the suitcase, caressing it with his hand. "He never came around that much anyway. He was always drunk when he did."

Mickey Katz stared up at Paige over the oxygen mask that covered most of the lower half of his face and his eyes glimmered through the pain. With one hand, he pulled the mask to one side so he could talk. His voice came out in a broken whisper.

"I made it for you," he said and pointed to a black vinyl toilet kit on the nightstand next to the bed. "Last night, before . . ." The words broke off and he shoved the mask over his mouth and nose, held it down tight with his hand and breathed deep. Paige unzipped the bag and removed its contents one at a time.

There was a small leather case containing a set of chrome Leary picks. Paige had seen them before and he held them in his hand for a few seconds, trying to remember the first time Mickey showed him how to use them. There was a worn copy of the Talmud with a leather binding and faded gilt lettering. Beneath it was a pocket watch on a chain and a small ring case.

The ring was gold with a large square-cut diamond in a flared setting. Eight smaller stones surrounded it. Paige looked at the inscription on the inside: TO MICKEY FROM DANNY. Mickey nodded at him and waved his finger at the case.

There was something stuffed down in one of the inside pockets. Paige reached in and pulled it out with his fingers. It was a single tape. Mickey pointed to the nightstand drawer. Inside it was a small tape recorder. Paige reached for it, thinking he would listen to it some other time. Mickey pulled the mask down and grabbed his wrist.

"Listen to it now," he said and pushed the mask back in place.

Paige slipped the tape into the recorder and adjusted the volume as the tape began to play.

He heard Mickey's labored breathing, a harsh gurgling noise like water running into an empty well. The sound was frightening. There was a cough, the shuffling of papers or maybe his feet in the cheap cardboard slippers he liked, then Mickey's voice. He sound tired and weak. I don't want him to die, Paige thought.

"You hear me all right, Pat?" Mickey said. "Archie got me this thing. I can hold it right in my hand and talk into this hole here. I guess they don't make the kind with wires anymore. The fucking Koreans, what do you expect?"

Paige turned off the tape and looked at Mickey. "Can't this wait?"

Mickey pulled the mask back. "No more time," he said.

Paige started the tape again.

"I tried to write some of this down," Mickey said on the tape, "but it hurts too goddamn much. The main thing is if you're listening to this, then I must be dead or damn near it. There are worse things. They say there isn't, but they don't know what the hell they're talking about. You watch an eighty-five-year-old shit in his pants every couple hours and break down crying and you'll see right through it."

There was a racking cough on the tape and more shuffling of papers and the sound of a door opening and closing.

"One of the nurses came in and told me to keep my voice down. Screw her. Now you listen to me, Pat. I'm going to tell you what I know about Tom Ferris and your old man and when Connie got killed. I knew most of it, the rest I put together, a bit here and a bit there, you know how it is. I want to make sure you know what happened, so it's going to take a little time.

"I told you I worked for your old man, Pat. That was back when all the new guys used to wear them shitty gray uniforms right out of the academy and drive the Red Terrors around. Rizzo wasn't a politician then, just another wop. I got myself in a jam and before you know it, I'm getting passed up the line. Back then I was scared. It was just me, sitting in this holding room, watching the faces change every hour or so. Somebody must have thought I was worth the price of admission."

On the tape, Paige heard the sound of a door opening and then Mickey said, "Will you give me some fucking privacy, please?" The door closed and Mickey breathed into the microphone. "It's like a pay toilet in here, anybody that's got a quarter thinks they can waltz in with their pants down. Don't get old, Pat, don't get old like this. It don't pay." More coughing. "Anyway, the last one come to see me was Tom Ferris. He didn't say too much, asked how I was getting along, whether I wanted something to drink.

"I'm a real picture. I got one eye closed where some shithead punched me just in case I get the idea I'm living in a democracy. My hands are handcuffed to the bottom of the fucking chair, so I can scratch my nuts with my elbow if I want to, and here's Tom Ferris asking me if I want a cup of coffee. Why, I ask him, so I can steam clean them, too? Tom likes a sense of humor and cuts me loose. I get the coffee, my hands are so fucking blue they shake like they do now, coffee's going every place, Ferris is pissed I spilled some on his new black brogues, they cost sixteen dollars he tells me and I'm impressed, somebody pays sixteen dollars for shoes that look that bad has got to have some kind of talent, and then he gets down to business.

"I figure he wants me to do some snitching for him and I'm all set to sign up but no, he asks me if I need some extra work every now and then breaking into places."

Paige listened hard now. On the bed, Mickey nodded in rhythm to his own voice. His eyes glistened.

"The jobs weren't much, really. I'd go into a place, make sure there were no surprises and leave the backdoor open, never took a thing, never was asked. They were all politicians, not all big shots, either. I stayed around to watch one night, just so I'd know, might come in handy. Car pulls up and it's Tom Ferris coming in to do a plant on some poor schmuck thinks he's going to run for councilman or something. Fat fucking chance.

"I got paid, you know, a couple hundred every now and then, but there was never any real money involved, that wasn't the point. I never did time, never got caught. I met your father about a month or so after I started doing it. He liked me. He brought me out to Margate, gave me a fruit basket for Christmas, he must have thought I was a ward case. I think he got a charge out of being around a real thief. He told me to talk to you when you got to be somebody, when you made detective, he said.

"Tommy taped everybody for your old man, that was his job. He did the dirty work, he even did it to cops. He and your old man used to sit around listening to people screwing or going to the bathroom, that was the big deal.

211

"Once I opened the door for him, Tommy'd plant that stuff everywhere, in the toilet, under the mattress. He said that the Catholics were the best. They'd be screwing and talking about Jesus doing this and holy fucking Mary and you wouldn't believe it, he said. What was even better was this one tape of the cardinal they had. The cardinal's so fucking constipated he would pray before he took a shit. You should have heard him. Your old man used to do imitations."

There was a break in the tape, a four- or five-second gap that startled him, so he backed it up and listened for a minute. Then he realized that Mickey was only getting himself ready.

"One of the other things I used to do was help Tom Ferris collect the pay offs from the fences. That was his other job, to get the money and turn it over to your old man so he could hand it out when he needed to. That's why Ferris was so scared when I gave you that list of dealers you asked me for. Hell, he took money from damn near every one of them.

"You remember I told you about the dealer who got the crap beat out of him? His name was Hazen, and that Peterson guy used to work for him. Tommy knew him, too. He's the one who took him to the hospital. The guy's thumbs were bent back to his fucking elbow, hands all smashed to pieces."

Mickey motioned for him to turn off the tape.

"I know what you're thinking," Mickey gasped. "Why didn't he tell you? You listen now."

Paige turned the tape back on.

"So I'm getting to my last point here, Pat. A few years go by and I'm getting older and not so interested in running around the rooftops, so Tom asks me if I can find somebody who can help out a bit. I knew one or two, so I think about it and I think the best I can do is this kid, he's got some smarts and he wants to do good for himself and his family. This was before he got into smack."

Paige's mouth went dry.

"I gave him Sonny Ray, Pat. Sonny was our secret, Tom's, your old man's, too. I don't think anybody else knew about him except the three of us. It was like the fucking Masons, swear an oath and that kind of shit except that you don't think about getting expelled if you fuck up.

"Maybe that's what Sonny didn't figure, not that junkies

have to have a reason for anything, they don't need reasons, they got holes in their arms for reasons. He screwed up a couple times and Tom calls me on the phone and says to talk to Sonny, see if I can straighten him out because Danny is getting teed-off at his mistakes. So I got a hold of Sonny and spell it out for him, but it's like talking to a fucking taco. The next thing that happens, Ferris gets him sent down to one of the district tanks and turns a couple of the brothers loose on Sonny just so he knows what it feels like to get really fucked, but you can't teach a junkie anything."

A few more seconds of silence.

"There isn't much left to tell you, Pat. I don't know what Sonny was doing at your house. Maybe he just wanted to get something of his own back, maybe he thought your old man was going to be there. I don't think he meant to kill Connie, I think she just happened to be in the wrong place, but who knows? Once it happened, your old man didn't have any choice, did he? You were nuts, beating up on guys, trying to find out who did it. Your old man was scared shitless you were going to find him. So Danny gave the job to Tom Ferris and he goes out and does it.

"I ain't proud of this, Pat, but I ain't crying, either. I didn't fuck things up the way your old man and Tom Ferris did. I'm telling you this because I'm dying and I don't owe them nothing anymore. When Tom came by the other night, all worried that you were looking in the wrong places and maybe going to find out, I almost told you then and there. I don't know why I didn't. Maybe because you're still a cop and I'm still a thief. But fuck him and fuck your old man, it's time you found out the truth. There's nothing more to it than that. You've had a tough time of it, but you come out all right. You want to know any more, you ask Tom about it."

The tape ended. Paige reached down to turn it off, trying to shake off the tension that seemed to hold him in place. The sounds of the hospital rushed into his ears and the last of Mickey's words faded into the place where he let his memories hide. He slipped the tape into his pocket.

"Whatever you're going to do," Mickey said, "be careful."

30

Ferris's car was in front of his house. Paige circled around the block once and parked near the end of the street. He went into the house through the backdoor, easing it closed. A radio played quietly in the front room.

Marion was there, sitting by herself on the couch.

"I saw you drive by the first time, Pat," she said. She had on her work clothes and there was a newspaper spread over the table in front of her, an empty coffee cup holding it down. "Now you come sneaking in through the backdoor." She shook her head disapprovingly.

"Where is he, Marion?"

"I told you he's not here," she said.

Paige headed for the stairs. Marion stood up.

"You leave him alone!" she yelled and started for Paige. She crossed the room quickly, surprising him with her swiftness. He caught her and held her, feeling her heart pound, her breath hot against his shirt. She went rigid in his arms and then pushed him away.

"It's too late for that," Paige said.

"What are you going to do? I want to know, Pat. He came

home last night and locked himself in the spare room and I want to know what he's doing there and what you're doing here. For God's sake, we're friends! Why can't I get an answer from you?" Her voice moved faster and faster and rose in pitch until it was a shriek and she was crying and flailing at him with her arms.

Paige held her again, enveloping her until she stopped moving and stopped crying. She pushed him away again and straightened herself out, fixed her hair, and wiped her face with her fingers.

"Can you just tell me what's going on?" she asked. "I just want to know if everything's going to be all right."

"I can't tell you."

"Is it going to be all right, Pat?"

"Why don't you go to work, Marion." He started up the stairs. Marion picked up her purse from a chair in the living room and then walked past Paige to the front door.

"Why don't you go to hell," she said and slammed the door behind her.

Paige climbed the stairs. The door to the spare room was unlocked. Paige pushed it open. The room smelled dry and clean, just a hint of scent from the pine tree-shaped air freshener dangling from a hook on the wall to mar the effect.

There was a single bed in the room, a small desk with a black folding chair in front of it. On the desk was a tape player and about two dozen tape cassettes stacked next to a large notebook and a manila folder with a note from Jimmy Wu clipped to the top. He stuffed the folder into his coat pocket and sat down to look at the tapes. Each of them was marked with a name and a date. The first one had his father's name on it. The date was a week after Connie's murder.

Paige crossed the hall and looked in the other bedroom. Tom Ferris lay sprawled on his back across the bed, his arms spread out in a drunken welcome. Paige closed the door quietly.

Paige found a shopping bag full of tapes in the closet and dumped the recorder and tapes from the desk in with them and carried it to the backyard. He filled Ferris's grill with charcoal, lit it, and began to sort through them while the coals got hot.

The smoke from the burning tapes was heavy and black, like plumes of ink jetting into the sky. Bits and pieces of charred plastic drifted through the air, settled on leaves and grass, and speckled the backs of his hands. While they burned, he listened to his father's voice telling Tom Ferris that he just didn't give a good goddamn anymore. Paige wondered where Tom had hidden the microphone.

"I do love the doctors," Danny was saying. "I've got a heart the size of a football and they stand around in those nice white uniforms that make them look like they haven't taken a piss for three weeks and they tell me that my prognosis is good. If somebody in the wards could talk like that, I'd run him for senator first chance I got, teach that asshole from Pittsburgh a lesson in public speaking."

Tom Ferris spoke up, but the words were too indistinct for Paige to hear. His father's voice seemed to bristle.

"Do you honestly think I care what they think of me anymore, Tom? Haven't you seen through that after all these years? That was never any concern of mine. I let them hate me all right if that's what it took to keep a grip on things. It doesn't matter what they think of you but what they'll *do* for you. Christ, I should be writing a book." The scrape of a chair leg across the floor. "Where are you going? Bring me some aspirin, would you? I keep it next to the sink." The tape came to an end.

Paige removed the cassette from the machine and tossed it in the fire. It began to melt, bending in the center, then the tape caught fire and burst into flame, spiraling around like a snake gone mad. He took another one from his pocket and read the date. Connie was dead a little over a month. Paige remembered that her murderer was dead by then, too. His father in another year. Paige put the tape in the machine and listened.

"I thought we ended it," his father said. He sounded tentative, a thought still unformed at the moment of its birth. He spoke reasonably, the way he always did whenever he needed time to think of a new angle. Danny Paige worked fast on his feet. "The dead bury the dead and all that poetic crap, so why all this, Tommy? Busy doing your sums, haven't put enough away from skimming the payoffs over the years?" A muffled voice in the background, the words unclear but the sound was one of pleading.

"Oh, Jesus, is that it, Tom? After all these years you want to be a policeman again?" his father said and laughed. "You're

216

not feeling guilty about Sonny, are you? I wish I could have done it myself. That's what I kept thinking about at the funeral home, how I wanted to drag him out of the coffin and kill him all over again." There was a pause, the sound of something moving in the background. Then his father continued.

"No? Do you think being a cop again will clean the guilt off you? Is that why you're thinking about being a cop again? Your brains have turned to shit, Tom, you were always a lousy cop, that's why I picked you to work with me. If you keep this up, next you'll be doing bingo night at Saint Theresa's, pulling white glove duty for all the funeral boys."

Paige leaned forward as if he were sitting across from his father instead of Tom Ferris.

"You drunken fuck, you think I didn't know about her condition, you think I didn't care? How the hell was I supposed to know you were going to sic the niggers on him? That's why he killed her, you son of a bitch. You're worse than he ever was because you should have known better."

Tom Ferris started to argue with his father. A hand slapped on a table like a bone crack.

"Keep your mouth shut while I'm talking," Danny Paige yelled, "just keep it shut and listen. I don't care what you think you know, I make the rules here. Sonny hurt one of mine because he thought he could hurt me. Well, he's dead, isn't he?"

The voice filled with smooth menace. "You think you can scare me the same way, do you, Tommy? Think that's the smart move to get what you want? I give you the best deal of your sorry life and then you threaten me. I don't even know what to do with you anymore."

Paige stopped the tape there, rewound it, and listened to his father's words again, listened carefully, and when he was certain of what he'd heard, he ignored the warning from his own heart and let the tape roll forward, wanting for his past to finally play itself out.

"I'll give you what you want, Tommy, I don't write off loyalty cheap even when you throw it away in the end. But I tell you this, you'll only get so far, I'll see to that. Will detective keep you happy? Think you'll be satisfied with that? You're cheaper than you look, Tommy."

Paige half expected it when it came but it still went through him like a fire storm. "I'll pay your fucking price, just to keep the stake out of my heart. I've paid everyone else's, even the Mole got paid. But if Pat ever finds out what we did or that Connie died pregnant, I swear I'll kill you myself, I'll string your guts around your neck like ribbon."

There was the sound of footsteps coming closer, then his father's voice once again, in a whisper as dead as stone.

"This is the end of it, the case goes no further, not for as long as you're alive, not as long as Pat's alive." A long pause. "I don't have to shake your hand on it, I'm not buying a pig."

Neither man spoke, and then into the silence the bitterness of his father's voice.

"You're the one who really killed her," his father said. "I told you to leave Sonny alone but you had to teach him a lesson, show him what you could do. Well, we've all got lessons to learn now, don't we, Tom." Then his voice cracked and Paige listened to something he had heard only a few times in his life, the sound of his father crying.

He turned off the tape and sat still for a moment before tossing it onto the fire with the rest of them.

The backdoor of the house opened up and Tom Ferris stepped onto the patio. He carried a beer in one hand and drank it standing by the door.

"Hell of a mess," Ferris said. He watched the black smoke spiral into the air. "Where's Marion?"

"She went to work," Paige said.

Ferris pulled a rusty lawn chair toward him and dropped awkwardly into it. "Mind if I sit down?" he asked. "Already it's starting to feel like a long day."

Paige felt like he was sitting next to a stranger in a bus station.

"How'd you find out?" Ferris asked. His voice was sloppy and belligerent.

"Mickey Katz," Paige said.

Ferris smiled and shook his head. "A Jew thief's revenge," he said.

"Maybe it was overdue," Paige said.

Ferris grunted. "Who cares? You come here for an explanation, Pat?"

"Can you give me one?" After all the years, Paige found that his anger was like a point of light, bright and hot, but very small. "Didn't you think I deserved to know about Connie or wasn't that part of the big picture?"

Ferris closed his eyes and sighed. "There never was any big picture. We got caught in a bind. Your old man was worried about you, I was worried about you. You were running around the city like some kind of avenging angel, you remember that? We thought you were going to get yourself killed or kill somebody else, so what the hell good would it have done to tell you the truth?"

"What the hell good would it have done?" Paige said. "Is that some kind of magic phrase that makes it all right?" The years caught up to him suddenly, his grief wasted and spent, like the passions of some dumb beast, ground down and ruined by the casual brutality of what they'd done. Paige pulled Ferris from the chair and shook him. It was like shaking a corpse. There was no feeling left at all.

"I had a right to know," Paige shouted, his words falling like ax blows, cutting away to a heart of dead wood. "She was my wife. She was pregnant. She was *murdered* because of what you did!"

The tears came suddenly. Paige felt them fall on his hand. Tom Ferris cried silently to himself, as close to an apology as Paige would ever get. Paige didn't know whether to believe them or not. His father had cried at all the wakes for people that he hardly knew. The tears there were real, too; at the same time, as phony as prayer.

He looked past Ferris, and suddenly he had a vision as clear as a photograph. He saw Connie and a little girl standing together beside the backdoor of their old house. The girl looked like his wife, small and composed. Paige stood behind them, one hand reaching out for his daughter's hair. She turned to take his hand and her fingers felt as light as a breath. His father came into the picture. Danny tried to sweep them up in his arms but Paige pushed him away with all the force he could muster. He wanted to hold his daughter close, to feel the softness of her hand on his but she was gone. The vision grew brighter and brighter until it burned itself out.

He looked down. Tom Ferris had stopped crying, his mourning over as quickly as it had begun. When Paige released him, everything else went with it.

"We did what we thought was best, Pat," he said. "They were talking about taking your badge away, for Christ's sake. Maybe you forgot about that. You think about what you'd have been like if you'd known. Danny didn't want to see you go down. Neither did I."

Paige looked at him in sad amazement. "All his life, my father used people and told them it was for their own good and he got away with it and that's all it ever was. It was just his way of keeping his foot on somebody's neck and being able to shake their hand at the same time. Look what he did to you. He's been dead for years and you're still his boy, more than I ever was."

"I'd do it again," Ferris said, but there was no force behind his words.

Paige took out the report from Jimmy Wu and opened it to the last page. Halfway down he picked out the Lucky Seven Import Company and Lindor Peterson's name next to it.

"You knew about Peterson from the first day," Paige said. "You could have given me that."

"I wanted to keep you away from things, Pat," Ferris said. "Sloat's already talking about a suspension. He's serious. I tried to keep him off your back as long as I could."

Paige took out his shield and held it in his hands, feeling the weight of it. Not much there, he decided. Paige thought he might drop it in the fire, bury it beneath the ashes and the clouds of oily smoke where it belonged.

He could not bring himself to throw it away like that. Instead, he tossed it to Tom Ferris who dropped it in the dirt, then fumbled around to pick it up, brushing it off on his pants, trying to give it back to him.

"You keep it, Tom, you're so worried about me losing it."

After tonight, Paige thought, if there was anything left, he could always come back for it.

31

Grant hated wearing the bandage in public but the situation being what it was, didn't see that he had much choice. He just needed to know whether Caroline King was still at the hotel and then he could decide what he would have to do to get to her. Even if they had her surrounded by police, which was what he expected, he was prepared to deal with it. He could wait. He touched the bandage on the side of his face and thought about the scar it was going to leave and decided he could wait a long time.

Grant found a maid at the Hershey who was willing to talk to him for twenty bucks. Her name was Leana and she smiled and flirted with him when he told her he was a reporter for the *Inquirer*. She acted like he was going to take her picture. Grant wanted to shove her down an elevator shaft. She stopped smiling and turned cagey when he asked her about prostitution in the hotel.

"Why you want to know something like that?"

"We heard some cops were renting rooms and using them for hookers," he said.

"I never heard nothing like that," she said.

221

"Then what about the cop on six?" he asked. He'd walked right past him twenty minutes earlier, a young cop in a uniform reading a paperback novel. Grant kept walking and took the stairs down to the next floor.

"You mean the skinny one?" the maid asked. "He's too tired for that. Been there most of the night, watching that woman."

"Who is she?"

"I don't know. Somebody said it was Grace Kelly's niece but if that's her niece, I'm Tina Turner. I seen her when they brought her in. She was *all* fucked up."

"Were there any other police around?"

"Some other detectives but that was last night. They left the young one to watch her. They ain't been back since then."

Grant thought that would work out beautifully. Now all he had to do was plug Lindor into this new equation and he might have a solution to his problems. The maid touched his arm and pulled back suddenly when she saw the look on his face.

"You planning on coming back here soon?" she asked.

"Why?"

"Because maybe I can watch the place for you, then you'll know who's in there with her. Maybe I can find out who she is or whatever. Those other detectives come back, I can let you know that, too."

Grant thought about it.

"That's worth another twenty," she said. "Me watching out for you."

Grant took some money from his pocket and peeled off a ten-dollar bill. The money felt like cellophane in his hand, all shiny and smooth, making crackling sounds like a fire when he snapped it out straight between two fingers and handed it to her.

Times like these, he thought, you either had to kill them or pay them and right now it was a lot cheaper to give her the money.

"The rest when I come back, okay?"

She took the money, folded it several times, and slipped it into her shoe.

"I'll be here," the maid said. "I ain't goin' nowhere."

He called Peterson from a pay phone in the rear of the lobby. The dealer picked it up on the third ring.

"You busy tonight, Lindor?" Grant asked before Peterson had a chance to speak.

"I beg your pardon?"

"I said, are you busy tonight? You know who this is?"

Peterson didn't answer right away, then in a rush. "Of course I know who this is. Are you serious?"

"I'm very serious."

"It's just that you sound different."

"Stress," Grant said. "It's a very stressful profession."

"What time?"

That's good, Grant thought, hearing the excitement finally coming into Peterson's voice. I like eagerness in a student.

"You just hang around the shop. I'll call you later and let you know everything."

"Okay," Peterson said. "I'll wait right here. I didn't think it would happen so soon."

"Me, neither," Grant said. "Ain't life wonderful?"

32

Paige took the alarm system out at the junction box. He'd done it so many times in his life that it had the comfortable feel of routine.

He worked his way methodically through the wire maze. Every alarm system he'd ever worked on had a series of false leads, some were hot, some were cold, some tripped an internal switch that set off the alarm. The thing was to keep your eye on the main lead and ignore the rest. Once the main lead was cut at its source, the others would fall.

Paige used a pair of crochet hooks to fish out the wires. He hooked on to the hot wire and followed it through, clipping it off with a black metal binder clip every few inches to keep it from becoming tangled.

At the end, the hot lead split into three. The ground wire was fitted into a precut slot on the side of the junction box, the other was the feed from the main power line, the third was a false lead.

Starting with the false lead, Paige snipped them off in succession, then waited. Sometimes there was a secondary trip switch hidden in the system that tripped the alarm if the power flowed out of sequence. Once or twice he'd cut the wrong wire. He counted to twenty-five. No alarm.

Paige unscrewed the plate on the door and slid the steel bar between the door and the jamb. He pushed up with the heel of his hand. The bolt gave way. He told himself again to be careful because anything was possible now.

The storage room of Peterson's shop was dark except for a single yellowish light over a desk to his left. The door to the showroom was directly ahead, not more than twenty-five feet away. On his right were several pallets loaded with large wooden crates. Behind the crates in the right rear corner was another door, probably a bathroom, Paige thought. There were a few other crates on pallets immediately to his left. On the desk was a computer, a telephone, a Rolodex, and a pair of stacked in-baskets filled with invoices. On the other side of the desk, next to the showroom door, was a tall metal cabinet. The cabinet was locked.

From the showroom he heard classical music and what he thought might have been laughter. Was Peterson talking to a customer or was he on the phone? What was he going to do if Peterson brought the customer into the storeroom? Shit. Don't just stand there and wait for him, Paige thought, move. He hurried toward the other corner.

Peterson burst through the doorway, his huge arms raised above his head. Paige ducked down as Peterson rammed into him. The dealer drove one knee heavily into his side. Paige sank to his knees on the concrete floor and fought to catch his breath. Peterson battered him with his fists. One blow struck Paige in the eye. It teared up instantly. He fought back, half-blind.

Paige brought his fists together, swung up hard, and struck Peterson in the center of his chest. He struck him again, aiming for the heart this time. Peterson kept pounding his back and side, but the blows weren't as strong as before. Paige hit him again rapidly, once, twice, three times. The blows slowed the dealer down but didn't stop him. Paige hunched his shoulders to protect his neck, took a deep breath and swung up as hard as he could. The blow caught Peterson just below the neck and knocked him backward. The dealer groaned and toppled over. He stayed that way for only a few seconds, then he began to crawl toward Paige.

Paige took out his gun and leveled it at Peterson's head. The dealer stopped moving. Paige caught his breath, then he stood up and backed away slowly until he felt the cold metal of the cabinet.

"Get up," he told Peterson. The antiques dealer stood slowly, clenching and unclenching his fists. Paige motioned with the gun.

"Put your hands in your pockets and walk over here." He pointed to a place on the floor a few feet from the desk. Peterson did what he was told. "Sit down, keep your hands in your pockets."

Peterson glanced furtively at the cabinet. Paige smiled. "You keep your goodies in there, Lindor?" he asked. "Where's the key?"

"You can't do this," Peterson said. "You're a cop."

"Not tonight," Paige said. "Where's the key?"

Peterson remained silent.

"You right- or left-handed?" Paige asked. "Come on, easy question."

"Right," Peterson answered.

"Hold it up," Paige said. Peterson looked mystified. "Hold it up in the air. I want to show you something."

Peterson raised his hand.

Paige pressed the barrel of the gun into the palm. He spoke calmly.

"You tell me what I want to know or I'm going to blow a big hole through the middle of your hand, Lindor. You'll be able to suck your lunch through it but not much else." He cocked the gun. "I'll count to five."

At four, Peterson made up his mind. "There's a key ring in the top drawer," he said.

"Good. Now you can put your hand back in your pants."

Paige found the keys and opened the doors. One side consisted of several open shelves, mostly empty. On the other side was a series of drawers, none of them more than three inches high. Paige chose one of them at random and pulled. He pulled too hard. The drawer fell out. Peterson gasped.

A dozen or more small ivory carvings spilled on the floor by his feet. Paige picked one up. A small boy being sodomized by two men. "Very nice, Lindor," Paige said. He looked from the carving to Peterson and then threw it at the dealer. Peterson ducked. The carving missed his head by inches and left a gouge in the crate behind him.

Peterson bolted. Paige caught the back of his shirt and pulled hard, swinging him head first around into one of the crates.

"Where is he?" Paige yelled. Peterson struggled to get away. Paige swung him into the crate again. "Where is he, you piece of shit?" He threw Peterson against the crate. Paige saw a crowbar on top of one of the crates and grabbed it. The dealer covered his head with his arms.

Paige lined up several of the ivory carvings with his foot and then bent down. He smashed them with the crowbar, the ivory splintering, white shards spewing off in all directions.

"I can do this all night," Paige said. "Tell me his name."

"Stop it," Peterson said. "Stop it now." Paige pulled another drawer down. It crashed onto the floor, scattering more ivory figures and dozens of photographs. Paige picked up one of the photographs. It was a man and two small girls. Paige dropped the photograph and struck at the figures. The floor was covered with pieces of ivory and bone, like the wreckage of some primitive burial ground.

Peterson started to get up but Paige swung the crowbar at him and he stayed down. Paige pulled another drawer out, several leather-bound books and more carvings tumbled onto the concrete and something else, a thin red binder, the color vivid in the light. Paige picked it up, opened it. Peterson seemed to curl into himself.

"Clients?" Paige asked, but he already knew that. He scanned the first few names, some more prominent than he might have guessed. Next to each name, delivery dates, money, notes on preference. Marlene Trombly's name was on the list. Julia's name appeared toward the end, two purchases over the past year.

"Did you give him the names first or was it the other way around?"

In the back of the book, he found a list of payoff figures, over two hundred thousand dollars in the last year.

"You've been a busy boy," Paige said. "Did all this go to him?"

"I don't know who you're talking about," Peterson said. "They're legitimate expenses." Paige knelt down in front of the antiques dealer and wasn't entirely certain what he might do next. It was a new feeling for Paige.

Paige slapped him, not hard, but sharp and quick. It was meant more to humiliate than anything else. Color rose in Peterson's cheeks and his eyes shone.

"I don't have a lot of patience left," Paige said. "I can keep asking questions and you can give me the answers or I can tear this place apart looking for them. That might take a little longer but we'll end up in the same place in the end." He aimed the gun at Peterson's right hand. "I want to know his name and I want to know where he is right now and don't tell me you don't know who I'm talking about because if you do it again I'm going to turn you into a fucking cripple."

Peterson pursed his lips. "He's not in there," he said, nodding at the binder.

"That's a good start," Paige said. "Where?"

"In the Rolodex," Peterson said. Paige looked at him in disbelief. "Why not?" Peterson said. "It's so obvious no one would think of it." The dealer gave him a little smirk. "He told me that."

Paige tossed the Rolodex to him. "Take the card out, put it on the floor." Peterson spun the wheel, selected a card, and placed it between his feet. "Kick it over here." Peterson pushed it to Paige with the toe of his shoe.

The name on the card was Edward Grant. There were two addresses, one was nearby, the other was in Chestnut Hill.

"Is that his real name?"

"I haven't the faintest idea," Peterson said. "We do business, we don't discuss our life histories."

"No," Paige said. "You just exchange clients." Disgust swept over him. He tried to shake it but it crept into his voice. He looked down at Peterson. "Then he goes out and kills them. But you already know that, don't you?"

"So what?" Peterson screamed at him. "You think I care?" Spit dribbled across his chin and he wiped it away with the back of his hand. "He promised to let me come with him tonight, but now you've ruined it!"

228

"Where is he now?"

"I want my lawyer."

"Where is he?" Paige raised the gun.

"Fuck you," Peterson said. "I want to talk to my lawyer."

"Fuck your lawyer," Paige said. He aimed the gun at Peterson's hand and pulled the trigger, jerking it to the right at the last second.

The shot was loud in the room, a sudden sharp crack that split the air. One corner of the crate next to the dealer's hand exploded. A large splinter of wood embedded itself in the side of his arm. Peterson screamed and pulled at it frantically. The piece of wood came away bloody.

"You're crazy," he screamed at Paige.

"You're right," Paige said and aimed the gun at Peterson's leg. "Your kneecap is next. Where were you going to meet him?"

Peterson stared at his arm. "God," he said, "look at the blood." There was a note of astonishment in his voice. Paige glanced away momentarily.

Peterson came after him. He was still surprisingly quick. Paige heard the scrape of the crate as the antiques dealer pushed off from it. He tried to bring the gun up but Peterson hit him first, knocking him into the cabinet. Paige pulled the trigger from reflex but his aim was wrong and the shot exploded into the ceiling. Plaster fell over them.

Peterson picked up the crowbar and swung it at him. Paige saw it coming and rolled out of the way. He was too slow. The crowbar struck hard on the edge of his shoulder and the pain came hard and fast. He dropped the gun and watched as it spun into the corner by the desk.

Peterson swung at him again, missed and smashed into the concrete floor. Paige went for the gun. The crowbar struck the side of his knee, and his leg went immediately numb.

Peterson pulled back for another swing. Paige kicked out hard with his good leg. His foot caught Peterson in the middle of his chest and flung him backward. Paige reached the gun and swung it around. He fired without aiming. The bullet cut a furrow along the side of Peterson's scalp and tore off the top of his ear.

Peterson didn't stop. The crowbar descended. Paige raised

his injured arm. He could barely feel it, wasn't even certain that he could hold him for more than a few seconds. Peterson slammed the crowbar down and Paige felt the pain tear through him. He looked up at Peterson and saw the rage in his eyes and felt his own strength slipping away.

It was only a question of moving the gun six inches to the left. Paige did that. He pressed the barrel against Peterson's chest and pulled the trigger twice. The first shot burst through Peterson's rib cage and blew away half his heart. The second tore out what was left. Peterson jackknifed onto his back and lay still. The crowbar clattered and spun in a half circle on the floor beside him. Paige let the gun drop. His arm was covered with blood and tissue and there was a spray of red across the front of his jacket.

Paige lay back and waited for the pain and the noise to stop. When he tried to stand, the pain in his leg was too much and he had to grab the wall to keep himself from falling. He waited a few minutes and tried again. This time he made it. The pain in his shoulder cut through him and he sat down again. The door to the bathroom was about fifteen feet away. He would give himself a few more minutes and try for that.

By the time he reached the bathroom, he was sick with nausea. He slammed the toilet lid closed and eased himself down on it. The pain pounded in his ears, a relentless drumming. It felt like his bones were being broken one by one.

He stood awkwardly at the sink and turned on the cold water and washed the blood from his hands and face. He drank a few handfuls of water and splashed more on his face until the nausea went away. In the medicine chest over the sink, he found a bottle of painkillers. He ate half a dozen and shoved the bottle in his pocket.

Where was the Rolodex card? He searched through his pockets but couldn't find it. Then he remembered it was still on the floor with Peterson's body.

Paige found it, hidden beneath one of the broken drawers. He brushed away some dirt and tried to read both addresses. The words wouldn't hold still. They jumped around in front of his face. He covered his eyes with one hand and breathed through his mouth.

The air tasted like blood.

I've got to get out of here, he thought, and looked at the first address on the card one more time. It was around the corner, just a few blocks away.

In his condition, it shouldn't take him more than two or three days to get there.

33

Caro worked in her underwear because it was easier. Nothing got in the way. The hotel room was totally dark. She enjoyed that; no sight, only touch. She stuck the fingernail file underneath the faceplate of the door leading to the adjacent room. The door was next to the dresser and she braced herself against that for better leverage. She wanted her knife. Somebody, maybe Ferris, maybe Paige, had taken it and now all she had was the file. It would have to do. She worked the file around under the faceplate of the lock until she found the spring lever. She popped it with one quick upward thrust and then went to work on the dead bolt.

Except that somebody'd forgotten to lock the dead bolt. The door swung open. She heard music from a radio and water running in the shower. There was an open bottle of wine on the table and two glasses. There were some clothes laid out carefully on the bed, a man's light blue seersucker suit, a pale yellow shirt and a yellow tie. Next to that, a cream-colored cotton dress. Caro looked at the dress and decided that the woman who wore it was about her size. She gathered up her things and slipped into the room, closing the door quietly behind her.

In the closet, she found another dress, a short dark blue knit that she put on, wrapping her own dress in a tight ball and folding it under her arm. She heard laughter in the shower and decided she had a little bit of time.

Standing in front of the dresser mirror, she brushed her hair back over her head with her hands and took a deep breath. She hadn't really seen herself since the attack and now she wished she hadn't. She looked horrible. One side of her face was covered with a dark malignant-looking bruise that spread across her cheek and up into her hairline and swelled the flesh around her eye. When she touched her skin, it hurt like crazy, sending out flashes of pain. It hurt so much her knees trembled and she thought she might collapse.

She took another deep breath and ignored the pain. It wasn't hard if you worked at it and she worked at it now, hearing the shower go off, the voices from the bathroom filling the void. Caro moved silently toward the door. She opened it quickly, realizing at the last second that it had been chained and stopping suddenly before it hit, lifting the chain and stepping into the hall.

It was all luck now. She kept her face away from the cop in front of her own room, turned, and walked off in the other direction. The hallway took a sharp right turn about forty feet away. If he was going to come after her, he'd do it before she got to the end of the hall. She started to count the feet under her breath, marking each one as she got closer to the end.

When she was six feet away, she thought she heard someone call her name but she kept on going, making the corner. She ran down the hall toward the exit sign at the other end, not expecting to make it. But she did and took the stairs two at a time until the pain in her head forced her to slow down.

There was nobody else on the stairs. She looked up and waited but she was alone. She got off on the next floor and took the elevator to the parking garage and went from there to the street. At the first pay phone, she phoned Jack at his office in the Bourse and waited impatiently while his secretary went to look for him.

"This is a surprise," he said when he came on the line.

"Listen," Caro said, cutting him off, "I need your help right now. I mean it."

"Well, sure," Jack said, "anything you want." He listened while she told him.

Grant couldn't keep track of the time. The pills kept screwing things up. They either made it go very fast, sped it up so that everything moved past him in a blur, or they slowed things down so much that he felt like he was walking around under water. He didn't mind it so much; in fact, he liked the feeling. He just had to make sure he checked his watch every fifteen minutes so he knew what the hell he was doing.

Right now he was in the Hershey looking for the goddamn maid, and he could swear he'd been looking for half an hour but it was only about ten minutes. When he saw her cart, he got the idea that she'd been hiding on him but changed his mind when it turned out to be the wrong maid.

"Where's Leana?" he asked.

The woman answered him in Spanish.

"Leana," he said again. "She's a maid like you except she speaks fucking English."

"Leana, *si*," the woman said and pointed her finger toward the ceiling. Grant figured that one out.

One floor up, Leana was loading her cart up at the supply closet.

"She ain't here," Leana said.

"Where the hell is she?"

"I don't know. I saw her running down the hall about a half hour ago. I didn't chase after her or nothing."

Grant's mind did an angry little jump and he felt like breaking something. Like maybe the maid's neck. The pills didn't help this situation but they could make it a lot worse if he let them. Now he had to think, figure out what to do next.

"Was she by herself?" he asked.

"I didn't see nobody with her. But maybe she was going to meet somebody."

"But she was running away?"

"She moved her legs pretty fast, looked like running to me."

"The cop know she's gone?"

Leana grinned.

"He don't know shit about that," she said. "He's still up there reading a book."

Things started to pick up, the world moving fast again. Grant handed the maid another ten and headed for the elevator. He was hot now, his mind bouncing around with possibilities, knowing exactly which one was going to bring him the prize. He was so fast now, he couldn't even wait for the elevator. He took the stairs, two at a time, hardly breaking stride even when he reached the first floor.

34

Paige saw a car parked on the right-hand side of the garage, directly in front of the door into the building. He could see that much in the dark but little else. His shoulder ached but not as much as his leg. His knee was swollen and he had to drag it along when he walked. He took the aspirin bottle from his pocket and ate two more. The pills were bitter and chalky and they sucked all the moisture from his mouth.

What if Grant was here already? What if he was in the car or between the car and the wall? If Grant was there, then Paige was already a dead man. He bent over slightly and worked his way down the wall until he was three feet from the car, close enough to read the license plate.

It was Marlene Trombly's car.

Paige waited for a moment, then stepped around to the driver's door and looked inside. The car was empty except for a small white shape on the passenger seat. In the dark it looked like a dog that had curled up and gone to sleep.

Paige threw open the driver's-side door. The light came on and he saw that the shape was only a rolled-up bed sheet. It was smeared with blood. Paige leaned inside. Lying on the passenger-side floor was something small and pale. It glittered in the light. Paige looked away briefly, a conditioned reflex, and reached down for it.

And pulled back.

The object on the floor was a human finger, a diamond ring still on it.

Paige took a deep breath, then another, and felt for the ignition. The keys were there. He pocketed them and walked slowly toward the door.

The door to the building was unlocked. He opened it and saw the elevator just a few feet away.

It was out of service.

It took him nearly ten minutes to reach the third-floor stairwell. The pain in his leg had become a continuous flood that engulfed his whole body. But he forced himself to move through it. He opened the door and looked into the hallway.

The hall was deserted. He guessed that Grant's office was on the right, toward the front of the street. He guessed wrong. The office was on his left next to the stairs. The lock looked simple but wasn't. It took him seven minutes to open it.

Paige turned on the light, in too much of a hurry to worry about the consequences. There was no one there. The room drew him in, welcomed him with its cold embrace. There was a small reception area, as narrow as a coffin. At one end, another door led into a larger room. There was a desk, a chair, and a bookcase. The desk was angled into the corner away from the windows.

There was nothing in the desk, just a few insurance papers, a box of canceled checks, some indecipherable scribbles on a pad of gray paper. It was as if no one had been there at all. Paige was ready to leave. I want to see where he lives, he thought.

He drove Marlene Trombly's car. When he bore down on the clutch pedal, the numbness in his leg made it feel curiously hollow as though someone else were doing the driving. At a traffic light, he glanced down at the floor.

Jesus.

He pulled over as soon as he could and looked for a clean rag or something to cover the severed finger. But he couldn't find one and finally pulled the bloody sheet down over it just to keep from having to look at it again.

35

Caro was upstairs packing, tossing some clothes into a suitcase when she heard a car pull up out front. Cautiously, she stood to one side of the window and looked through the curtains. It was Jack's Mercedes. She'd been gone from the hotel for forty-five minutes and kept expecting Paige to show up. Another ten minutes and she'd be gone and none of them would find her.

Jack had a house at Longport just south of Atlantic City. Actually, he had *two* houses in Longport, one right on the beach, the other a few blocks back. He hadn't rented it, he told her, so she could use it as long as she needed it. How about a month? No problem. That would take her through August, time enough for her to decide what she was going to do about the rest of her life. She wasn't living long like this, not anymore.

She went out to get the keys and directions. Jack was standing at the door, dangling a set of keys.

"Good Lord, what happened to you?" he asked. He looked at her face, twisting his head from side to side so he could see everything.

"I was in an accident." She wanted him to give her the keys

and go. It was all she could do to keep from snatching them from his hand.

"Are you all right?"

"You mean aside from the fact that I look like shit. I'm fine, Jack. I really appreciate your help but I'm in a hurry."

"That's all right," he said as if he hadn't heard a word she'd said and handed her the keys. "The small one is for the garage. I can't remember if there's anything in it or not. If it's empty, you can use it. The other two are for the house." He took out a typed sheet of paper and a one-page copy of a map. "I had my secretary type this up. These are the directions and a few things you might need to know about the house. Here's a map, showing where it is. I marked a few other places, the grocery store, things like that."

Oh, for Christ's sake, I can find a goddamn grocery store, she thought. He's being nice because he thinks I'm a helpless female and he wants to come and visit.

"This is wonderful, Jack," she said, plucking the papers and the keys from his hand and kissing him on the cheek. "Why don't you come and see me in a couple weeks, okay? Right now I've got to get going."

She pushed him halfway out the door and he stammered a good-bye while she ran back upstairs. He stood there for a moment, feeling more than a little foolish, then started to close the door.

Grant stepped beside him. He was wearing Paige's freshly washed uniform with a light blue jacket to cover up the rip in the sleeve.

"You know you're double-parked out there," Grant said. He was smiling his winner's smile, all teeth, the one that looked like he was going to tell you that you won something nice.

"I was just leaving," Jack said. Grant watched him leave, tracking him until he stopped in the middle of the sidewalk.

"Is this about the accident?" Jack asked.

"Yes, sir," Grant said and touched the side of his face. "It was a bad one. She's lucky she got out of it alive. We're all lucky." He liked the way Jack sobered up when he heard that.

"I can see that," Jack said. "Well, I'll be going now."

Grant waited until he was in the car. "Have a real nice day," he said as the Mercedes drove off. Then he closed the door behind him and went hunting for Caro.

He was moving in slow motion now, the pills pulsing in his veins as he swam through the house. The late afternoon sunlight played tricks on him, turning the walls into silver waves. He started for the living room, heard a noise from upstairs and climbed toward it. As he went, he took off his belt and wrapped it around his hand, thinking how it was going to feel, especially when it moved real slow.

When he came to the top of the stairs, he saw Caro at the other end dragging a suitcase toward him. It took her a few seconds to recognize him and then she was running for the back of the house and Grant was coming after her.

It was great. He was sailing through the air and laughing because it was just like a dream when no matter how fast you ran you couldn't get away. He watched her legs fly as she reached the stairs to the third floor. They were like pieces of white bone, all smooth and shiny. She couldn't hope to outrun him.

Grant caught one of her ankles and snapped it up sharply. Caro flipped forward and fell face first on the stairs. He could hear the crack when she hit and started laughing. Everything was under water again and the sound echoed all around him. He caught her other ankle and dragged her down the steps toward what he figured was her bedroom.

She tried to kick him but he twisted her leg and kept twisting until she stopped. Inside the room, he picked her up roughly and stood her in front of him like a punching doll, hanging on to one hand, and slammed his fist into the middle of her chest, knocking the wind out of her. When she fell toward the bed, he pulled her back and smacked her hard across the face. Her eyes bulged out and she dropped against the edge of the bed and slid to the rug, Grant laughing at her all the way down. She didn't move.

Grant left her there and picked up the phone to call Lindor Peterson. He let it ring a dozen times but there was no answer. He waited five minutes and tried again but Peterson still didn't answer.

Caro began to stir. He rummaged through her closet until

he found a leather belt and a pair of clothes hangers, took the leather mask from his jacket pocket and went to work.

She came awake a few minutes later. Grant used the clothes hangers to bind her hands and feet together behind her so that she was bent backward at a painful angle and tied them tight with the belt. Then he dumped her on the bed and got down beside her. He put his hand inside the mask and pressed it down her mouth. The taste of the leather made her gag. He put his face close to hers.

Caro didn't get really frightened until she saw his eyes. The pupils were like two pinholes filled with dark light. Grant brought his other hand up. He was holding a pair of scissors.

"There's been a few changes," he said. "I guess we'll just have to improvise." He pressed the scissors into her cheek and she heard the faint pop as the point punctured her skin.

She began to scream but Grant didn't notice.

He was far too busy.

36

Paige ran across the yard toward Grant's house. The ground was hard, the grass dry and dead beneath his feet. Small clouds of dust exploded with each step. Paige felt as if he were crossing over into some unknown land. He thought he saw something move on the porch and dropped behind some bushes on the other side of the drive.

On five, he thought, shut his eyes and went through the slow count, the numbers feathery light on his lips, then popped up quickly, the gun stretched over the leaves, pointing into the darkness near the door.

Nothing moved.

He jerked the gun back suddenly, a reflex action, surprise and anger mixed together, then aimed it at the door again. There was nothing there.

Paige stood awkwardly, his damaged leg cramping up as he straightened it. He could hardly feel the pain anymore but the stiffness made it difficult to move. His vision was split between the door and the side of the house. Grant could come around the side and Paige would have only seconds to react. He walked slowly up the steps, keeping the gun pointed toward the side because that's what he feared the most. He kept wondering if it was a setup, a bit of play before the real thing jumped out at him.

The front door was unlocked and slightly ajar, enough that he caught the edge of the wood with his fingers and swung it open. He locked both hands on the gun and stepped through the open doorway.

Paige moved through the empty house, moving the gun in front of him like a weight. It took him into the dining room. Candles still burned on the table, a plate of food, half-eaten, lay abandoned. A handful of pills lay scattered on the kitchen floor.

He searched the rest of the house, starting with the attic and moving to the basement and the long tables half-filled with merchandise. The guy must have had a fire sale, he thought, and then it dawned on him maybe that's exactly what Grant was doing. He was moving and selling everything off and somehow Julia got in the way of that. All the rest happened because Paige had forced it. It made as much sense as anything.

The openness of the basement angered him, the tables laid out like some kind of flea market. Where the hell had he been while this guy was doing business?

Then he found the back room. He dug his heel into the dirt floor and his mouth went dry.

There was the chair and the knives, spread out like a fan on a small side table. And next to the knives, a tape recorder.

Paige didn't want to touch anything, so he took a tissue from his pocket, rewound the tape, and pressed play.

He heard Julia Weinstein; she was screaming the word "No!" She stopped screaming abruptly and he heard the sound of the first hammer blow and knew what came after that. The tape spun around and around and the next voice he heard belonged to Marlene Trombly, telling Paige that she had decided to stay in town and why didn't he come over to see her after the Patrons' Ball.

Paige closed his eyes. Grant had been in his house. Marlene Trombly's voice ended. He stabbed at the stop button.

There was something else beneath the tape recorder, a photograph. Paige fished it out with the tips of his fingers. He flipped the picture over. It was Caro, the one from his file. Paige went upstairs to call the hotel.

It rang ten times before O'Neal answered.

"Is she there?" Paige asked, already knowing the answer.

"She's gone. I don't know how the hell she got out. Wait a second." Paige tried to call him back but O'Neal had already set the phone down. He returned in a few minutes. "She broke through into the room next door and went out that way. That's the only way she could have done it."

"All right," Paige said. "I want you to get some backup units to her house." He gave O'Neal the address. "You stay at the hotel."

"How do you know she went to her house? Maybe she just took off."

"Don't argue with me," Paige yelled. "Just do what I tell you. I think Grant's gone after her and if he misses her at the hotel, he's going to look for her at home. I'm going there right now."

Paige hung up. He called Caro's number and let it ring a dozen times before slamming the phone down. Then he hurried to the car as fast as his legs would let him.

O'Neal tried to decide what he should do. If he called this in and it turned out to be nothing, his ass was going to be in a lot of trouble. On the other hand, if it turned out that Paige was right, he was going to be in a lot worse shape. He needed to clear this with somebody who could handle a thing like this.

He called Tom Ferris and talked to him about it. Ferris told O'Neal to sit tight and not to worry because he knew exactly what to do. Ferris sounded like he was drunk but that's how he sounded most of the time anyway.

Which was fine with O'Neal. What bothered him was the other thing in his voice that O'Neal had never heard before.

Ferris sounded really excited.

O'Neal decided it was his imagination. He stopped worrying and went back to reading his book.

37

Ferris decided to go in through Caro's front door because he wanted the other guy—was his name Grant?—to know he was there so he wouldn't do anything stupid. Ferris thought he might just knock on the front door and stick the gun right in the guy's face and tell him to lay down on the floor. They could chat after that.

Maybe Paige was wrong, maybe this wasn't the right guy. Wouldn't that be a big surprise for everybody? But Ferris wanted it to be the right one, wanted it more than anything he could remember. He wanted to hand him over to Paige just so he could draw an end to everything, finally mark their lives even. That was one thing Danny had taught him, that things had to be square, an eye for an eye, a dollar for a dollar, that was the important part. After that, it was just so much sand down the rat hole.

Ferris kept the gun at his side and walked toward the door. He felt surprisingly calm, as if he'd been rehearsing for it all of his life. It came to him that he hadn't done anything like this in years. Running around the Art Museum didn't count. He was sorry about that, too, sorry about the screwup with the transmitter. Hell, he might have done that on purpose, too. He couldn't keep things straight anymore. Drinking turned everything into a blur, and he'd grown used to it that way.

He was just glad to be back on the line, doing his duty as he saw fit, helping Pat out. Danny Paige had been wrong. This was the only thing he ever really enjoyed. Maybe that's why killing Sonny Ray had been so easy for him.

When he knocked on the front door and no one answered, he waited a few seconds and then pushed it open. He was a little surprised that it was unlocked but he went in anyway. It was dark inside the house, so he stepped into the living room to find a light switch. He found one and flipped it on. The light didn't work.

The light went on in the hall and Ferris spun around, dropping low and aiming the gun at the empty doorway.

He heard the footsteps from the other side of the room before he heard the voice but in his mind they ran together, the soft rustle of the carpet and then the voice, full of purpose, a cop's voice. "Can I help you?" the voice asked and it sounded so much like Patrick Paige that Ferris found himself turning to greet his old friend before his natural caution slowed him down. He swung the gun and started to bring it up. Only when he saw who had spoken to him, did he hold it down.

It was a cop dressed in a uniform. The cop was holding something shiny in his hand. Ferris couldn't see it clearly. The cop was walking toward him very fast. If he didn't slow down, Ferris thought, the cop was going to walk right into him. The cop looked so much like Paige it was amazing. They could have been brothers. He still couldn't see what the cop had in his hand.

Ferris smiled and the cop smiled back.

The first time the scissors went into him, Ferris didn't even feel it. When the pain finally came, it was too late to stop it anyway.

Ferris was still alive. He was lying on the living room floor, his eyes half open, eyelids fluttering, staring up at Grant's face like he recognized him. Grant knelt down beside him.

"So where the hell did you come from?" Grant asked. Ferris didn't answer, not that Grant expected him to say anything.

Grant moved in closer, the scissors snapping through the air.

"What's the matter, cat got your tongue?" Grant started to grin. "We can fix that right away."

When he finished, Grant didn't wait around to see who else was going to show up. He checked the street to make sure no one else was around. When he was certain of it, he bundled Caro up in a blanket and hustled her out to his car and tossed her on the floor between the seats. She struggled but he slapped hard and covered her with the blanket and she didn't give him any more trouble.

Then he drove off to find Lindor Peterson to let him in on some of the fun.

The lights were on in the gallery and Grant could see the open backdoor. That was the first bad sign. Nothing was going like it should except for the girl. She was working out just fine and that made up for the rest of it. Maybe Lindor caught a burglar, but he decided that probably wasn't the case. Lindor couldn't catch a cold. He locked the car and went to take a quick look.

He smelled the blood even before he opened the door, then saw Peterson sprawled on the concrete, a puddle of red beneath him, and couldn't make up his mind what to do next. The pills seemed to wear off and he was suddenly sober. The idea that Peterson was dead hit him hard and he stepped back from the door and leaned against the wall to catch himself. There were half a dozen pills left in his pocket, all mixed up so that he couldn't tell the speed from the Percodan. He said to hell with it and ate them all, covering his mouth with his hand and licking them off with his tongue. That was something the cop back at Caro's wouldn't be doing anymore.

Grant waited a couple of minutes and felt the first rush as the new pills started to work. He looked over and saw the cut wires on the junction box and it came to him through the rush that Paige had gotten to Peterson first and that was even better because dead he could still use Lindor and make everything look like Paige went a little crazy and cut up the dealer and the girl. By the time the cops got around to figuring it all out, he'd be halfway to Texas.

But now he had to think about dragging the dead dealer across the floor and Lindor wasn't exactly small. It took him a few minutes to get the body in the trunk, but the pills helped. Peterson's legs wouldn't fit, so Grant just bent them backward and stuffed him inside.

He got back into the car and leaned over the seat, the scissors in his hand.

"I'm going to make him watch what I do to you," he said to her. He reached down and cut her, once, twice, three times. Caro didn't scream this time.

It was impossible to scream through the mask.

38

Where were the other cops? Paige stopped the car at the end of the block and looked down both sides of the street. He recognized Ferris's car parked in front of her house and he hit the accelerator hard, covering the distance in a few seconds, skidding when he hit the brakes and bumped into the rear of the other car.

The front door was unlocked. He turned the handle and shoved it open, catching it with his hand as it bounced off the wall. A light was on in the hall, so he swung around the doorway, using his good leg to carry him through.

Paige saw Tom Ferris with his head thrown back against the wall of the living room and he knew instantly that he was dead. He jerked the gun up suddenly, a reflex, surprise and sorrow mixed together, then swept the room until he realized he was alone in the house.

Grant had made only two cuts. The first one to open him up, the second to make it easier to pull his guts out. They lay in a puddle in his lap, one of his hands still tangled in them. Ferris's mouth was wide open and filled with blood. It spilled down his chest into a pool on the carpet. Ferris had his hand dipped into it. The ends of his fingers were caked with it.

Paige stepped back and saw the writing on the wall.

Ferris had written the word HOME in his own blood.

Paige looked at the writing again and then at Tom Ferris. There was something in his hand, something hidden behind his other fingers. Paige knelt down, his knee sinking into the wet carpet and pulled his fingers open.

Paige's shield fell out. He wiped it off on his pant leg and stuck it in his pocket.

Then he got himself ready for the long ride home.

39

Paige stood before the front gate and stared into the silence of the old house. He lifted the latch and the gate swung open.

The house welcomed him back.

Paige hadn't been inside it for seven years.

He worked his way slowly toward the side of the house. His leg had gone numb on him again and he rubbed it hard to bring some feeling back. The leg stayed numb.

The backdoor was wide open. He went through the open doorway, toward the kitchen table in the center of the darkened room. The years vanished in an instant. To his right, he could see the refrigerator. Next to it, the counter and the sink. Beyond that, the stove and the door into the living room. When he reached the table, he ran one hand down the thin chrome legs and out across the cracked linoleum. When he looked up, he half expected to see a pot boiling on the stove.

He moved around the table and his foot touched something slippery. Paige reached one hand down and it came away wet. He squinted through the darkness and saw that the floor was smeared with blood, the trail leading toward the living room. Grant had dragged somebody behind him.

The smell of blood hit him suddenly and he breathed through his mouth to keep the stench away. Then he followed its trail through the house.

The living room was empty, just as he knew it would be. He was sweating, the salt stinging his eyes. He blinked hard and wiped one hand across his forehead and then down his face. He smelled the blood again, the coppery taste coming alive on his tongue. The house pulled him in, dragging him through his past all the way to the present. He moved like a robot, holding his stiff leg with one hand as he inched it forward.

He reached the bottom of the stairs. His hand touched more blood on the wall and he pulled his fingers away quickly. How far away was Caro? On the stairs? In one of the rooms? Was she even alive?

Where was Grant?

There was a rattle from the top of the stairs. Paige put his back to the wall and tried to see through the darkness above him. Were the windows open upstairs? Suddenly, he couldn't remember. The house smelled of mildew and dead air, so they must have been closed. Did he close them? He couldn't remember. Paige climbed the first two steps, stopped and then moved to the other side.

He continued that way, back and forth up the stairs until he reached the landing, waiting for Grant to come for him at any time. But he made it safely to the top. Once there, he crawled to the corner of the landing and sat back, his gun aimed straight down the hall. The pain in his shoulder began to nag at him again. He had to brace his left arm with his knee to hold the gun up for more than a minute.

His eyes slowly adjusted to the cobweb of darkness and he saw what lay ahead of him.

The hall was nearly twenty feet long, two rooms on the left, a bathroom on the right, his bedroom straight ahead at the end. A short rope for the pull-down ladder to the attic hung from the ceiling in the center of the hall. He felt a breeze. It touched his face and fluttered away. The door at the end of the hall rattled and moaned.

There was a flicker of light beneath his bedroom door. Paige leaned forward. There it was again, a thin line of fire just beneath the door. If he looked carefully, he could see the trail of blood led straight to the end of the hall. That's where Grant had taken her.

Paige remembered the light the night he found Connie. There was lots of light then and he wanted darkness instead; he wanted to close his eyes and bring on the night but he couldn't do it.

The memory churned around in his stomach. His hands were sticky with sweat and blood, and he wiped them on his shirt to get them clean. He thought he might throw up, and he laid his head back against the wall and waited until he was calm again.

The door swung open a few inches, pushed by the wind. Paige stood up slowly and wondered if Danny had had the walls washed before he closed up the house.

He tried the first two doors but they were locked. The bathroom was open, the shower curtain gone. There was enough light from the small window to see that the room was empty.

The door at the end of the hall slammed shut. Paige jumped at the noise and dropped to the floor, pressing his shoulder against the cold tile. The gun felt heavy in his hand and his leg hurt. The pain didn't stop when he stood up again. He moved carefully toward the end of the hall.

One room left. He reached for the handle, afraid of what he might find.

The attic ladder dropped down behind him. The support chains snapped straight and cracked like lightning. Paige threw himself to the floor, rolled quickly and came up again, his finger tensed on the trigger. Shoot, shoot, shoot. The thought screamed through his head.

A rush of hot air poured through the opening into the hallway. Paige took a deep breath and smelled the dust. Seconds went by, minutes. Nothing happened. The hallway remained as empty as before. He eased his finger off the trigger and stood up, his nerves on edge, the pain worse.

Without waiting, he pushed open the bedroom door. There was a man kneeling in the corner. Paige instinctively braced himself against the doorjamb and fired.

254

Lindor Peterson's body fell over onto the floor, the pale face gazing up curiously at Paige. He swung the gun around toward the bed. A candle burned on his old dresser and he followed the soft arc of flickering light. The bed lay stripped and bare except for a small coil of rope tied to one leg. The rope angled upward through a large metal hook that was screwed into the ceiling in the corner near the windows.

Caro stood on a chair beneath the hook, the end of the rope twisted around her neck. Her hands were tied behind her, her feet balanced precariously on the seat of the chair. Paige looked beyond her. The windows were open. The flame of the candle danced in the wind. Caro began to struggle against the rope. The chair teetered to one side.

"Don't move," Paige whispered. She struggled even more. The chair tipped back. One leg rose dangerously high off the floor.

"Don't move," Paige said again. This time she stopped.

He stepped toward her, watching the hallway and the windows. A few feet from the chair, he could hear the sound of her sobbing through the mask. He checked the windows first, leaning out far enough so that he could see on either side of the roof. He saw nothing and began to untie her hands.

"It's going to be all right," he said.

Grant swung down through the open window behind him and smashed into his back. Paige hurtled forward, knocking over the chair as he staggered into the bed.

Caro swung free. One leg hooked onto the back of the chair but Grant knocked it away and came after Paige with his bare hands. The rope tightened around her neck.

Paige held onto the gun and tried to bring it around. Grant kicked him in the ribs and sent him toppling over the other side of the bed. The pain was astonishing. He tried to raise the gun but Grant was already on top of him. One hand raked across his face, missing his eye and closed around his throat. The other clawed for the gun.

Grant squeezed Paige's throat, harder and harder. Paige felt the breath die in his lungs. White fire flashed across his eyes.

Paige swung his right hand up from the floor and slammed into Grant's face. The burglar kept his hand on Paige's throat and pressed harder. Paige tore at his face again, feeling the flesh begin to break beneath his fingers. Grant screamed and released his hand. Paige pushed hard and Grant fell backward.

Caro's body swung back and forth in front of Paige's eyes. Her kicking was less frantic now. Her body seemed to twitch in place.

Paige brought the gun up.

Grant scrambled toward the door and swung it shut behind him. The edge of it struck Paige in the leg. The pain tore through him and he fired. The bullet punched a hole through the top of the door, scattering bits of wood before ploughing into the wall. Grant kicked the door shut again. Paige spun out of the way and rolled toward the back wall.

Grant climbed through the window and hooked his arms on the edge of the roof. As his feet swung free, Paige aimed and fired. The effort took nearly all the strength he had left. The bullet tore through Grant's wounded arm, the force of it pushing him farther out the window. Paige tried to raise his arm to fire again but couldn't. Grant hung there momentarily, then swung himself onto the roof. Paige struggled to his feet.

He grabbed Caro around the waist, holding her with one arm while he tore at the rope with the other. The knot finally worked loose and he pulled it off her neck.

She slid down the front of his body to the floor, struggling hard to breathe inside the mask. Her eyes were closed. Paige fumbled with the buckles, ripping them open finally with numb and bloody fingers. He pulled the mask off carefully and threw it away.

The skin of her face was dark and covered with blood. Her hair was soaked with it, too, and it stuck to the sides of her skull. He ran a finger over one cheek. She'd been cut. She breathed heavily through her mouth. Paige undid her hands and held them in his.

Then he sat her up against the bed and went after Grant.

Paige climbed the attic ladder slowly, his left arm dangling uselessly at his side. The heaviness of it weighed him down. In the dark attic, he made his way toward the window at the far end.

The window wouldn't open. Paige found an old chair stuck

under one of the eaves and dragged it to the window. He held it in his right hand and rammed it through the glass.

The window exploded over the slate roof. Paige pushed the chair the rest of the way through. It landed on the roof, slid to the edge of the heavy gutter, and tumbled off. Paige kicked away the remaining glass from the window frame and climbed onto the roof.

From where he stood, Paige could see the entire back of the house. Directly ahead was a brick chimney, six feet high and nearly as wide. To the right, ten feet from the chimney, the roof ended sharply. On the left, it sloped gently toward the narrow side yard. Behind him, the rest of the house rose at a sharp angle to a high peak and down again on the other side.

A spattered line of blood ran along the right edge of the roof to the chimney.

Paige balanced awkwardly on the roof. He moved a few feet at a time, then a few more. The window was ten feet behind him. He stepped carefully, leaning slightly forward, like a man walking against a strong wind.

A piece of slate crumbled beneath his foot and broke away. Paige dropped down quickly, putting his right hand on the peak to keep from falling.

He stopped a few feet from the chimney.

"Give it up, Grant," he said.

There was no answer.

He moved another foot.

"You're going to die," Paige said.

"You first," Grant said from behind him. He held a piece of slate in his hand and sent it spinning toward Paige's face. Paige raised the gun and fired. The shot went high. The slate struck him on the side of the cheek. He grabbed for his wounded face and lost his balance. The gun fell and slid down the roof. Paige heard it strike the gutter before it disappeared into the darkness. A light went on in the house next door, then another across the street. Grant seemed not to notice. He smiled at Paige and started to cross the roof. Blood poured down his arm and dripped onto the slate.

Caro crawled out through the shattered window. Her face was pale white and she held something in her hand. She kept it in front of her as she danced down the roof toward Grant. He turned at the last moment. She raised her arm and brought it down in the center of his chest. Paige saw the piece of glass flash once as it fell. Grant staggered backward, and she struck him again.

He grabbed for her as he fell but she pushed him away. Grant slid heavily down the roof toward the edge. One foot struck the gutter and he rolled off. He caught the gutter with both hands and hung on.

Paige climbed down the roof after him, crawling alongside the final few feet of gutter before he reached him. Grant raised his wounded arm and Paige took it. The arm was slick with blood and it slid through Paige's hand all the way to the wrist. Grant let his good hand go and it dangled in space. Paige gazed down at the spiked top of the fence directly below and then into the burglar's face, knowing what he'd find there.

Grant smiled up at him, a mad delirious grin.

Paige smiled back.

He let go.

40

Mickey Katz was no longer in intensive care and nobody could tell Paige where they'd taken him. So he took the elevator upstairs and discovered for himself that the old man's room had been cleared out. Instead, he found a woman in a flowered dress putting some clothes away in the dresser.

"I'm Gladys Sikes," she said. "They called and told me there was a vacancy. I just moved in here. I don't know where your friend is. I hope he's all right." She pointed to the bag in his hand. "Is that food?"

"Yes," Paige said. "Bagels and lox."

"I see," she said and went back to putting her clothes away.

At the nurses' desk they told him that Archie was down in the employees' locker room. Paige found him, emptying his locker. He had everything in a cardboard box. He sat alone on the bench, staring at the box.

"Hello, Mr. Paige," Archie said. "You come looking for Mickey I guess." Archie looked at the box again and shook his head. "He's dead."

Paige sat down next to him, the bag of food on his lap. "When did it happen?"

"Last night after dinner," Archie said. "I brought him some magazines and we was looking at them together. He was sitting up in bed. Then he died. Just like there was nothing to it."

Archie closed the locker. His eyes were red and rimmed with tears. "I called your house but didn't get no answer. I thought you had one of those answering machines."

"I took it out," Paige said. "I got tired of listening to it."

"I never liked them myself. You bring his breakfast again?"

"Yeah," Paige said. "You hungry?"

"Sure am," Archie said and smiled. They ate quietly for a while, then Archie spoke.

"Mickey liked you bringing him breakfast," Archie said, "wanted you to do it more often but wouldn't ever say so, you know how he was."

"Where'd they take him?"

"Grossman's out on Broad, but he's ashes by now, that was his strict orders. Said he didn't want some place where people would come and mourn over his passing. He said you'd understand that." Paige was silent, so Archie continued speaking. "I read about the trouble you had, leaving the police and all."

"There wasn't any trouble," Paige said. "I took an indefinite leave of absence."

"You know what you going to do?"

"Haven't the faintest idea."

Archie shrugged. "There's something to be said for that, having no plans, nothing to tie you down."

Archie ate quietly.

"I read about your friend, the policeman who was killed," he said.

"Tom Ferris."

"I guess you two were pretty close, him being friends with your father and all."

Paige had nothing to say.

"I don't like to speak ill of the dead but the man drank too much." Archie's face was gentle and composed. "I could never abide a drunk," he said with great dignity. "I'm sorry."

Paige handed Archie another bagel.

"Me, too," Paige said.

Paige parked his car across from Caro's town house. There was a gold *For Sale* sign hanging over the door, the lettering on it small and elegant, like an invitation to an expensive dinner party, Paige thought. He turned on the radio and waited. An older woman in a navy blue blazer and cream-colored slacks opened the front door for a middle-aged couple. Paige couldn't hear all of what they were saying but they seemed very excited, pointing to the house and laughing. The couple walked off down the street while the woman waited on the step.

Caro appeared in the doorway behind her. From where he was sitting, he could see that most of the cuts on her face had healed. There was still one bandage left, a thin crescent of adhesive tape just above her right eye. Like a fighter, she favored the eye, squinting slightly when she spoke to the woman. The woman shook Caro's hand and followed the couple up the street.

Caro started to close the door and then she saw him. She stopped. Paige turned off the radio. He had no idea what he wanted to say to her, only that he wanted to say something. The words wouldn't come. For a moment, a few empty seconds, he was trapped by his own silence, and then everything was lost.

Caro shut the door.

Paige could hear the sound of the lock snapping into place all the way across the street.

Paige was on his roof, getting ready to try another jump. His leg had healed and he'd been working out, so he felt strong enough to make the last one this time.

He took the first two jumps quickly, leaping the short distances between the roofs with ease. It felt so good that he took his time with the next one. His foot barely touched the edge of the roof and then he pushed himself into space, soaring high for an instant before coming down hard and solid on the rooftop. He took the next one the same way, holding himself back for that final jump across eight feet of open space.

He started out fast, digging his heels into the gravel, his eye fixed on the edge of the roof less than thirty feet away.

Then something happened. His shoes scuffed on the gravel, slowing him down. When he was ten feet away, he gave up running and walked to the edge of the roof.

Paige looked down fifty feet, only this time he didn't see himself lying down there, didn't see anything except the cracked pavement and the piles of garbage.

He scooped up a handful of gravel and tossed the stones over the edge, watching them fall. They scattered on the pavement, the noise coming back to him only faintly, like the echo of some desire already forgotten.